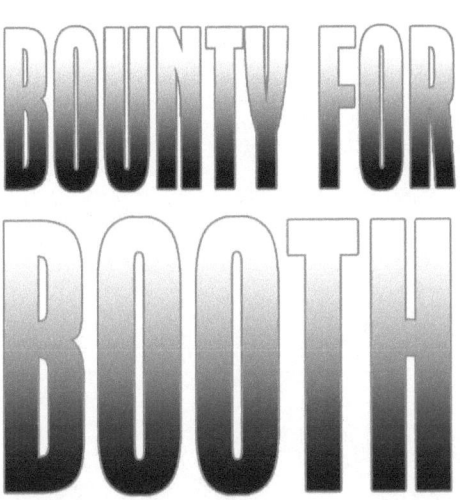

BOUNTY FOR BOOTH

A NOVEL BY

SCOTT WESTMORELAND

Advanced Praise for
BOUNTY FOR BOOTH

"Scott Westmoreland presents an unusual, alternate view of the famous Lincoln assassination in this thrilling 'what if?' story....his dialogue and historical knowledge add flavor and depth to a tale of intertwining decisions, choices and destinies that will delight readers who love a good page-turner!"
---Marie D. Jones, Best selling author, screenwriter, researcher, radio host

"Imaginative, bold and daring....It's themes of triumph and tragedy will stay with you long after you finish this book of alternative history."
---Michael Coleman, author

BOUNTY FOR BOOTH

Published by New Stage Media, P.O. Box 17087, Anaheim, CA 92817
info@newstagemedia.org * www.newstagemedia.org

ISBN-10: 0578120720
EAN-13: 978-0-578-12072-0

Printed in the United States of America
Cover illustration by Scott Westmoreland, graphics by José Rodriguez

All art inquiries direct to: scottfineart@sbcglobal.net,
or visit www.scottwestmorelandart.com

*For Karen, Cooper, and Gracie,
with love…*

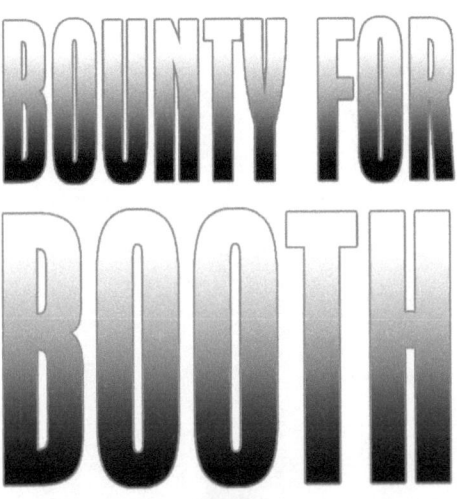

BOUNTY FOR BOOTH

A NOVEL BY

SCOTT WESTMORELAND

NEW STAGE
MEDIA

PROLOGUE

JEUNE VISAGE CONVALESCENT HOSPITAL
Metairie, Louisiana, 1928

Steady rumbles unfolded over the Gulf, announcing a sudden shift in the weather. Matron Sarah Van Percy burst through the annex doors, and descended the shorn green glade. White-clad nurses with pointy shoulders and winged caps followed like a line of army ants. Southern storms struck quickly, with gusto – not much time to gather the wheelchair-bound patients strewn about for art hour.

Within seconds, gale-force gusts bowed the bordering willows and magnolias, scattered yard debris, toppled easels. A bolt of lightning ripped through the eerie afternoon sky. At a count of *four Mississippi*, the earth shook with a deep, thunderous boom.

An elderly gentleman with "Stone" taped to his seat back, lurched and grabbed his masterpiece, tumbling in a bundle beneath the canvas. Drops dotted his slacks and cardigan, then came the downpour. "I's fine," he shouted, "help the others." Adrenaline surged as he summoned the strength to right himself, pushing his "own damn chair" up the gradient slope.

Back inside Room 111 (a river-view suite he crankily refused to share), he mopped his face, and leaned a nearly completed portrait of Abraham Lincoln abreast a multitude. Each Abe a different size and pose, skillfully rendered. There were seven, last count.

Flash – *one Mississippi, two Mississippi* – boom!

A voice spoke as he wiped the drops from his brow with a dry towel and watched the ensuing torrent. "You okay, sugar?" Soaking wet nurse's aide, Onyx Robinson, checked in. With a history of head trauma, there was cause for concern.

"I said I's fine, dad-blame it, now git." His words were liberally dunked in a blend of bayou twang and delta drawl. The Stones harvested sugarcane and owned slaves during the antebellum era. The African-American woman reminded him of his nanny, Isa Brown. Same eyes, same smooth chubby cheeks. He episodically believed she *was* Isa, asking Onyx to cook and clean, and summon her son, Griffin, for some fun in the fields. The delusions could last minutes, even days. He'd remember none of it. So, for safety's sake, he remained under constant care and supervision.

Jeremy Gabrick Stone was an ornery 86 years old, going on 17. A fervid storyteller if the notion struck, he kept mostly to himself, and secretively sketched and wrote in his journal. People would ask, "Whatcha got there?" He never disclosed.

"Looky here," said Onyx, eyes wide in awe of his talent. "Lovin' dem Lincolns, but don't ya paint nobody else?" She tended to pry. "D'utha' presidents prob'ly gettin' jealous. Coolidge makes 30 now, ain't he?" She appeared only as a head and hands around a paint-peeled doorjamb.

Stone sat at the edge of the bed, combing finger-nails through his still-wet locks, saying nothing.

"What pictures ya workin' from?" she puzzled. Even after she scoured every inch of the sterile cham-ber – including his knicker drawer – she never found a single photo of the 16th President.

Don't need 'em, I knowed that face like m'own.

Entering the foyer, she adjusted the thermostat. "Say, you's raised in Jefferson Davis country, ain't ya?" Vacant nod. "So...why Lincoln? Not bein' nosy, jis curi-ous is all." She searched for a stepstool and adjusted a vent on tippy toes. "Dis ole sweat box could use some fresh air and a good cool down."

He came alive and griped, "'Bout time I ain't gotta smell people's piss." When temperatures escalated, so did a moderate urine stench.

"Jis tell yassef it's fresh baked punkin pie," she advised. "Dat's what I do." Always a ray of sunshine lurking right below the surface. "Mmhmm, America sho' needs mo' men like Lincoln. Saved de union, freed de slaves." Flat-footed again. "Right befo' he was kilt by dat terrible Booth at Ford's Theater. Dat's de way of it, if mem'ry serves."

No words whatsoever.

"C'mon now," she rambled, "join de conversation. You s'pose to be de Civil War expert, ain't ya?" Silence. "Well, ain't ya?" Onyx puttered about, cleaning and straighten-ing a moderate mess: half-eaten bowl of milk toast, candy wrappers, soiled stockings, bifocals, a so-called *Tijuana Bible*. "You been lookin' at nekkid funnies again, honey?"

"Nope."

"What's dis?" She produced the crass comic from under his pillow, triggering an episode.

"Brushes, where are my brushes? And paints? Go get 'em, Isa...*now!*" Stone was suddenly and sincerely agitated. They were his lifeline.

"You missin' some kernels off yer cobb, darlin'," she tossed the lewd booklet in his lap, "but you delicious." He cracked a slight smile. "Back in a bit."

The old-timer turned his attention towards the window.

Onyx lumbered down the hall, white orthopedic shoes squeaking with each shuffle, thighs rubbing together, making fabric-on-fabric swooshes. Just then, a meek voice sounded from behind. "No it ain't."

Backpedaling, outside #111 again. "What was dat?" she asked.

"No it ain't," Stone flatly repeated.

"No it ain't...*what*?" She peered around the corner.

"No it ain't happened like that...Lincoln and Booth."

A confused expression. "Sho' it did."

"Nope." He was curt, assured. *Reckon it's time y'all knowed the truth.*

Onyx sauntered up to the belligerent old man. "Looky here, you rascal," she traced the well-worn path in the linoleum. "Arms up." She removed his clinging shirt, plastered like snakeskin, and then the pants. "I'm no scholar, but I knows my history. Abraham Lincoln was kilt by John Wilkes Booth on Good Friday, 1865, at Ford's Theater in D.C. Don't be messin' wif me now."

Flash, flickering lights, *kaboom!* Stone didn't flinch. Steel blue eyes, glassy and distant.

"Lawd have mercy! Dat's close, not even a *one Mississippi!*" The storm was bearing down on the building. "Now take care and rest," she advised, lowering blinds, cold wet clothes draped over her bent arm. "Be sure to tell me or Nurse Sarah if dem headaches or dizzy spells return, y'hear?"

Helping him to bed as if he were a child, she hovered over his frail frame – corpulent arms sagging, paunchy neck strained against her starched white collar. She fluffed the pillow, tucked the sheets, and gently kissed his forehead.

"Isa, you fat."

"I prefer de term *pleasin'ly plump*," she said, a little defensively. "But I hear ya, honey. Diet starts Monday," she sighed. "And guess what? You senile." She bent, and whispered in his ear, "Life's a bitch for us bofe."

Back out the door again.

Stone stared blankly as the squall continued to blur the landscape, lightning flashing every few seconds like artillery fire. No art hour for the rest of the weekend, maybe all week if the *Herald* weather column held true.

Drapes drawn, the room was dark and serene, textured by the buzz of an oscillating fan and the sweet sounds of a Victrola playing "Davenport Blues" down the hall.

The old man shut his tired eyes and pictured his boyhood home, a magnificent manor between Jeanerette and Thibodaux in the St. Mary Parish: oak allies, white-columned galleries, and lavish parties. An era long gone by.

Several moments passed. His breathing gradually slowed.

The atmosphere turned icy as a subtle vapor wafted with each shallow exhale. Then, in one final act, he rose and reached to the ceiling. His hands clutched empty air as if he saw something no one else could, and fell gently back, lifeless. With hazy definition, like looking through dissipating swamp fog, the spectral image of three women in period gowns materialized before him: one, matronly; one, a radiant beauty; and one, a small child with corn silk pigtails. All four grabbed hands, and walked straight through the wall in a wisp.

Moments later, Onyx returned with a flourish, wielding paint tubes and a fistful of brushes. Flipping the lights, she cried, "Looky here, honey, found yer... honey...?"

No reply. The room felt palpably vacant. He had a disconcerting bluish-gray tinge to his skin. Beneath the sheet, his abdomen was as still as a plank, no rise or fall for *10 Mississippis.* Her lip quivered as she gripped a wrist and found no pulse, then pulled the covers over his head and crossed herself.

The guardian of the greatest secret in U.S. history was dead.

Van Percy had her hands full with 50 beds. She instructed the trustworthy aide to remove Stone's personal items, alert the coroner, and ready the room for the next. It was Robinson's last duty of the day. Not that Van Percy was uncaring, but this was a busy facility with a laundry list of patients, all requesting privacy.

With no known will or next of kin to notify, Onyx was tasked with preparing the confines. In doing so, her foot clipped an unassuming box under the bed. Navy blue, it was held together with a thin elastic chord tied around the top. She pulled the string, lifted the lid, and uncovered several items: a plaid-rimmed Scotsman's cap, a framed photo of a bride and groom (*must be Stone*, she saw a resemblance), a combination lock, a bag of salt and pepper hair clippings, and a diary titled *Bounty for Booth* – hand-scribed in a gradient of ink, faded to fresh. In addition, she found the unfinished likeness of none other than John Wilkes Booth, never having noticed this one before, at least, not at art hour.

Freeing the diary, Onyx was careful not to drop additional loose-leaf pages wedged between the entries. Countless addendums and afterthoughts were scrawled on every blank surface. Some were lucid, and many, muddled. Most were undated, written at random moments throughout his life. The entire mess was bound by rubber bands that snapped at the furst tug, brittle from heat and age.

Van Percy eased in. "Did you telephone for an ambulance?" Her eyes were bloodshot and weary, her typically taught bun now a disheveled bird's nest.

"Yes, dey on de way."

"Good. I've been frantic," Sarah prattled. Her gaze narrowed to the shrouded corpse.

"I'm sorry, Onyx. I know you were fond of him."

"Thanks," she sniffed, and laughed through tears. "Y'ole fool. You in a betta' place." *Polite for, dead and gone, never coming back.*

She casually concealed the manuscript behind her wide buttocks. Van Percy cracked a curious smile, then shot down the hall at a clip. Room 118 was whining for a bedpan.

When she opened the cover, a discolored cocktail napkin fell to Robinson's feet, emblazoned with the moniker, "Palace Hotel, San Francisco." She bent to retrieve it, grimacing as she rose back onto swollen, aching ankles. The portly nurse had a history of high blood pressure and diabetes. "Diet starts Monday, Mr. Stone. I promise." Her empty, ongoing pledge.

The wall clock ticked towards five. It was the end of a draining shift, and the start of a long, wet weekend. She placed the journal back in its vault and secured the cord, then tossed the whole box into a satchel, snapped the clasp, and threw it over her shoulder. She then slipped the Booth painting inside a pillowcase, and took one last look back. "Rest in peace, sugar," she forced a tired smile. "Your secrets are safe."

CHAPTER ONE

STONE'S MEMOIR
Bayou Teche, Louisiana, 1852

Being a rascal would make me famous. Or get me killed. Or both. The world was full of rascals, reckon I ain't no exception. Always had my own version of things, a tad dramatic with a dash of cayenne. In this here story, I ain't a-gonna dwell on historicity, claim no authority. That's for textbooks. But I'll stick you smack-dab in my boots and speak the truth, as I experienced it. You can take it or leave it.

The name's Jeremy Gabrick Stone. Don't never call me Jeremy, call me Gabe. No more than 10, I's clever, curious, and always in and out of the skillet. Pap said I come to live out loud, like my mama. She died birthing me, so's I don't know firsthand, just stories. I do

1

know she was loved and missed something power-ful. Pap blamed me for killing her, but hell, I's only a newborn. No more my fault than the negro baby's for being birthed dark-skinned. Folks don't think ratio-nal like that, I guess. That's why they's such pain and suffering.

I woke one oppressive Louisiana night – way be-fore waking up time – to the faint smell of smoke. Parting the mosquito drape, I tumbled from bed and leaned out a second story window. The air was as still as a possum, with that just-finished-rainin' feel. The buttery moon was blurred by twisted ribbons of ashy plumes, rising a million miles up from yonder treetops of Vermilion Bay.

Them spooks was back!

I fished for trousers amongst the surrounding clut-ter (Pap said I's a big ole slob, and probably had a point). Then I fetched the dummy I fashioned from a burlap sack stuffed with shirts and shit, and shoved it beneath the covers to look like I's sleeping away. Told you I's a rascal.

Nimbly tossing one bare foot over the sill, then t'other, I slithered down the trellis like some kind of snake or something. Vanished into the still dark of night. I'd done this before, tons of times. Reach-ing the bottom, the moist grass cooled me as I scam-pered along the creekside trail. My brow beaded with sweat almost instantly, as I carved a path through the heat and humidity. Viscous mush squished be-twixt my toes, traversing the swampy corridor. They's reeds and thicket head-high, all around me. Closer I got, the more I slowed, stealthily avoiding detection.

Who knows what them spooks was capable of doing if'n they seen me. I called them spooks not because they's black (reckon that'd be wrong), but on account of they's all covered in blood, or war paint – like ab-origine head-hunters and suchlike.

I'd come about two miles, now just 30 yards from a raging fire that seemed to be the center of atten-tion. Looked like mostly coloreds, except this one lady leading the ceremony, she was Creole. I allow the rest was runaway slaves. They held torches and danced in circles, cavorting and a-chanting the most peculiar phrases. They's bottles clustered all around, filled with I don't know what. A big X was drawed in the dirt, covered with flaming sticks and branches like a fu-neral pyre. Bunch of little dolls tossed on top, burning in effigy. Got the feeling them dolls represented white men, maybe local growers. I recognized some of the names they's shouting. "Moore, Brandeis, Richardson, Stone!" Now I's terrified. That meant me! Well, Pap and Granddad, anyhow. My heart was a-hammering, and I's shaking something fierce.

They'd torch a doll, and then holler the name as if to say, "Screw you, ya miserable massa. Y'all can fry in hell!" Couldn't rightly blame them.

Land, I should be in bed, safe and asleep. Then I seen sights I still ain't forgot. My eyes was drawn to that one woman, the Creole hostess with the gown all torn to shreds, feathers around her wrists and belly. She wore a turban, and when she unraveled the cloth, a bunch of black snakes came spilling out the bottom! They's snakes in her hands, too, and beads. She'd holler some-thing, and the rest would repeat it. She'd sing a line, and they'd answer in kind, like them Catholic Mass' Pap dragged me to.

Though perspiring and sweat-soaked like I'd spiked fever, I's actually chilled by what I witnessed. Them spooks was snapping necks and ripping the heads right off some roosters with they teeth! I'll be dad-fetched if them chickens ain't even putting up a fuss, like they's hypnotized or something.

A twig snapped. I prayed it was an animal. I'd have been okay with that, I s'pose. But as it turned out, a child spook done snuck up face-to-face, staring me right in the eyeballs, chicken bone shoved clean through his nose, in one nostril and out t'other! Swarthy little sucker, all buck naked, painted with blood like the rest. Needless to say, I turned tail and took off fast as feet could carry a fool...like shit through a goose! He hollered, but I ain't stopped until I seen the outline of our house. I made muddy prints up the trellis, through the window, and I's finally safely under covers. Don't think Pap ain't noticed come sun-up, neither. He beat my bare behind with a belt like I's a disobedient slave. I opened my mouth to cry, but nothing come out. Probably better, as I ain't interested in giving him the satisfaction. Couldn't sit comfortable for days. Lawd, how that blistered! I s'pose that's why them slaves wailed so when they get they lashes. Only, blacks is thrashed with whips, different animal entirely.

By and by, Pap gave me more chores and homework, saying I needed extra schooling since I talked like a darkie. I admit speaking uneducated for a long while, even though Pap – or "Father," as he insisted I call him in front of people – had a scientific tutor lady come learn me all kinds of things, including proper English. But I spent most of my time around slaves and Creoles, so's that was the talking I's comfortable with. I'd speak a tad more regular down the road.

I knew I ain't no lowbred, being a white of privilege, but if folks heard my thoughts, they'd likely lynch me from the nearest cottonwood. I didn't understand the way things was with the coloreds and all. Looky here, I played with they kids, and found them no different in the heads and hearts than the rest of us. Just the skin. Sure, they was simple minded, but that's because it was a sin to read and write. They'd get punished something serious if they's caught learning. Can you imagine? I mean, blacks bled and wept when hurt, craved to love and be loved, laughed when they was being funny, and sang and danced with joy at the simple blessings. Just like me. And yet, Granddad, Pap, and Uncle Cal treated the *dogs* with more kindness. Always wanted to play a part in fixing things, just ain't sure how. Like I says, I's only 10.

First introduced to theatrical shenanigans at age 7, maybe 8, I spied the slave children on our plantation singing folk tunes, patting juba, and prancing about with reckless abandon. This made me chortle with delight. They's a brick fireplace in the servants' kitchen, and after supper, the youngins would take turns using the hearth for a stage. They play-acted the stories the elders passed along, emulating performances they heard about in New Orleans. They wore silly hats and did hilarious voice impressions. Ain't knowed it, but I'd watch for hours from the bushes by the window.

I always had a penchant for theatrics, putting on accents and such. But I's a natural artist, too. My bedroom was stacked with sketches and paintings of all kinds of subjects: manor houses with giant columns, George Washington and his minutemen from the American Revolution, even portraits of some of our slaves. A wide variety. I's way more interested in them things than boring ole school subjects like math, science, and so forth. Some said I's the best drawer and painter they ever knowed – so I s'pose if'n I combined the two interests, I'm best suited to design scenery. They don't get the applause, I reckon – scenic painters and the like – but I bet it made for a better show if'n the backgrounds were expert.

Most amusing and talented was an endearing little black kid named Griffin, roughly my same age, maybe younger. We was pals. He could sing on pitch, do flips, and turn cartwheels. Made comical voices, too: Mammy's, crotchety geezers, and whatnot. I never laughed so loud in all my days! I heard his lifeless corpse was found floating in the pond the slaves used to make bricks. That was long after I'd run off. Never knew how or why. Hope he ain't a victim of foul play. Granddad said Griffin was a sass-mouthed little smart-ass. Once, when Pap asked why he so short, Griffin replied, "T'ain't nobody's bidness but me and Jeeeezis." Then he genuflected, pounded his chest thrice, pointed skyward, and grinned from ear t'ear. We made it our secret code until the end of our days. I cried big ole gator drops when I heard he's dead. He was so gentle, trusting.

We played out back all the time. Hide and seek in the cane fields, mostly. Lawd, you could get lost in there. I remember once when the troughs was full of water after a great rain, Griffin done stepped right into a wasp's nest. Them buggers flew up his pant legs and stung him but good – hundred times, I reckon. He puffed up like a balloon. Got real, real sick, poor tyke. He was scared of water after that, even the knee-deep variety, but I knowed how to swim, so's he was safe... until I left, confound. Can't talk no more about it. Hurts too much to ponder.

In happier instances, I recall Griffin and me went to New Iberia on an outing to a lumber mill. He was chained to the other slaves, but I walked free beside him the whole time to keep him company. We talked, and whistled our way along. I worked it with Pap so's Griffin became my personal property once arrived, and the slaves were unbound. Blame ridiculous notion, ain't it? They's this celebration going on. Some kind of Independence Day, only it ain't even Fourth of July. They had a marching band, firecrackers, and red, white, and blue banners everywhere, draped over the buildings. Folks were firing guns and hollering, carrying on, singing "Hurrah, hurrah, Southern rights forever."

We wandered down a back alley into a tent. Griffin seemed to know right where to find it. Don't know how. The sign out front said, "Fortunes Told, 25¢." We held hands going in on account of it was so creepy: skulls, candles, giant playing cards with strange pictures on them, and such. After a minute or two, a woman entered and sat behind this great big glass ball. Her head and face was covered by a fancy handkerchief with moons and stars. As she wrapped her hands around the crystal, her nails clicked against the curvature. Them nails was as long as earthworms, only they's painted black and gold with some sort of pictures, like Egyptian symbols. She unwound the headdress, and a host of black snakes done toppled to her shoulders. It was her, the lady from the voodoo ritual! Only they wasn't snakes at all, just locks of hair all twisted and bound. Guess I's a trifle brought down, so's I told folks they's snakes, anyways.

"One quarter, please," she said, holding her palm out. I dug a coin from my pocket and sat on a low wooden stool with three wobbly legs. Griffin stood behind. I could see right up his nose. Damn if it don't look like he got a gap betwixt his nostrils, just like that child spook with the chicken bone! You don't reckon...? Nah, never mind. Can't be.

Anyhow, a quarter seemed steep for a bunch of nonesuch and make-believe. I mean, she could've told me anything (trust me, I done it all the time). Oh well, guess she had to earn her keep somehow. Spinning tales was as good a way as any.

"Queen Yvette is pleased you come," she uttered in thick Cajun. I could hear Griffin swallow hard. I shot him a quick glance, then front again to the witchy-lady. "I see de play of paradox," she continued, candle flames a-flickering in the glass. She's burning some sort of stinky-stick, too. My eyes stung me, but good. "Abundant joy, abundant grief. You from Dixie, yet you be North. Gray, yet blue. Betrothed, yet you wed another. You de restless rascal, always wriggling like a worm on a hook." She turned over more cards, rubbing the ball like they's a smudge or something? "Great bloodshed," she shook her head, solemnly. "De beastly beating spares your life."

She's as crazy as a rabid cur. Imagine, saved because I take a terrible licking? Don't make no sense.

"Now you be East, befriending brothers: one in favor, one in fury. You shock people with your art."

In a good way, I hoped.

"Also aligned with de burdened giant, you introduce mustache to beard for an epic clash. Only in death can come life. Shame de girls don't survive to see…" Long, troubling pause.

Witchy-witch done dropped the cards, and shoved back from the ball, face all screwy like she's sucking lemons and sugarcane simultaneous. "Enough," she proclaimed. "Queen Yvette has seen enough. Now go." She pointed stiff-arm to the slit in the canvas.

That's it? I thought, ducking through the crease, back into the blinding sun. That's all I get for my money? Good thing they's plenty more where that came from. What was it she was seeing? T'weren't nothing in that glass ball that I could detect. In my estimation, she seen this wealthy whitey sitting there and stuck it to me good. *Mercy sakes. Making monkeyshines for a living!* My scheming mind churned with all kinds of possibilities. I long dreamed of earning my fortune self-sufficient, without the need for slave sweat. This could be the ticket.

"You undastanz what she tells ya?" Griffin tugged on my sleeve. "All dat 'bout headin' noth, lovin' somebody ain't yo wife – den east, gettin' tween a family feud? Seem fah-fetched."

"Don't it? Well, no matter, we seen stuff we ain't never seen today. Met a real live witch, ain't even turned us into toads!" I nudged him with my boney elbow. Griffin got bug-eyed, then finally caught on and joined me in a guffaw through the slit in them big buck teeth. "Better than slavin' fourteen hours in the fields," I reminded him. "Stooped at the waist, trudgin' through the stalks and quagmire. Blazin' heat makin' leather outta yer skin."

"Sho' 'nuff," Griffin agreed.

The fortune-teller had peered deep, collecting details that revealed not only my fate, but the fate of the whole nation. The following day, she took down her lean-to and ventured southwest, far from the thunderclouds a-gathering beyond the horizon. I often thought of that woman. She was mighty accurate with her predictions, like shooting an apple at a hundred paces.

The 1850s, though chockfull of horrors that afflicted us all, was a time of grace and grandeur in the South. Our fathers and sons were safely doing they business; our soil, still unstained; our columned manors, erect, and untouched. She'd somehow caught a glimpse of the impending storm, something even voodoo can't fix. Only thing was to hold on tight, and ride it out.

By and by, I realized how good I had it. Yup, we should live life backwards to appreciate the thing proper. Oh, they's times I detested for certain, but all in all, them pollywog years was mostly simple pleasures, innocence, and high adventure.

CHAPTER TWO

END OF ALL INNOCENCE

It was a hot, moist, midsummer's eve – July 21, 1858. I'll never forget. Odd what you recall in life and what you can't. No matter, I'm right about this'n. The crickets and bullfrogs were all warmed up for an overture. Guess I was a man now. Almost 16, I sprouted to five-foot nine and refined my phraseology (tried to anyway). Father still refused to recognize that I'd swapped the backwoods talk for a more respectable drawl. Funny thing about that, I spoke exactly like he spoke. Where'd Pap come off being so critical? We were from Saint Charles, Missouri, after all. Perfectly natural for them parts. T'weren't until I's six or so we came south to the bayou on a grand paddle wheeler. Oh, how I love them riverboats. Just thinking out loud...

Upon my return from the livery, I clopped along and turned the corner to the manor. It was a splendid structure, yet simple, replete with eight towering brick-between-post Doric columns, smoothed over with plaster stretching two stories high, splitting a second story gallery wrapped halfway around the exterior. There was over 40 acres of sugarcane crop, with smaller sections of rice, indigo, and corn, lined with trees and outlying slave cabins. The aforementioned pool, originally dug to provide water and clay for bricks, was now used to irrigate fields and cool the home.

There was much to love about living in the deep South: the culture, the genteel ways. But the dark side had grown ever-present – the mosquitos and the diseases they carried (we'd lost a number of blacks that year to illness). Then they's the oppressive temperatures, and worst of all, the evils of greed and slave ownership. I'd made even better friends with them coloreds, cringing in horror when I seen the whippings and other ghastly goings-on. One day, I took to wandering over to Culpepper Grove, just a hop, skip and a jump. I came upon two negros dangling from ropes, all bloody in the crotch. They been lynched for harassing a farmer's daughter. They's notes pinned to the trousers saying, "Castrated for kissing a white," and "Lost my pecker spreading the clap." Necks squeezed tight, heads flopped sideways, limp like ragdolls. Made my spirit sink. A couple of pasty-face rednecks looked on with big ole smirks. I wanted to blast them smiles right off with Pap's Springfield musket, if'n I had it with me.

I loathed them hard-hearted sumbitches, probably as much as they did the two poor fellas, hanging there like fowl in a meat shop window. There was no future for the blacks, no voice, nor hope. On occasion, I passed the auctions. There I witnessed unimaginable atrocities: slaves stripped down naked to show a history of obedience (less scars meant better behavior), and grown men made to leap and dance like monkeys to display endurance and value. They were poked and prodded such as a butcher inspects the day's delivery. I heard there were nearly 31 million inhabitants in this land, and one in seven was owned by another man. America's dirty addiction. Read somewheres that even founding father Thomas Jefferson hisself said, "It was like holding a wolf by the ears; you hated to do it, but you daren't let go." My word, the way we humans treat one another.

On a moonless Wednesday evening, the air was suddenly alive with offensive, foul language, gradually a-growing in volume and intensity. Windows were open due to the dreadful heat, and I stood with my ear pressed against the parlor wall, listening to Pap and Granddad quarrel on the porch. Angry accusations sung loud and clear above the bullfrogs and crickets.

"I'll remind you that I am master here. My house, my rules."

"But why stripe him so?" Father protested, brim-full of piss and passion. "He's one of my very best slaves. Now he'll be no goddamn good for weeks, ya durn leatherhead."

"Don't curse me, kid. I'm warnin' you. That nigga stole---"

"Lester don't steal. Isa gave him the extra food." Isa Brown was Griffin's momma, caretaker of the master's quarters. She was like an auntie, pretty near had the run of the place.

"Then she embezzled, as well," Granddad accused. "How long, Lawd only knows. Cash box was ajar. Fifty dollars gone missin'."

My stomach was knotty as a pine.

"Isa had access," the ole tyrant continued to collect venom. "She'll be punished powerful. Dozen lashes 'cross the back and face."

"No...not the face!" I pleaded, slipping past the foyer, out the door, and down the steps, voicing my contempt every step of the way. This was an unbearable notion. Isa helped raise me. I loved them sweet, unblemished cheeks. "We blinded a slave once with just such a floggin', 'member?" No response. "The Lawd despises you for this," I bellowed, full throat, "and so do I!"

"Dishonor!" he roared. My opinion was never welcomed. "This Lawd of whom you speak calls for obedience. I know my scripture, boy. I don't see *your* sorry little ass in that pew on Sunday – which raises another point we ain't yet remedied. Now either you're with me, or agins' me."

"So be it. I's agins' ya, cussed blame imp! Soddy quim of a screw devil!" I cursed him in the coon slang that Griffin taught me, and when I's finished spewing all the filth I could conjure, I expectorated, punctuating my oration on his brand new boots. Uncharted territory for sure. I let out down the path, then froze dead in my tracks and turned around, a-digging my own grave. "Looky here," says I, fanning half-circle with open palms. "All this abundance compared to the scarcity in them folks' lives. As if we can't spare some extra meat and bread for a desperate man and his kin. Shame on you, sir!" I pointed a stiff index finger right in his face. He grabbed and squeezed the sap out of it – then let go. I expected an onslaught. Reckon he could've licked me good, four ways to Friday, but he ain't. Got a slow, seething build up instead. Almost worse.

"How dare you? I am a man. A just, hard-workin' man. Me! That nigga's no better than the mangy mutt in the road." I reckon the only way to justify slavery was to make them less than human. "Conform your thinkin' boy, or skedaddle north, where such notions are tolerated.

Now I's foaming at the mouth. "It's the *just* who tolerate the likes of *you*." I returned fire, tensions reaching a climax. I chased that jackass indoors, just in time to witness Uncle Cal and some rednecks dragging Isa away as she belted cries of consternation. They tore her blouse clean off, exposing a pair of bulbous brown globes. She instinctively cupped them with her hands, but they outmuscled her and bound her wrists behind with a cord. A quick semi-circle formed. Uncle Cal cocked his arm. Collective inhale. Then... *crack*! The whip released its venom on her bare back as she shrieked, begging for mercy. *Crack!* Another gut-wrenching scream. Then another, and another. Twelve total.

I absorbed every sight, every sound.

The other wrongdoer, Lester, was forced to witness the whole thing, knowing he's next. Poor man wriggled and thrashed under rope restraints and a two-man stronghold, wincing with each bloody lash. The other slaves were hiding in terror. We whites watched while they flipped Isa face-forward. Her back been filleted open like a catfish. Crimson streams stained the ground until they's practically puddles. Thank God the whip was mercifully tossed aside for the time being.

Next round: open, bare hand to the face.

Griffin came a-running, shrieking in fear for his momma's life. He was quickly scooped up by his cousin, Clemmie, and hid in the smokehouse.

That was it. No more. I darted down the central hall and out the front door to a bridled rig teamed with horses, plugging my ears best I could. As I mounted the wagon, muffled cries crammed the thick evening air. *Please, almighty God, save that po' woman's life.* I snapped the reins, kicking up dust clouds, and took flight down the narrow alley of oaks.

Granddad chased after me, but stopped at the steps. "Where you goin', ya foolish little ingrate?" The words stung me. "Senseless little shit!" I remember Granddad's wrath like it was yesterday. "You'll never amount to nuthin'," the bastard trumpeted. Adrenaline coursed through my every organ and limb – wind in my face, spokes a-spinning like they's coming right off the axles.

Life as I knew it dissolved behind me. *Finally, the sweet smell of freedom without the burden of family finances!* Like ole Lucifer hisself was hot on my heels, I never looked back.

Don't rightly recall when it struck me, daybreak maybe? My stomach rumbled for Isa's heavenly tatercakes and grits breakfast. Then again come supper, I's craving her savory crawfish jambalaya. But surely she weren't cooking today, or any day in the foreseeable future. Hell, I ain't even certain she survived the night. My appetite soured considerable pondering the brutality she'd faced. I had a dark secret to confess, a secret that might've changed the course of history if'n I'd acted different. See, I was the one who convinced Isa to sneak the extra food. She refused time and again, but I insisted. I's also the thief who stole from the cash box. Reckoned I's owed it for all them tongue lashings and emotional abuse. Wouldn't blame you for hating me, hated myself for what I done, or didn't do. Sometimes, folks do stupid shit. Shoulda fessed up, I knowed. Shoulda intervened with a fury, and jumped in the way of that whip, but I didn't. Wished a million times it was a dream, but it ain't. I'd die of shame if'n I dwelled on it. Alrighty then, I've said my peace. God alone be my judge.

Now then, my intent was to cut all ties, no debts or encumbrances. But right off, I realized I'd stole the family rig. I promised myself to pay it back when the opportunity arose. I had nary a possession to my name, 'cept the clothes on my back, the rig, a blanket, a shovel, and a coil of rope. Should've thunk it through a smidge more, but in my moment of destiny, my fate unfurled.

Unsure if'n I'd been followed, I hastened the pace, looking to reach Bayou Goula by nightfall. The team was depleted and hungry. I'd spent the better part of 24 hours heading northeast to the Mississippi River. A hundred mile stretch of passable road meandered beside the banks. Easiest route. I'd venture into Arkansas, then on up through Missouri, my birth state.

Cloud cover provided cooler conditions overnight, on into late morning. In spite of my wickedness, I sensed God had an eye on me. His love proved purer than any of my calamities.

Now, I best have a proper plan. Top priority was escaping. But where? More in search of a life than a specific destination, it would be weeks, maybe months before I arrived in the Northern territories. The notion sprung to visit a most prosperous gentleman named John Randolph. He had the largest sugarcane operation I knew of – one of the true dynasties of the South. We acquainted whilst I'd accompanied Pap to an industry meeting in New Orleans when I's about 11. Randolph said he was gonna build this place called Nottoway. (We all had names for our homes; ours was Cypress.) He extended an open invitation. Claimed you could fit over a half-dozen normal manor houses inside. Based on his description, I had to see it with my own two eyes.

T'was common coin he'd been a cotton planter turned sugarcane magnate. Folks called him "Captain of Industry" because of his position and stature. I said I's done with greed and opulence, but why not go out with a bang?

The mammoth white edifice was visible for miles. Just in time, too – the horses needed relief. Its towering roofline topped the surrounding trees. I thought for a

minute I'd reached the Executive Mansion in Washington, only that'd be shortchanging this place, a dad-burn
castle! Looked sort of Italian in design, different from
the Greek-Revival style of most plantation structures.
I counted 21 squarish columns supporting two main
stories, with ornamental iron-railed galleries on both
floors. They's a brick-supported basement level, too.
Reckoned 50 or 60 rooms, and some 200 windows. The
closer I got, the more I shrunk in its shadow. In a word:
grandiose.

My arrival was recognized as the second-story gallery doors swung wide to an assembly of gals, filling
the thrust section of porch to capacity, all prim and
proper like they was on display. I tied the team to a
fencepost and announced myself. "Greetings ladies.
The name's Jeremy Gabrick Stone. Is your pap...uh,
father available?"

"Business or pleasure?" the eldest hollered down,
after a brief deliberation.

"Pleasure, I guess." No sense revealing my current
circumstances.

"Just a moment."

The younger ladies tittered before disappearing
back through double French doors. I made certain the
horses were secure, and then continued up the path
towards a pair of stately, curved granite steps. Felt like
I's meeting some kind of European monarch or something. Guess I was, in a sense.

Visible through large windows to my right was a
breathtaking grand ballroom, ornate as a wedding cake.
T'was white as bleached cotton, including the floor-
boards. Illusions of waltzing women and gentleman

filled my mind. I pictured lavish socials with music, laughter, and high spirits. This was the South y'always dream about.

"Good afternoon," a rather authoritative female spun me. "Awful presumptuous peerin' through windas before a proper welcome is extended."

"Sorry, ma'am."

"My name is Emily Randolph. To what do I owe the pleasure?" She extended a courteous paw.

I took her hand and bowed, nearly touching my forehead to her knuckles. This was the South, and politeness went a long way. "Jeremy Stone from Cypress Plantation in Bayou Teche."

"And what's your business, Mr. Stone?"

"Oh, nuthin' much. I knowed I come unannounced. Real sorry, but your husband and my father met in New Awlins a while back. He offered to show us your magnificent home. Happened to be passin' by, so's I thought I'd take him up on his offer."

"And where is the gentleman?"

"Oh, it's just me, ma'am."

"Very well, let me see if Mr. Randolph is at liberty."

In her absence, I soaked in as much of the 400 acres of highland as my eyes could swallow. To the front was an unobstructed look at the Mississippi, replete with passing steamboats and barges one would expect on the main waterway to the Gulf. To the sides, acre after acre of fruit trees, flowers, and gardens: roses, strawberries, vegetables. Plenty of shade, too, beneath an abundance of live oaks.

"Greetings, Master Stone. You made it," said Mr. Randolph in a soft, Southern dialect. "I'm only sorry your father was unable to accompany you." John Hampden Randolph was a clean-cut gentleman with wavy black hair and shiny shoes. Hospitable, assured. The son of a judge, he'd moved his family to Iberville Parish from Mississippi. He met and married Emily Jane Liddell, a woman of wealth, herself, with a substantial dowry of $20,000 and 20 slaves. They was raising 11 children. Eight were girls, many of whom I's just encountered on my approach.

"Please, do come in."

"Much obliged."

The entrance was sublime: elegantly appointed with soaring ceilings, and massive brass and crystal chandeliers. The white ballroom was to the right. I hoped to see it first, but was escorted to a gentleman's study on the left, instead. Being an artist, the filigreed crown moldings first caught my eye. They were arrestingly intricate, and ran the length of each 15-foot-high wall. One could only imagine the craftsmanship, patience, and expense!

"How's business?" he asked, straight away. "And how is Jeremiah Stone?" (That was my Pap.)

"Oh, uh, fine," I hemmed and hawed, noticing the fireplace had pipes (I's told for burning natural gas made right on property--- ain't no hogwash!). Anyhow, I'd come for food and a good night's rest, surely he needn't know my family dynamics.

"You were such a little shaver last I saw you. Fine young man, now. Helping manage the operation?"

"No, I..." An assortment of lies raced through my noggin. "I'm headed north to finishin' school," I blurted. There goes that blame tongue again. "Studyin' art and design."

"Oh yes, I remember now. I seem to recall you had an artistic flair from a very young age. I think your father showed me a rather sophisticated sketch of a riverboat you'd rendered. The architectural accuracy was uncanny. Glad to hear you've kept it up."

"Thank you, sir."

"Now then, finishing school. That's just fine. Which one?"

Oh boy, I thought to myself, *here we go.* "Uh...um, Minneapolis...Polytechnic."

"Minneapolis Polytechnic?"

All I could think of being under the gun.

He nodded, uncertain. "Sorry, I'm not familiar."

"Yes, well, it's new," I says with aplomb, praying he wouldn't press the matter.

"Bully, then. I sent my eldest to Academy in Cincinnati." He handed me a scholastic brochure. "Design you say? You know, Nottoway was built by Henry Howard, most revered builder in all of New Awlins. You two simply *must* meet. Perhaps I can arrange…"

"Oh uh, no, sir," I stammered, clearly up a tree. "Drawin', paintin', theatrical scenery, perhaps. Portraits, too." At least I'd sort of tumbled back down to the truth.

"Splendid. Come with me." I followed him through the entrance corridor, and into the glorious ballroom. "I wished this section to be pure white to showcase the beauty of my ladies," he said, peacock proud.

"Most magnificent sight I've ever seen," I offered, feeling like I'd entered the Pearly Gates.

Traversing the milky-white wood, I trotted like a high-stepping horse to ensure my boots ain't leaving scuffs. Isa always scolded me for dirtying her cleanly mopped floors.

"Look at this portrait, here." Randolph pointed to a fine rendition of his eldest daughter hanging above a glorious, hand-carved marble fireplace. "This was commissioned to announce my Ella to society. On first glance, it garnered the attention of Mr. Lovik Feltus of Natchez. They shall be married next year."

"Wonderful news. Congratulations."

"Yes, it is. Only, the artist has since returned to Paris. I'd intended to have one done for each of my daughters. Mary Augusta is 14. We shall announce her debut in the near future. Standard protocol – portrait first." He thought for a moment. "How would you like the opportunity to capture her on canvas?"

Job's mine, straight through the buttonhole? No other try-outers?

"Being a student," he advised, "I'd have to see a finished product first, of course."

"Of course." I choked on a clump of spittle.

"If it is to my satisfaction, I'll pay you handsomely. Say, one hundred dollars?"

A hundred! I'd build my own damn finishin' school! "Yes, I'd like that very much. Only..." and here's where I mighta overstepped, "I'd need lodgin' and a stipend for materials. Whether you end-up buyin' it, or not." Greed came natural to us Stones.

"Yes, of course. Now, any idea on a time frame?"

"I don't know, 10 days, tops?"

"Bully. Welcome to Nottoway." He firmly shook my hand, clapping my shoulder with the other. Just like that, I had work, accommodations, and true blue independence. Of course, as with everything, they's quandaries. Being homeschooled, t'weren't much opportunity to fraternize with the opposite gender. Oh, I had the occasional ecounter visiting town or attending neighboring socials, but nothing you'd call substancial. I'd seen bosoms, and bare behinds and such on naughty playing cards Pap brought back from Bourbon Street, but that was about the extent of it. Here I was, not only eating and sleeping under the same roof as eight lovely young ladies, but I's being paid to stare at one of them for a couple weeks, all day long, scrutinizing her delicate features. Granted, Mary was just 14, but she was the prettiest of all, if'n you asked me. I'd fallen prey to her beauty from square one. Weren't right letting personal feelings taint this moneymaking opportunity.

I commenced my project the following day, after a night of fascinating conversation and delicious roast beef. You know, I ain't barely needed to exit my chamber to empty my bowels, flush it away! I's used to a little porcelain commode box by the bed, but never a whole separate water closet! What a miracle of convenience. T'was modern America, invading rural Louisiana.

Personal hygiene aside, I'd done a slew of portraits for fun, but never like this. To say I was nervous was like calling the mighty Mississippi a creek.

"Can't wait to see it, Jeremy," my subject chirped, tucking her chin all pinch-lipped, drawling out the side of her mouth so as not to wreck the pose. "How long you been painting?"

"Oh, professionally, a few years." The lie tripped ever-so-lightly off my tongue. "By the way, please call me Gabe."

"All right, Gabe," she squeezed the words out one side again.

"You can talk regular," I giggled. "I'm workin' on your hair at the moment." Soft, silkybrown tresses pulled tight in a bun, with just a few rogue locks cascading to her delicate shoulders. A magnolia blossom was pinned above her left ear. Lovely. Her alabaster skin was smooth, and them big brown eyes was nearly black – peering right through to my very soul.

"Besides painting, what do you fancy?" she inquired.

"Oh, I don't know, dramatic arts, I s'pose."

"Me, too!" she livened. "Daddy and Ella saw Edwin Booth in *Hamlet* at the St. Charles Theatre in New Orleans. He was a triumph, they claim. Patrons showered him with crowns of laurel and sacks of gold like an emperor."

Edwin Booth was the most revered actor of the day, son of the legendary thespian Junius Brutus Booth, brother to lesser known, but wildly popular matinee idol, John Wilkes.

"Fine!" I said with genuine enthusiasm. "I heard of them Booths. They's theatrical royalty. I reckon Junius died a while back, but I hear the sons picked right up where he left off. Why, I'd give my left testic..." I urgently refrained, plumb forgetting my manners. "I'd give *anything* to see one of their productions."

"Ask daddy about it, he said Edwin Booth was most captivating. J.B. Wilkes – that's how the other brother is known in the Playbills – is rumored to be coming to New Orleans. Maybe we..."

"Maybe we...what?" I asked knowingly. I could tell she's fished-in by my boyish charms.

"Never mind. Say, when we're done here, may I escort you around the mansion?" Her voice was a most pleasingly proper one. "We have a music room and a bowling alley..."

"Bowlin' alley!" I bellowed, nearly dropping my brush. I'd barely moved beyond the hot and cold running water, gas fireplaces, and flushing chamber pots. "I would like that," I exclaimed, mixing ochre and sienna, rendering the highlights in her tresses, now bathed with afternoon sun. I fantasized about living in this here utopian enclave. Taking walks in the gardens, sipping juleps on the veranda, watching paddle wheelers ease by. It was all so intoxicating. I confess I had notions of sampling Mary's affections – holding hands, sneaking kisses behind the rose bushes. Probably not the smartest idea, but t'ain't no crime, neither. They's something about painting a pretty gal that makes you just, well, become involved, like an actor fancying his leading lady in a theatrical production. Hard to separate fact from fiction. That's the way of it, anyhow.

My imagination ran rampant. I could picture myself as a son-in-law, setting up a permanent art studio, making money hand over fist painting portraits for all the neighbors. I'd learn to hunt, bowl with the brothers, and smoke them big ole Cubans after dinner in the men's study. Perhaps I'd even sample a nip of brandy.

Got to studying how I'd made this place a paradise in my head. *Even the slaves were happy here*, I daydreamed, all the while a-whistling and painting away. Surely, the fanciful notions would only bring me grief.

I let out a magnificent moan as I unbuttoned my trousers and flopped down on the bed, patting my convex midriff. That evening's dinner was one of the finest meals I could ever remember: blackened catfish, sweet potatoes, collard greens, cornbread muffins with a drizzle of honey, and apple crisp with a small slice of cheese melted on top for dessert. Nary a detail had gone neglected. I ain't knowed who cooked it, probably a slew of slaves helped, but my compliments went out to the whole lot. Made me think of Isa. Had I done right leaving her? Should I return to check on things and protect the nanny I'd grown to love? Sometimes beatings turned into murders. Frightful, but true. No, says I, my decision was final. Reckon I'd eventually get over the memory of the beatings, but the sight of them deep, permanent stripes would haunt me. No amount of worry would change that. I couldn't feel bad enough to remove a single wound. Not a one.

Strange how Nottoway had over 500 slaves, yet things seemed so peaceful, so calm. Not that I was rethinking my stand on the slavery issue, but there was a vast range of experiences from plantation to plantation, based on the temperments of the folks involved. They's evil owners and nice ones, t'weren't so black and white. Many shades of gray.

I addressed the mirror over the washbasin. My long, cornsilk hair practically covered my eyes. Always liked my steel blue eyes. Is that strange to say about your own puss? Some parts weren't so pleasing – my ears was a pinch of the stick out variety – but I's thankful for my eyes and nose, 'cept for the smudge of paint I'd neglected to wipe, smeared at the tip. (No wonder them gals kept giggling in my general direction, all through vittles.) Looking at myself, I seen a man standing there. How'd that happen? I used to be a boy without a worry or care, surrounded by folks that loved me. Least I thought so. In fact, many a care and concern came a-creeping in my mind that particular evening.

Main supper table topic was the increased likelihood of secession, and the muttering thunder of a threatening war. Tensions between North and South had growed ever intensified. Mr. Randolph was opposed to it. "We could never emerge victorious against a monstrous, mechanized North," he insisted. The boys, on the other hand, seemed almost eager to take their aggressions to the battlefield, teach them Yanks to mind they business. I just sat and nodded. What if war did break out? Where would my loyalties lie? My roots were Southern, but my convictions were decidedly Northern. This family exemplified all that was gracious about Dixie. How could I share my eagerness to head towards territory that better suited my ideals?

My mind swirled with conflict.

Then they's Mary sitting over there. Dad-fetch if she don't look more endearing with each stolen glance. I saw her sneaking looks at me, too, in my periphery. I'd better hurry and complete this durn portrait, collect my keep, and move along. I had no business complicating things for her, nor me. I's a loner with no ties, headed North. Them Randolphs was different; they was the South personified. So much invested, so much to lose. Before bed, I prayed something powerful that everything would work out for the best. For all us folks, and the country I loved.

❧

Day 12 commenced to a hint of sunrise, and the cry of a peacock. Most plantations had them. Sounded a natural reveille to welcome the dawn, a shrill tone for such an exquisite creature. His tail feathers were an intricate work of God. All them other birds must've been envious. A large variety of winged critters called Nottoway home – there were flocks of all kinds on the grass, grazing on a breakfast of fresh seeds and worms. Mr. Randolph loved the abundance of local fowl. He even had a collection of original art prints from the famous naturalist, John James Audubon. I marveled over them one night after dinner, joining Mr. Randolph in a smoke. My tongue tasted like leather for days, sort of erasing the notion of making a nightly habit of it.

A terrific electrical storm had rolled through during the bewitching hours, dropping buckets. I listened wide-eyed as the thunder literally joggled the joint; real sockdolagers that prompted tiny footsteps to seek sanctuary in the master suite.

With a still-rising sun, I stood a-gazing down from the window overlooking an outside kitchen, built separate from the main structure in case of fire. A servant was carrying a whole hog worth of ham and smoked sausage, and John Jr. (a son my age) toted a mountainous skillet of hash towards the house. The savory aroma hung thick in the morning air. Seems he was up early in preparation for a day of hunting. Some of the youngins must've awakened, as well. Individual bell tones jingled in their chambers, calling for assistance getting dressed. Each had their own distinct ring, so's the help could tell them apart. Right clever system.

I threw on my new clothes, graciously donated by one of the boys, Moses. Felt strange wearing hand-me-downs, weren't no end to my airs. I's an only child with plenty of money for new clothes (articles that may or may not still be hanging in my bedroom closet). I ain't never had cause to wear another man's duds. I admit to a moment of homesickness for my old room, my things, but only for a moment, mind you.

John and Moses were heading into the woods for deer, maybe even bear. I wished I was going, but I had business to complete. The portrait was nearly finished, most likely my last day. After gobbling the last of the hash – best in the whole of Louisiana – I sat alone in my own world, putting final touches on the intricate lace collar of Mary's frock.

"I do declare, this is exquisite," she whispered over my right shoulder. She'd snuck up in silence. "Father will love it. I know I do." She placed her delicate hand on my back, sending a warm current through me like smooth, Tennessee whiskey.

"Thank you," my voice wavered. "Don't know if it does you justice, but I'm pretty pleased with the result." Knowing this painting was to be presented to suitors, a twinge of envy arose, as did a randy tent in my trousers, different from being piss-proud with a morning mast. "I hope it serves you, Mary, as it did Ella," I said. "You certainly deserve the happiness she has found." My tone was awash with ulterior motives.

Disappointed, she pouted. "Don't you like me, Gabe? I know I like you." She walked her fingers up my arm, and pressed the tip of my nose like a button. "Boop," she said, in a flirtatious way.

"Well, yes, but..."

Our eyes locked. I felt pulled like a magnet towards her rose-petal lips. Durn my undirected ways! "Mary, here's the thing, I'm a restless rascal. Always wrigglin' like a worm on..."

She closed her peepers and puckered. I wanted so badly to taste the nectar of her sweet mouth. There'd been a kiss wafting in the air betwixt us for days. In a moment of divine clarity, I veered starboard and dropped a peck gently on her cheek, of my own volition. Timing was everything, and twitterpated or not, it was my time to git. Ain't right cajoling with the gal I's supposed to be helping find a respectable mate. I judged my intentions was impure, considering. Blast it all to Hades, if I weren't becoming honorable.

Draped in a black velvet cover, the portrait was finally unveiled. Them Randolphs were tickled to death, the whole congregation.

"No fair, where's mine?"

"Looks exactly like her."

"Paint me next!"

Best I ever done, if I do say so myself. Mary was a beauty, and I'd achieved a most flattering likeness. Mr. Randolph counted off five crisp twenties in my palm, offering a final, firm shake. "That ought to cover it." This time, it was I who felt like a captain of industry, full of piss and vinegar. One hundred dollars may as well been a million in my clammy clutch.

"Won't ya favor us by stayin'?" Mrs. Randolph offered.

"We've planned a grand garden party for next weekend," John added. "There'll be several suitors in attendance, as well as numerous neighboring families. Perhaps you'll secure some additional commissions?"

"Yes, will you?" Mary urged, batting them lashes all butterfly-like. Firmly resolute, I declined. Fine as them two weeks was, I knew I couldn't stay. Didn't trust myself.

"Good luck to you, Gabe." Mr. Randolph smiled and fetched a map that would surely benefit me on my long journey. "Say hello to the boys at, what was it now, Minneapolis Poly?" Somehow, I knowed he ain't buying it, and yet he'd given me the break I sorely needed, no hassle. A kind and generous man.

So, let's tally it up. On the debit side, the whole chapter's predicated on a lie, and I nearly let my devil-ish whims get the best of me. On the credit side, I fattened my billfold (and waistline) considerable, proved my worth with an honest job well-done, and left things alone with the daughter. Figured I's surely come out on top.

Silent thanks to heaven for weighing in on it.

With warm farewells (especially from Mary, more mature than her years), I threw a canvas sack of clothes and provisions onto the buggy, and took one last look at Nottoway. As I ambled down the dirt path to the levee, Mary blew a kiss that hit my heart, dead center like a bullseye. Most gals would've been troubled at the outcome of our unrealized romance, but not she. Raised right by exemplary parents, this woman was the very fabric of Dixie, as were all them folks. Yessir, no finer family in the United States than the Randolphs.

As for me and my *urges*, it'd have to wait a while. Oh, I retained my irrepressible rascality, no doubt. Just made a good decision to lay off this time. Guess they's hope for us all.

CHAPTER THREE

SEPTEMBER, 1859

With the sun high on the horizon, my pits were spritzing powerful, throwing malodorous smells back out to the atmosphere. You knowed you stink when you can smell yersself. Good thing Mary ain't around. Curious how one day you be this little hairless, scrawny child, folks doing everything for you – wiping your dirty face, cleaning your messes, cutting up your vittles and such. Then, all of a sudden, you this sweaty, stinky, hair in the pits and pecker...man. Good land, gotta find food, a house, money, and a wife. I allow it's just too much for a feller. S'pose that's why ya only live a day at a time. Thinking out loud again...

I welcomed them speckled stars come nightfall. They meant relief. Daytime temperatures was taking a toll, mercury hitting the high 90s by 10 in the morning.

With a generous roll of greenbacks, I had occasional accommodations and more than my share of meals from city diners. Places advertising "Good ole Home Cookin'." You know, the entire plate's golden brown because it's all been deep-fried. Costs seven cents, comes with what they call pie a-la-mode-ee. (That's fancy French for *includes a lump of vanilla ice cream.*) Food seemed to change a tetch as I continued. I loved the culinary variety, once you got beneath the standard beige coating. S'pose I weren't no skinny, Southern stick of a lad no more for certain. Eating was something I's fairly adept at.

Isa was a downright admirable cook, always at my beck and call. She'd make a blame cow pie mouth-watering if'n it's doused in her special gravy, her secret blend of herbs and spices. Told her I's gonna open up a restaurant right there at Cypress, charge a quarter per plate. One memorable November harvest, she prepared a feast for the slaves made only of items found on our property: raccoon, roasted goat, wild Tom turkey (including the balls!), fried tomatoes, and okra. She done captured, kilt, and cooked it all on her lonesome. She ain't even squeamish about chopping the heads off. I ate two dinners that day, preferring the slave version to the traditional one we had in the formal dining room. Took a powerful long nap afterwards. Something about turkey makes you wanna snooze, even if it's smack dab in the middle of day. I generally dislike daytime naps. I always feel like a lifeless sack of cornmeal when I wake – like I can't move, like I been tarred and glued to the bed. Yup, eating the turkey is the best part, I allow. Especially the way Isa done it. Don't mean to sound like cooking's the only thing she's good at. Isa was a dear, dear friend with a rich philosophy, gentle humor, and tender ministerings. Just really craved the cooking part I allow. "Lawd, chile," she'd laugh heartily, "ya cuts yassef and gravy gun come out 'stead of blood!" I can still hear that warm, wonderful cackle. Man oh man, I missed her. Griffin, too. Large lump in my throat as I write this.

With such immense ground to cover, I spent many an overnight out in the open, vulnerable to any number of things: bugs, animals, the elements, and no good thieves and beggars. I felt so alone. Probably part of me liked it better that way. Just the incessant hoofbeats and katydids to accompany me all through Arkansas and Missouri.

A person can learn a lot about theyselves when there ain't nobody in their ears telling them how to be, what to think, or who they are. Still, I bumped along every dirt road and ballast cobblestone street, pondering my stay at Nottoway. The rendezvous with Mary, in particular, stuck in my mind. Pleasing as she was to spy, it's them conversations that sparked me most. Seemed to be interested in the same things, like theater, art, foreign countries, and cultures. We spoke frankly, often well into the night. I knowed she ain't the true one for me, though, because she's so attached to her Southern roots, and here I was on the runaway trail north. Reckon I would've been more dedicated to Dixie, too, if'n I'd have growed up in that wonderful Nottoway household. Made me miss Mary even more. But I met her, ain't I? They's gonna be others, such was the claim.

I used a pen and stationery from a hotel bureau and started scrawling this here book – the one you been studying ('least I trust they's a you). Made a long list of attributes I'd like in a gal. Filled the page black with ink. Described how she'd look, what her voice'd sound like, even the clothing she'd wear. Pictured her folks and siblings, even the smell of her breath and perfume. Whole ball of wax. Then, I took this ole lumpy mattress been discarded in the back alley, and loaded it into the wagon. Not just for sleeping, but bouncing, too, like I done on my bed at home. I fastened the paper to a tree and hopped like a toad, over and over, looking at the list the whole time, picturing this gal in my mind. Folks'd think I's crazy I knowed, but that's what I done, almost nightly. Seemed if I made things clear enough in my mind, lo, they came to be, no matter how far-fetched. Like voodoo magic!

"Looky here, God," I prayed, fireflies swirling around like embers from a campfire, "please get this gal's attention. I don't know who she is, or where she's at, but whisper in her ear to find me." Envisioned the sweetest, most kind-hearted little filly. Brown hair, fancy French braid, dark eyes as large as saucers, thick eyelashes, red cherub lips, and a pleasin' slender chasse.

I bounced ramrod for nearly an hour on the thing, until it was burned in me like a brand on a bull's backside. That ole mattress was flatter than a flapjack once I got done jumping. I tried to plump it back up by stuffing the thing full of Spanish moss, since they's such abundance dripping from every oak. Big mistake. See, they's this little red chigger bug in there that'll bite you fierce. I looked like I had the pox or the Great Siberian Itch! Lasted pretty near a week. I paced all night long like a durn caged animal, itching and a-scratching. Live and learn, I s'pose.

I snuffed the campfire, choking like a dumbass because I forgot to get downwind. Then I crouched on that mattress beneath the surrey and fell into a deep sleep, dreaming vivid. I was back at Nottoway in the midst of a glorious party. The white ballroom was replete with well-dressed gentleman and hoop-skirted dames, waltzing and a-whirling like ballerinas on top of a music box. We's all drinking and conversing in grand merriment. They's a long line of suitors studying the portrait I done, dressed to impress, boasting to one another about money, stature, and prowess.

Funny thing, but the actor John Wilkes Booth was in line with the rest of them, patiently waiting his turn. Got the odd impression he's gonna try and kidnap her, all because Mary and me were talking about him once. Funny the things that pop-in when we's asleep.

Oh, well, dreams are dreams. That's all for now...

I stood and stretched, feeling rejuvenated, but anxious to git. Ate a hardy breakfast of fried beans, and wild berries. Gave me the winds like mad. No matter, ain't nobody around but us squirrels. I's free to let 'em rip, and did so liberally.

St. Louis was within a day or two, according to the map. I'd cross ole Muddy Water and make a sharp right turn towards Ohio. Maybe I'd follow another river for a change. I might be repeating myself, but I's actually born in Missouri, St. Charles to be exact. The capital of the whole state at one time. Pap moved us south to Louisiana when I was around six or so, saying it was too much for him to earn a living plus look after me on his own. But I knowed it was on account of he'd lost everything to a scam artist. He bought a fortune in land grants that ain't amounted to more than a few acres of sand and cactus. Probably a wealth of snakes and scorpions, too, if you took to studying it.

Pap seemed to get hisself into legal fixes left and right. One time, he's brought to justice when I's around 5 or so. If'n memory serves, he was a tetch too closely acquainted with a bunch of con men who were swindling folks on street corners with betting tricks. He was the plant of the operation, the innocent guy on the street. He'd let you win the first few times, boosting yer confidence. Then *whammo*, you'd go on a painful unfortunate losing streak. That's how they done it. Finally, he got found out and had to face Justice Clemens up in Hannibal. No jail time or nothing, just ordered to leave the state with a fine and a severe hand slap. I think those was Pap's words. Good times for me, though. I sat on the curb outside the court, talking to the judge's

11-year-old son, Samuel. He's the only friend I ever remember making in Missouri, a colorful young guy with a lively imagination and a wealth of trivia. Said the street pavers we's sitting on was once used on great ships from Europe to help balance in the waves. Told me marvelous tales of pirates, riverboat captains, highway robber gangs, and cave explorers. I's too young to remember the details, but his uncommon large head and infectious humor stuck with me good. I heard his pap, the judge, died some months later of pneumonia. Shame. Reckon y'all know what became of Sammy, though he eventually changed his name.

Thanks to God I's surviving the trip unscathed, safe and sound in the Northern territories come late fall, just before the snow. Yessir, I seen a heap on that journey: folks building barns, farmers farming, men smoking pipes on benches outside country stores. I seen places of worship with magnificent stain-glass and peaceful gravesites. I seen a dead animal or two, or a million. I seen schoolyards with children playing stickball, marbles, and hoops. I seen corn and wheat, waving like they's saying hello. I seen cool, babbling streams, waterfalls, and endless woods offering solace from the rays.

And one more thing, in a parish they called Mansfield, Ohio, I seen a real live angel from Heaven.

Nobody in Franklin County ever died from a deer attack, yet I lay comatose, eye sockets bearing deep shades of charcoal purple from the blows of that cranky buck. I was barely discernible, folks said. Bandages concealed my bygone button nose, the one I loved so, now as compressed and crooked as a bend in the mighty Mississippi. Eyes sealed shut like a streetbrawler on the short end of nasty fisticuffs.

I'd advanced all the way up into Ohio's unincorporated farmland, bordered by vast, dense wilderness teaming with wildlife. I figured I'd set a spell on my way to Cleveland, where I planned to petition classes at the University. Seems with the help of them topographic diagrams, I pointed myself north and just kept going and a-going. The further from home, the better.

Anyway, I's on the tracks of a male white-tailed deer traversing a trickling stream. I'd acquired a rifle and became an adequate yet reluctant hunter. I's distracted by a flock of Canadian Geese flying in a steady "V" overhead, but they disappeared beyond the tips of the timberline.

Just behind an adjacent cedar grove stood a young lady of around 12. No more than five yards from the brim of her bonnet stood the majestic creature. Startled, the robust animal turned and stared her down, nostrils flaring, antlers sharp and 20-point, flowering from stems like magnificent spring bouquets. The little gal hid her hand behind her back, foolishly enticing the creature with a make-believe fistful of eats. Bad idea. Suddenly lowering his head, the bull charged the miniature matador, pierced her sternum with a powerful thrust, and drove her backwards into the thicket. She shrieked, top-tone. Before you could say "George Washington," she was curled in a fetal position in the tall grass, repeatedly struck by the deer's powerful hooves.

I rapidly approached the aggressor from the rear, kicking mightily at its hindquarters to distract the incursion. My tactic proved successful. The girl was able to roll to safety in the waist-high weeds. Why I ain't just pumped that beast full of buckshot, I'll never know. Maybe I's mesmerized by its beauty, or maybe I feared endangering the girl. Firearms ain't exactly my forte.

Anyhow, hair on end in a crouched posture, the six-foot, 200-pound male flexed his hind legs, pushing down on me with a series of hardy blows to the head, and knocked my rifle clean away. First, he struck the front of my cranium as I squirmed in avoidance, then the side and rear. The animal beat the living Jesse out of me. Motionless, I finished facedown as the incensed stag suddenly and mercifully ceased his onslaught.

Perhaps he lost interest. His sparring partner done gave up. Nonetheless, he turned and scampered deeper into the thicket, leaving us victims in its wake. Me, most severe.

A silver dollar-sized circle of blood stained the front of her frock, yet she managed to right herself and dash to a neighboring farm. Fortunately, a pair of farmers were on hand, tending to some horses. She called to them mid-gallop in a state of panic, then stumbled and collapsed at their feet. One stayed behind in her aid, the other darted towards the woods. She thankfully recovered without measurable distress. I wasn't so fortunate, suffering intense head trauma. It took me weeks before I even recognized my own reflection in the mirror. Town folks was real nice, though, parading through the bedroom with homemade family dishes to help make me strong. It was right comforting to see the same kindly faces every afternoon. Not sure if I actually began remembering things, or just relearned them, but no matter. T'was a frightful, confusing time.

I have cloudy memories of puking my guts out, spending what seemed like weeks in bed, unable to do more than sleep, take the occasional sip, and piss in a pot. In my slumber, I had the most realistic, foreign visions. This once, I felt I's at the banks of a large river, wider than the Mississippi and more dry and desert-like. I was wearing the oddest scarf and shorty-short skirt with pleats, yet I's a fella. Gold and jewels hung around my neck and wrists, too. Strange. Then I's part of some kind of coronation in a river. Huge crowds gathered and cheered, calling me "King" somethin-gorother. I seen them plain as day, exiting en masse, waving, and wishing me well. *Wonder what the hell that was all about?*

Next thing I knowed, I sped like a runaway cart through a long, dark tunnel with a light at the end, and was spit out like a wad of chewing tobacco. Scarier than them voodoo rituals, by golly!

This unbelievable fog had swallowed me, yet each time it got light (and when I say light, I mean blinding), I see'd things sharp and clear, sure as I'm standing here. Lasted for a month or more. Folks must have thought I'd plumb gone bats.

Most dedicated nurse of all was Katie Wilmington, the gal I rescued. She sat at my bedside, religiously wiping my brow with a cool cloth, hour after hour. She'd sing and read her poetry, and I allow she kissed my forehead and cheeks more than once, too. My brain would wake from a deep spell of slumber, eyes glued shut. "I'm going to marry you," she'd say, figuring I can't hear, but I was listening to that little angel the whole way. I's aware of everything that was happening, I just couldn't move. I honestly believed it was her loving energy that helped me heal.

Finally mended, I learned the lay of the land, fortunately took in by the Wilmingtons. They ran sawmills on the banks of the Black Fork River. Ben, the husband, let me help out three days a week. I always appreciated the things he done for me. He's a barrel-chested British gent with whatcha call 'em, lambchop sideburns, taller waist up than waist down considerable. Paid me a dollar a day, which was mighty generous wages I guess, though I daren't mention making $100 for two weeks work at Nottoway. Did me well to get my mind and muscles working again, anyhow. Weren't the type of job I enjoyed (or's all that good at), but he let me take spare scraps to build sets and hard stage flats. I loved that part about working the mill.

I fashioned some of the smaller pieces into panels for my paintings. Kind of refreshing being in a different part of the country for a change. New subject matter to bring to life: cows, cornfields, and haystacks. North-type stuff. Only so many pillars and paddle wheelers to paint before you become stale and uninspired. A creative-type like myself needs a fresh perspective now and then to keep them juices a-flowing.

I stacked the sheets in back of the barn and built a 12- by 15-foot acting platform. We put on productions for the school kids. I reckon Ben Wilmington ought to get credit for teaching me how to draft my designs to paper, then erect them. He had many books on the subject, being he's in the lumber business and all. I used that barn as my theater, and even did a full scenic set of *Romeo and Juliet*'s famous balcony scene. To my surprise, several youngins showed interest in putting on a production. Kate, foremost, asking me if she could play Juliet to my Romeo. *Ain't took long to figure how come.*

The club we formed, The Sacred Coalition of Creatives, met Fridays at two o'clock in the mornin' in the loft. The motley gang consisted of myself, K-Dub (that's Kate), Owen (a neighbor kid born with one useless arm), and Butch Busby, budding musician. Oh yeah, and his brothers, whose proper names escape me (we called them Tiny and Stink). Kate and I nicknamed them Whistle, Plunk, and Boom, because it sounded like monkeys done stole some instruments when they played. Butch's pap spoiled him, so's he had all kinds of symphonic gadgetry: horns, flutes, cymbals, and drums. Oh, well, probably sounded perfectly fine in his ears. Strange, but I never saw no sheet music. They just played by ear, which might explain the dreadful racket they made.

Kate was a marvelous little poet. I, of course, was the child prodigy painter. And the others, well, wouldn't be much of a club with just Kate and me, now would it? Didn't have to be no expert to join. We snuck out each weekend, climbed up to the hayloft, and discussed all things creative. Stink brought moonshine. Butch smoked a pipe. It was real high society. You could show off your art, brainstorm an idea, or read from a work of inspiration. Pretty much anything you fancied during your allotted turn on the floor. I made burlap-stuffed dummies to ensure no bed ever appeared evacuated in the wee hours. Enjoyed pulling the prank too, using wigs, dressing the figures in nightshirts, and so on. Nobody got caught until one time, Butch tripped on his tympani whilst climbing through the window, sending a resounding crash reverberating through the still serenity of his household. Woke his pap, who of course smelled the smoke in his hair and clothes. Took such a switch to his little ass, he's bowlegged for a month. Looked like a walking parenthesis. We had to take a break for a good while till the smoke cleared, so to speak.

Yessir, Kate and me had precious good times through the years. Later in life, I's just so thankful for those times – prayed over it each night, short but honest. Many an hour we fished in the pond, skipped stones, and played in the yard with the animals. They had ducks, goats, pigs, chickens, kittens, and a dog named Digger. Sometime we tried to teach ole Diggie, so's he could participate in them plays we done in the barn. He only obeyed Kate, so she acted as animal trainer. When I weren't the director, I at least tried to be the harassing big brother, but I can't. Maybe we actually *was* more to each other than brother and sister. Reckon it was innocent enough. Hell, I heard of some folks from Arkansas that married they cousins. Bet the offspring ain't comed out too pretty. But enough, we ain't blood kin, so let's just let it alone. All I can say is watch out, intention is a right powerful force.

CHAPTER FOUR

MANSFIELD, OHIO, 1862

Ever been so sure of something, you'd bet your cotton-pickin' life on it, only to realize that ain't the way things was at all? Well, looky here, I woke that morning knowing exactly where my head would rest come slumber, and who'd lie beside me. There was few things a body counted on, but this was one of them, or my name ain't Gabrick Stone. So here's the story:

Nearly four years had passed since I'd left Cypress, and the world was a different place. Slow to recover from my brain swell, I's troubled with memory loss, and gaps of missing time and detail. Not completely ignorant, just ill equipped to keep every little thing straight. I fear my imagination may have filled in some spaces with *thinksos* and *mightahappeneds*.

The War to preserve the Union had erupted. Not everybody called it that, just us Yanks. I was unable to participate due to lingering trauma from my head injury. What seemed tragic at the time, actually served me well when the army come a-calling. As stated, I refused to participate, but did my fighting with my mouth and drawings, instead. Picked up some extra cash sketching for local papers and such. Satirical, political commentaries of our nation's new leader, Abraham Lincoln. He was simple to depict: lanky frame, beard, furrowed brow. My new hero, of sorts. I got to know his policies and intentions real well. He's gonna free the slaves, they said, and reunite the country. I struggled to draw the hypercritical pictures – ones that made him look bad. Ain't wrote them, just drew them. If I wanted the work, I had to put my own personal feelings aside. Anyhow, these was just pen and ink sketches. I'd paint a real fine picture of him later on.

It was during them Ohio years that I firmly took to portraiture. Instead of coming up with my own brilliant style from scratch, I copied the look of other painters I admired. Then, once it's mastered, I worked backwards and settled on my own uniqueness. I could only work a few hours at a time, though, until the headaches started in. You know, funny thing about that, it made me see life real up close. Ain't no such thing as advantage or disadvantage, near as I can figure it. Things just *was*. Lemme show you what I mean: Folks'd say to me, "How fortunate, Gabe, you bein' born to wealthy white farmers."

I'd say, "Maybe."

Then they says, "Shame you fell from favor, though. Defected North, no family, no friends."

I said, "Maybe."

"Fine thing," they'd soon see, "you lucky son of a gun. Meetin' them Randolphs, makin' enough money to finance things."

"Maybe."

In time, the opposite. "Bad luck, sufferin' such a terrible accident with that there buck. Tragic, boy, jis tragic."

"Maybe," I'd shrug.

Army come a-recruiting. "You can't fight 'cause of yer head injury, you say? Fortunate bastard."

That damn buck ultimately saved my life.

Get the picture? Lesson being, don't waste your time forcing your will on things. God knows what he's doing better than we ever could.

Benjamin and Martha Wilmington had a son named Ben Junior, killed straight off in the First Battle of Bull Run, early in the conflict. He was just 17. Got hisself trapped in a trench, ambushed from behind. The thought of that poor boy dying as he done, like a helpless chicken in a fox-infested henhouse, was too much to ponder. As a result, Katie and I became fast friends. I made it my duty to replace Ben Jr. in her life. We was never all that tight, Junior and me. I tried to get close, but it ain't in his nature to be friendly. He tended to push folks away. Artistic ones like me, anyway. He bent my feelers a few times calling me *sissy* or *Sally*. We did have a few irregular good talks, I guess, during the years I spent helping tend the mills. These was times when he was troubled. I s'pose I lent the emotional support he needed.

They's this one fix he got hisself into when he was hooked on pain-killing medication. He got bit by this black widow spider out at the woodpile, and I'll be damned if that thing didn't nearly take his leg! Little itty-bitty spider causing such a heap of strife? Who'd have thunk? Big ole bruise running up and down his calf, then this walnut-sized puss sack oozing poison and shit for days. Lawd have mercy! Anyway, so Doc Brady gave him some morphine until the thing ran its course. But he had to have more, and more. And more. He started stealing from the office when Doc was out on house calls. Ole Brady had the presence of mind to lock the door, but not the window. Junior figured that out, first try. When a person can't do without something, they find a way. It became a real, bona fide *sichee-ation*. Anyway, I helped break Ben's habit by tying him to the bedpost in his sleep, until he sweat the thing dry. Dad-burn, how he threatened to do me in! Ended up thanking me in the end, though. Ben was affable enough, I allow, but real into roughhousing. I just ain't subscribed to that newspaper. Even when we's on good terms, he'd come a-running up and tackle me from behind, and pinch my chi-chi's until they's good and sore. He wouldn't stop until I hollered, "Ben is my master, Ben is my master," loud as lungs could cry. I hated that.

By and by, it was Kate and I that formed the true bond. The precious companion I hadn't had since

Griffin. Katie saw us as sweethearts, I knowed, but since she was four years younger, we was more like siblings in my estimation. She ripened from girl to woman real nice, though, I must admit. Real, *real* nice. One time, we was swimming in the pond together come twilight, and I'm embarrassed to admit but we stripped down and exposed ourselves. Just our silhouettes. And no touching neither, just looking. Lots and lots of looking. I reckon it's only natural. Animal instinct tends to bypass the brain. 'Tween you and me, her parts was coming along splendid. Hooee-boy!

Nonetheless, on my 20th birthday, I was proposed marriage by this other gal named Millicent McGill. She was a bit older, 25 I recall. Yup, ain't no wax clogging your ears – she proposed to *me!* She made it somehow seem like I was the one done the asking, but it was her. She carried on about the family business, inheritance money, and wanting to start a family. Women can spin a thing like a spider spins a web – natural, almost artistic. You ain't even realized that *you* are what's for supper! Her daddy was a wealthy mill owner who worked with Mr. Wilmington. The whole thing seemed kind of arranged, if'n you ask me. Sort of planted in my foggy noggin. Her parts ain't near as nice as Kate's, but plenty of other fellers seemed to fancy her, and we been paired up in public for a while now. Broke Kate's heart. She never cried outward from what I see'd, but her eyes seemed red and puffier than usual, for a spell, anyway.

Millie was pleasant enough, I s'pose. And I admit the financial security sounded enticing. She had wispy strawberry hair, fair Irish skin, and an annoying sniffle

(kind of gnawed at you) on account of her dust aller-
gies. A real girly girl Millie was, with the most impressive doll collection y'ever did see. T'was worth a
fortune, I bet. Many were from Europe. Her folks was
originally from Dublin, and fiercely loyal to Lincoln,
which enamored me, so's I went ahead and bit the bullet so to speak. I answered "yes," and jis' like that, we's
betrothed.

After a short engagement, the white-veil moment
finally arrived. I felt a pang of sorrow for Millie that
fine autumn day. Ain't supposed to be that way; supposed to feel a rise of excitement when your bride appears at the end of the aisle. See, she woke with a big
ole stye in her left eye called a chalazion. That's a painful blocked gland that makes your lid puff like a pas-
try. All sore and closed-up, she wore a patch just to
look presentable. A big, black, pirate patch. It sort of
complemented my tux, and was the only color the doctor could get last minute.

"Dearly beloved," the preacher man said, "we
are gathered in the presence of our Lord on this day
of great joy and blessings, to unite Millicent Delilah
McGill..." the words were muted by an unforeseen
distraction. With boots firmly planted at the altar, moments before the "I do's," I noticed the arrival of a lady
in lavender. Elegant and lovely as a lily, she wore lacey
white gloves, a floppy hat, and carried a parasol. The
latecomer strolled down the aisle like some sort of dig-
nitary. A uniformed escort helped her to the pew. She

raised her head, and our eyes locked instantly. Embarrassingly so. (Dad-gum, them stunning eyes!)

At that very moment, I felt pangs the way I'd only ever dreamed about. Oh, I know, foolish talk but true. Millie kicked my shin like she seen the whole scenario developing through the one good eye in the back of her head. Quickly, I doubled over, faking a stomach malady. It's my leg that throbbed, but bellyaches somehow seemed more convincing. Ever the rascal, the plot bought me time to think, or run, or whatever one does in such a predicament.

The audience gasped, wondering what had befallen me. Was it food poisoning? Influenza? I could hear the murmurs clear. I dashed out the door as it slammed with a conclusive jolt. *All right, now what?* I consulted the clouds and reclined on some splintered white steps behind the chapel.

"Last minute jitters?" came a voice at my rear. It was her, the lady in lavender, Ms. Kate Wilmington. I stood, brushed the paint chips from the seat of my britches, and wondered what in the world I was going to say to the 72 guests inside. Not the least of which was the pirate bride, who must be worried I's somewhere regurgitating on the tuxedo and tails her daddy done financed.

"Why did you stop? You were doing wonderfully." Kate loosened the bow tie that deprived me of oxygen. She's taking care of me again, like always.

"You know full well why I'm out here, K-Dub." She loved the nickname I'd given from the git-go.

"Whatever do you mean?" She demurely loosened the top button of my collar.

"Looky here, I'm supposed to be gettin' married, and in you traipse, lookin' all...all..."

"All what?" She brushed the wrinkles from her frock.

"Don't play innocent with me. You planned this. This whole thing been in the works since pinafore and pigtails."

Kate twirled a matching parasol, resting on her shoulder. "Why Gabe, I haven't the slightest inkling. *Mr. Wilmington and guest*, the invitation said. I'm the guest."

"No it ain't," I insisted. "Read, *Mr. and Mrs. Wil...*"

"Lovely invite, by the way. Gold embossed? Nice touch. Your idea?"

"Millie picked it out. I can't afford niceties, you know that, now that I spent the last of things. She's the one..."

"With the high-toned airs?"

"Yup." (We always finished each other's thinking.) "Where's your pap?"

"Too troubled to come. We said our goodbyes this morning."

Stupid me, my compromised brain ain't caught the plot. "Listen," I said, "if I's to reveal somethin'...well..."

"Scandalous?" she inserted.

"Yes'um. Promise not to tattle?"

"I would never. You tell me everything, you know that. Sworn bestest friends." She ritualistically tapped her heart three times and pointed upward – the gesture we'd borrowed from Griffin.

"All right. Well, for one," I whispered, "I ain't so sure I want to stay here, work the mills."

"What do you want?"

"Go to New York, be a Broadway designer. That's my dream."

"Not so unreasonable. Millie is in love, she'll follow wherever life leads. And...?" She gave the parasol another brisk twirl, tassels a-flinging wildly. Women have a way of making you think you're steering the ship. "Go ahead, I'm listening," she said. "And...?"

"Oh, all right. I love you, damn it. You win, K-Dub. You're the one for me. Always been, always will be, so drop the act and..." the words nearly dried up coming out, "*marry me.*" There was defeat in my tone.

"Thank you...I think? Didn't realize it was a contest, but I accept. Ironic, you didn't even invite me, and now you..."

"I thought you'd be hurt."

"Apology accepted." She made a bright red lipstick mark on my cheek, then wiped it away quick. Probably ain't wise to wear kissy marks from a woman besides the bride. Kate had confessed her feelings many times, but I never took her for more than a kid companion. Somehow, God transformed this twiggy tag along into the embodiment of feminine finery, and now I couldn't imagine spending a single day apart for the rest of our lives.

"So, what now?" she asked. I leaned in for a better smooch, but the termite-infested handrail gave way, split in two, and sent me crashing to the ground. I struck my head and was rendered unconscious...again! When I woke, I's confused something awful. "Hey, did that mean ole buck get away?" I mumbled, seeing six of Kate.

"Gabe, it's me. You hit your head pretty hard."

"Where am I?"

"You won't believe me if I tell you."

"That bad?"

"Worse. We're outside a chapel, there's a wedding."

"Whose?"

"Yours. You just abandoned the bride at the altar, confessed your love for me, and now we're getting married!"

Just then, a piercing voice rang out. "Jeremy, (sniff-sniff), what in God's name is taking so long? (Sniff.)" Millicent came bounding down the front steps, calling for the absent groom. Bouquet in hand, missing some blooms. She'd had enough, whacking the flowers on her thigh as she scurried along.

Upon her arrival, there was nobody. Only knee-high grass in an abandoned field, swaying gentle in the breeze, and branches rustling in the thicket some 30 yards away. Kate and I hid until Millie had gone. We knew they'd come looking for us, so's we lit out like banshees, across the open field and into the dense woods. She'd packed a bag and hid it since early that morning, just in case. "Hope the raccoons haven't inspected my unmentionables," she chortled, trying to locate her luggage.

Was this ghastly of me, ditching Millie and her family? Seems I's always running away from somebody. I'd never been a bigger rascal. Remember when I said I was sure where my head would rest that evening, and who would be next to me? Reckon I's wrong.

After the initial commotion died down and the last bewildered guest departed, we waited a while before hopping a train for the Eastern Seaboard. Expecting to be on the 5:15 stage to Akron, we had an hour and a half to waste. Kate and me was committed for life, so's what came next seemed only natural. (If'n they's children or skittish Christians present, best skedaddle.)

I cleared a space in the soft grass beneath a grove of trees and shrubs. We placed an evening gown on the ground and lain in a lover's tangle. Very romantical. Her lips were soft, moist, and tasted unique to her. Not like honey, or mint, or nothing recognizable. Just...her. I couldn't get enough. I ran my tongue along Kate's perfectly straight tooth line, then nibbled her bottom lip. She took my tongue in full, slurping and a-panting, working up a generous lather. Sometimes gentle, sometimes aggressive, our emotions escalated until we's finally risin' to our knees, removing each other's clothing. First, my stockings and shoes, then the shirt, button by button. Next, the black tuxedo trousers and drawers. Good thing my unders was clean – a fella never knows for sure. Usually, nobody sees them but the one a-wearing them.

Soon I's buck naked, completely exposed right there in that open field! Freebootin', we used to call it down South. Good thing we's in a grove, obscuring the view. Ain't needing some stranger to get a free show.

Then, it was her turn. I slowly unlaced her lovely lavender frock and delicates, draping them over a branch so's not to get them soiled. The parasol and hat helped protect her pale, virgin skin from the dusty bars of sunshine that's a-spilling through the autumn foliage.

Kate's bosoms dropped and bounced firm: smooth, round, and just as I'd remembered that night in the pond, only fuller. A small scar was sandwiched 'tween her cleavage where she'd been lanced by that buck. (I reckon I didn't notice last time because it had been dark.) I grabbed hold with both hands, full fist, kneading and a-squeezing to the sound of her mellow moans. The more I fondled, the more intense our kissing became. She held tight to my proud protrusion. Before I knew it, I felt like a levee was ready to bust. *Ahhh! Holy Moses*, I effused all a-quiver as the flood gates opened. Happened so fast, with such intensity, I's a-feared Kate ain't shared in much of the proceedings. I reckon we technically did save ourselves until the wedding night after all – whole event was just a bunch of petting and pulling, come analyze it. Her folks would be glad of that. Ain't such a sin, I s'pose. I'd better figure out how to involve her more next time...

In recapitulation, here's how she shakes out. Again, I's on the runaway trail (I sense a theme), nothing but the clothes on my back. Couldn't help but think of that gypsy voodoo lady and her prophecy: You go north, sustain a whoopin' that saves your life, love a gal ain't your fiancée, and head east. Got to admit, not a bogie in the batch! But that ain't what turned that witch white, eyes a-bugging. What was it that shocked her so? Can't hardly imagine. Reckoned only time would tell.

I was tracking towards New York, *not* sharing a mattress with Millie, *not* married, *not* subject to managing mills all my life. Instead, I's on a hard, wooden train bench with my bestest pal, deep in love. Not just *a* love, *the* love. Selfless, doubt-free.

Like I's said, through it all, God had an eye on me.

CHAPTER FIVE

NEW YORK, NEW LIFE

F all in the Northeast was an exuberance of colors. I couldn't have done it better with my paintbrushes. The trees were a splendid array of yellows, oranges, and reds – all the way from Mansfield to Manhattan. Winter was fast approaching, and soon, a blanket of snowy white linen would shroud the autumnal splash. I'd miss the views from my window as the train whistled its way into Newark Station.

Just a quick ferry across the Hudson, and we was home.

My eyes could hardly accept what they seen. Reckon I rubbed 'em more than once. I's surrounded by so many bridges and buildings, 10 stories high! Back home, they's some structures of four or five floors, but nothing like this---practically smashing against the clouds. (Okay, slight stretch, but they was tall I tell you.) The constant commotion made my heart jump like a toad. My brain was uncommon ringing too, probably on account of the relentless clickety-clack cadence of the tracks as I'd lain with an ear out the porthole, days on end.

The trip took longer than expected. Kate and I ventured to a place called Niagara Falls, and got married beside trillions of thundering gallons as they rimmed the great ridge, punishing them poor pools below. Thick gray mist turned Kate's hair into tight-spun ringlets, but she didn't mind. No hairdo or nothing could dampen the day. "Best of our lives," we proclaimed. Course, t'weren't no gifts piled head-high like at my other wedding, but marrying Kate was well worth the trade-off.

Can't rightly say we did much sightseeing in Niagara Falls, since we barely made it outside the hotel room. Reckon I'd done a better job including her in things this go 'round. Man, did I include her, included the hell out of her...thrice daily! We'd take a proper honeymoon once the dust settled in New York City. Every respectable bride deserved one, a nice honeymoon, that is. The beach, perhaps? Always dreamed of dipping our toes in the salty sea.

I'd requested my money be wired, so's we could pay rent, buy some outfits, set up our new home, and whatnot. Didn't have much as I'd blown through most of it. Kate's folks kindly obliged, and tossed in some extra funds of their own. Mighty nice considering our rather unconventional departure and all. They was so supportive and loving, them Wilmingtons. Never could bring myself to call them *mom* and *dad*, but it felt like they was, anyhow. Reckon the rest of the wedding party wanted to skin me like a cat. Can you blame them? The wickedness of it. All's fair in love and war, such was the adage.

Looking back, they's deep fondness for that time. We's so young, so full of hope. Kate concurred, and convinced me we ought to write Pap in Louisiana, to share the news of our blessed union. "No," says I. It'd been such a long, tough row to hoe, and I preferred she didn't. But being kind-hearted with nary a grudge nor axe to grind, she did it anyway, scribing the most congenial letter:

Dear Mr. Stone,

You don't know me without having kept correspondence with your son, Gabe, my husband. We were married this week in Niagara Falls, New York. I knew you would be pleased. He is the most wonderful man I have ever known. Kind, caring, and talented. Please give blessings upon this union, as we are, and always will be, a family. We are staying at 324 Bleeker Street in New York City. More soon, *as details become available. Until then, be safe, be well, God bless.*

Signed, Mrs. Katherine Wilmington Stone

Honestly, he ain't deserved such consideration. *Like he gave a lick I'd found happiness.* Finally, he wrote back many years later. He'd taken the slaves to Texas to escape the immediate danger. Granddad stayed back to salvage what's left of things at Cypress, but the old bastard finally died of natural causes, Pap wrote. Weren't no more details about it.

Anyways, Pap talked mostly about hisself, which ain't no surprise. No inquiries about me or nothing. He said our home was used as a Confederate hospital, and then a temporary morgue. I shuddered at the notion of soldiers lying in my bedroom, having arms and legs amputated on tables and such. Or cold, dead bodies scattered about, they souls roaming the halls, confused. Gave me chill bumps all up and down. Best I block it out.

Speaking of death, Griffin had died from drowning like I's said prior. Poor, dear friend. I wanted to believe it was an accident, but I had my doubts. I seen crazier shit go down against blacks for simpler things. I just hope he ain't done in for smarting off. I studied about his mama, Isa, praying that wherever she was, God was taking tender care. That's all for now.

We found a cozy place on the corner of Bleeker and Perry, just a short walk to the theater district. In fact, mere blocks away was The Laura Keene Theatre, near Houston Street. Miss Keene was the reigning queen of Manhattan. She would write, produce, direct, and star in her own shows. She was so successful she built her very own venue. Glorious! White and gold with black marble floors, velvet seats, and statues flanking a towering proscenium arch. Some folks was opposed to a woman having such power, so they'd bust in and vandalize the joint. They'd cut up scenic drops, toss chairs, steal costumes and suchlike. *What the hell's the matter with people?*

Reports were, in the time between Lincoln's election and the Rebel attack on Fort Sumter, 250,000 tickets were sold to her song and dance spectacular, *The Seven Sisters*. Kate and I caught closing night of a revival, our very first Broadway show. What an eye-popper! Thirty-five nearly nudes with shapely gams and alabaster bosoms, parading about in transparent, patriotic costumes! I pretended to be enjoying the music, waving my hands like a conductor to the memorable melodies, but all eyes were on them showgirls. Kate kept looking over, somewhat questionable. She ain't just fell off the cabbage wagon.

The best number was called "Uncle Sam's Magic Lantern." The bearded icon was holding a bald eagle (his magic lantern), as chorus girls reenacted scenes from American history. They even depicted plantation life with slaves and all. Funny how she showed a more congenial, romantic version of it. Maybe she'd been to Nottoway. They's gals in blackface pretending to be negroes at the slave trade. Big ole ship called the *Constitution* sailed right across the stage, wiping out the so-called ebony wedge, symbolizing the black marketplace. Folks cheered wildly. Some reviews called it "patriotic nonsense," but Kate and I enjoyed it considerable. Well, I did anyhow. So much so, we waited backstage afterwards for an introduction. Keene's props, costumes, and colorful scenery were tops. I just had to say so in person.

I's mighty inspired to get a show of my own. Had the bug now, for sure. Perhaps I'd interview for a job in the future. I don't know if it was on account of it being the final performance, or what, but they's this huge line outside the stage door, military men and everything. I asked some folks why all the commotion, and they said the president and first lady was inside! "Old Abe, himself," I gasped, more excited about the prospects of shaking his hand than Miss Keene's. But such an immense crowd had gathered, we thought better of it and headed home for the night.

It was a crisp, clear evening. The air chilled our cheeks while we strolled the short distance from Houston to Bleeker by glow of the gas lamps. The bustling main streets were amply lit with the white lights of theater marquees, but the side roads were hushed and darkened considerable. Just the clomping hooves of the occasional surrey, and the boot-stomps of momentary passersby. I stepped on a discarded flyer, advertising the upcoming production at the Winter Garden Theater: "Edwin Booth is *Hamlet*," it read. "Six weeks only!" Performances began Tuesday, March 3. I couldn't believe my fortune! I'd see the legend after all.

Randolph had raved so. Maybe I'd even get a meeting. I reckoned I'd spend a week or two designing schematics in preparation. Surely, I's needing a portfolio of samples to take on interviews. Maybe they ain't made the scenery yet, you never know. What a greenhorn I was, looking back on it.

I felt a bolt of Hosanna rush through me. My Broadway dreams were nearer to reality than ever, just as I'd prayed whilst bouncing on that holy mattress. I almost felt guilty for my happiness, pondering the unspeakable tragedy going on all around the country. Brother fighting brother, buildings in ruin, families tored apart. I was thankful for the few hours of escape that the Broadway shows provided, and the opportunity that seemed to be presenting itself.

The following week I finagled a meeting with Mr. William Stewart, manager of the Winter Garden. Edwin Booth was still in Boston visiting his brother, John Wilkes, who's acting in *The Corsican Brothers*. Johnny weren't no good, Edwin told me once, but crowds roared in approval nonetheless 'cause he's riding the coattails of the family name. "Sour grapes," John Wilkes would fire back. The rivalry was intense.

One night during the Corsican run, Edwin was announced as a guest in the audience. He received such rousing cheers, and John was infuriated when he collected only polite, serviceable applause in comparison. This feud was an ongoing spectacle, as you'll soon see. Edwin even banished his brother to Southern markets, saying he was tarnishing the Booth name up North with second-rate offerings. Edwin was the real executor of the legacy, critically and financially. It was a stronghold John was desperate to capture. I gathered this gossip by eavesdropping backstage. Paid dividends to put a prying ear to the door once in a while.

Anyhow, as Mr. Stewart alluded, Edwin made all final production decisions. Stewart seemed to think he had his own backdrops and costumes from previous *Hamlet* incarnations, but I showed him my designs, anyways. He's mighty impressed, and said he'd make sure they got proper consideration once Edwin arrived.

First week of February, the elder Booth was finally in New York, oddly unaccompanied by his wife, Mary, who'd suddenly taken ill in Massachusetts. Folks said they's inseparable. They had a little daughter, too, and he missed them something crazy, I gathered. Truth told, my first impression of the star was mixed, to be kind. Edwin had a medium build, somewhat comely, with long, curly black hair, and an animated face. Too bad he was quite an epic drunk! "Don't be fooled," Stuart would say. "Booth's a genius, but he suffers the ills of an unraveling mind." I reckon stardom and constant travel weren't all they's cracked up to be.

I was dumbfounded (and a bit nervous) as to how he'd pull off performing for thousands without passing out cold. But that ain't no matter to me, he's probably never gonna use my designs, anyhow. *Served him right*, I sulked, watching in the wings as he slurred his words and stumbled about the stage. It was a far cry from the unanimous acclaim that preceded him. Here's a for instance:

"With bare-butt kin," he said one time, instead of *a bare bodkin*. Next came, "who would fart-holes bear?" (The word was *fardels*, but he twitched it.) The audience let out a raucous roar. "To grunt and sweat under a leery wife," – the line was *weary life*. Again, he got a huge laugh. Unfortunately, they ain't laughing *with* him, but *at* him.

He staggered aimlessly, as actors guided the guy through his blocking. Kind of sad, but I had to admit, it was mighty impressive that Edwin knew every word of Shakespeare by heart, no matter the play. He quoted passages at will. T'weren't always from the show he's supposed to be performing, but the audience ain't seemed to care. If he went dry on a piece of dialogue, he'd just make something up that sounded every bit as authentic as the rest. Either he had an unusually large thinker, or figured another way to store the recitations. Uncanny!

We got to know each other little by little, as I was present for nearly every performance. After initially chilly salutations, Edwin acted somewhat impressed by my creations and let me hang around permanent, like an apprenticeship. I had access to the theater, and frequently watched crews service the limelights, hammer flats, touch up drops, and whatnot. I's grateful for the chance to learn the ropes.

"Hey, scrub," they'd hand me a hammer, "make yerself handy. Standin' around with your finger up your nose, y'ain't worth a fart in a whirlwind." They's quite an eclectic collection, them technical crew: Irish, Italian, Greek, Jew, you name it. Stagehand stew, I nicknamed the whole stinking melting pot. Occasionally,

I's even asked to supervise in various capacities, so I's added Production Assistant to my mostly made-up resume. What the hell, t'weren't a total lie. I got to know that mishmash pretty well, settling they squabbles, keeping them focused. Felt like I'd earned a diploma in world social studies by the end of the run. They's a gang of rowdies after hours, too, I tell you. Kate used to joke, "Sounds as if your drinking buddies have a theater problem." She could always make me howl.

As if he ain't already struggling with circumstances, on February 19, Edwin received a letter at half-hour call that his ailing wife took a turn for the worse, slipping into a critical state. Putting it plain, she was dying. Edwin was frantic. I can only imagine how he felt, him being so far from her. By the time the curtain fell that evening, the last train to Boston had departed. He spent a restless night gulping coffee, sobering hisself for the 7:00 a.m. train, but when he reached Dorchester Depot, she was dead. I never seen such sorrow in all my days. He told us he prayed to join her in death's sweet release. Said Mary'd come to visit in the form of a ghostly apparition, the way his pap, Junius, had materialized to their mother. Don't know if it was the alcohol talking, but he was sincere as shit, far as I could see. Edwin's apathy towards me took a turn in the weeks following, as a result. S'pose I's a sympathetic shoulder again. A burgeoning friendship developed 'tween us. I reckon sometimes listening was better than talking. This was one of them times.

We also shared an interest in spiritualism and the supernatural. It was all the rage during the War Between the States, what with folks losing loved ones left and right, needing reassurance they'd see them again in the hereafter. I regaled him with stories of voodoo rituals, psychic readings, and a spirit visitation of my own. I could've sworn Mama was sitting at the edge of my bed one night. I seen her see-through body, felt the mattress compress, and sensed her gentle touch on my cheek. I swear it. Never told nobody until now.

This comforted Edwin, proof of the afterlife. However, his melancholy permeated for the remainder of the run. It kind of took the luster off the news Kate and me been itching to share.

Edwin's gloom persisted, but all was well on Bleeker. Me and my bride was expecting! Baby was due round about Thanksgiving. (By the way, t'was Lincoln that made it a national holiday during his presidency, but we'd always celebrated Thanksgiving unofficial, beforehand.) Booth offered cautious congratulations and cigars from his abundant private stash. I only puffed a few times, since I always hated that wretched aftertaste...like I's licking feet.

I saw Booth daily, as he let me paint his portrait alongside famed sculptor friend, Launt Thompson. Launt was a short, thin, Irish fella with a pointy beard. He had an uncommon knowledge of the human form, and said he developed the skill working for a Dr. Armsby in Chelsea. Launt was critical and cold at first, like Edwin, but I quickly learned under his tutelage and earned his respect.

Edwin adored art and sculpting. Reminded him of his pa, who musta been quite skilled at both. I was elated to be making the money, and got a heap of free advertising from it, too. Many an interested spectator watched through the windows (accessible from the sidewalk), keeping tabs on our progress. I collected a whole list of interested parties wanting portraits. Enough work for five, six months at least. This cheered Katie to no end.

Edwin began telling folks they's a waiting list, seeing how I'd be busy designing scenery. It done me good having him witness my popularity. For the first time, I sensed security. Learned a thing or two about sculpting, too – an invaluable addition to my repertoire. Matter of fact, Launt took me to Madame Tussaud's traveling wax figure exhibit in Times Square. We became obsessed with the process, the realism. If I ain't knowed better, I'd have sworn they's the real thing. Some statues even breathed from bladders hid inside the chest cavity!

Launt and I became friends aside from mutual relations with Edwin. I reckon he admired my paintings, and I was mesmerized by his mastery of the three-dimensional figure. He even did his own wax statues. I observed him on occasion at his studio apartment on 51 West Tenth. He shared it with a man named Pinchot who worked nights, slept all day. "Pinchy" ain't liked houseguests much, so's I was only invited every so often when he's away.

Edwin dropped his drinking, thank goodness, but commenced smoking a pipe nonstop. It gave me terrible headaches. I daren't complain, though, as he callously claimed even the worst physical discomfort couldn't match his tortured soul. Edwin had a way of speaking that was so eloquent and dramatic. Lent a certain validity to everything he said. T'was a shame I first knowed him during his dark times. He wasn't always like this.

A chronic insomniac, Booth conversed late into the wee hours (he called them his vulture hours), as he reminisced about boyhood travels with his dad. He was the favored son, I take it, accompanying his famous father on many a tour, domestic and abroad. John stayed back with his mother and younger siblings in Maryland. This incensed John something awful. Edwin was plenty outward with his fanciful descriptions – San Francisco sounded particularly riveting. It made me want to visit someday.

I reckon Junius was fortunate to have had a dedicated assistant to keep him motivated, organized, and sober. Edwin benefitted likewise from the worldliness and exposure. He soon grew obsessed with acting, and felt encouraged to take it up hisself. Good thing, the world would've never seen his genius otherwise.

"Baby brother Booth is ailing," Edwin revealed. John had cut short his current engagement in Cleveland because of a nagging neck injury. Seems he'd sustained a gaping gash from an ill-staged knife fight. A fibroid tumor formed, and he's returning to New York to have it surgically removed. He would reunite with the rest of the family at a rented mansion on Seventeenth Street whilst he convalesced.

"It will serve us well to reunite under one roof," Edwin remarked. "Meanwhile, I'd like for you and your expecting wife to use my cottage on Long Island. It isn't much, but the peace and quiet will be most pleasing to her."

"Much obliged," I said. "Most generous of you."

"My pleasure. You have done marvelous work, both at the theater and on my portrait. I enjoy your company. Perhaps you'll see a revitalized Edwin Booth upon your return."

As the family renewed bonds (Edwin later confessed it benefitted brotherly relations to act depressed and resigned to quitting the business), I took the opportunity for that short vacation on Long Island. With a cozy place to stay and a wad of cash burning a hole in my pocket, I had a wife to pamper.

Landlocked our entire lives, Kate and I jubilantly headed to the shore. Neither had ever seen the sea. A second honeymoon of sorts, as intended. First go-round in Niagara Falls, we had experiences of a *different nature*. This time, we actually surfaced for air and some sightseeing. She was my Heaven on earth: lustrous light brown hair, hazel eyes, radiant smile, and a beauty mark above her upper lip. Beauty by the bushelful, sure, but smart and adventuresome, as evidenced by our very first encounter with that buck.

Not to mention her stunt at the church, and leaving life in Ohio (with parents she loved) to follow this fool all the way to New York. I reckon we's *both* born to live out loud.

Eager to prove her passion beyond the mundane interests of most, Kate had definite opinions on politics, economics, woman's rights, social injustice, show business, you name it. She loved to write about it, and spent most nights penning poetry or personal papers while I worked at the theater. She said she had aspirations of getting published one day, but felt satisfied in the meantime with her growing pile of personal diaries. "Life worth living is life worth documenting," she'd expound.

The carriage ride went by in a snap. Notable how time passed so quick when lost in deep conversation. Katie and me could read the blame obituaries to one another and be satisfied.

We welled up the moment our toes touched the Atlantic, immediately grabbing hands and staring out at the sheer wonder of it. There's something about the ocean that puts things in perspective: alive and unspoiled, endless ultramarine in full panorama. The landlocked ain't knowed what they's missing.

Sand tickled our toes as we walked hand-in-hand, the foamy tidewater lapping at our ankles. Swarms of curious seagulls overhead, a-squawking and a-shrieking, occasionally landed to bid good day.

Kate gently rubbed her belly and sang a lullaby to baby as we strolled.

"Precious angel from above, I give
my heart to thee,

And vow to love the greatest
gift, t'was ever given me.

Can't hardly wait to watch you
grow, and someday you shall see,

A precious baby of your own,
and give your heart to thee.

Oh, Shepherd bless this tiny
child, and guard it tenderly,

For this is just the greatest gift, t'
was ever given me."

Hearing Kate's lovely serenade made me realize
Heaven weren't a place beyond the clouds; I's
there, right now.

Edwin's beach house was intimate, but charming.
Right snug to the sand. It was white with light blue
shutters with a weathervane to top it off, and had ivy
growing on the mailbox and porch posts. Once inside, we tossed our bags directly on the floor and took
each other right there on the supper table. Shades was
pulled, so's nobody could see. Got to a point where the
sofa seemed like a more comfortable host, so's we carried our passion to the parlor for the finale.

The front room was sparse but stylish. They's a coatrack, mounted pipe collection, some posters of Edwin's stage productions, and a cozy fireplace that seemingly ain't used much. (Three or four kerosene lamps were set inside the hearth.) The bedroom was six steps down a hall to the back, and was decorated in a sailing theme with pictures of clipper ships and a life preserver stuck on the wall over the bed. Perfect for what we had in mind. No kitchen, no indoor water closet, but a freestanding outhouse some 10 paces from the door was luxury enough.

The ocean was right across the way. Moonlit walks were the best as we pondered our place on this lonely little planet. I always seen the man in the moon, but Kate seen the face of a woman. Don't make it this nor that – just *is*. We never argued over it neither. That's what made us a perfect match. I reckon it takes all perspectives to make the world go around.

We'd stroll for miles, skipping stones, or picking berries and wildflowers. I made a wish on a shooting star and wondered what God thought of the mess we Americans was making down here: friends and families, suffering so. Patriot brothers, fellow countrymen, North and South, exterminating one another. Insane. I figured soldiers must be looking at the very same sky right this second, and yet, Kate and me was safe, secure. Don't seem fair. Their lives might end before they'd even have one more night to enjoy the magnificence. Reckon some probably wished it *was* their last night, just to put an end to the fear and pain.

On our final evening, we huddled together on the sand, memorizing the stars. "When we get back to the city," she said, "let's work on the nursery. You'll paint a mural or something, won't you, darling?"

"Yes, of course. What color?"

"How about yellow? She'll love that. You'll depict a sweet little girl in her Sunday best, holding a sunflower splashed with sunbeams. Bright and cheery."

"Wonderful, but what if the baby is a boy. We'll have one sore little soldier on our hands."

"It's a girl," she admonished. "I'd bet my life on it. Mothers know these things."

"How did we get so lucky, Kate? Findin' one another, chasin' our dreams to New York, far away from the bullets and cannon balls."

"I don't know." She stopped and crouched, picked up the most perfect cone-shaped shell, and placed it in her pocket. "Remember that nice Montauk Indian man we met today from the Hamptons?" What was it he said?"

"No tree had branches foolish enough to fight amongst theyselves," I said slowly, trying to remember it proper.

"Right, that was it. Wisdom for the ages. I wrote a poem this morning," Kate continued, "about walking hand-in-hand. Not just on this beach, but through life. Shall I read it?"

"'Course," I encouraged her, brushing wind-tossed hair from her eyes and mouth. "I love your writin', Mrs. Stone."

"Well, thank you. And I love you for loving it, Mr. Stone. And for our baby, and our life in New York." We grasped hands and clunked our foreheads together. Cross-eyed, we looked like them Cyclops from Greek mythology – lovesick ones, at that. "So such opportunity there in the city." She backed away. "Promise me we'll stay. You work in the theater, I'll be a journalist, and our children can be...anything their little hearts' desire."

We shared a tender embrace.

"You miss your folks back home?" I asked, looking moonward.

She itched her nose and uncovered a silver locket concealed under her frock. A small, heart-shaped reminder with her parent's initials engraved on the front. "Sure, but we'll write and they promise to visit. I just want to be wherever you are. That *is* home." She fetched a slip of stationery from her sweater pocket and read her words aloud.

HAND IN HAND
by K. W. Stone

A lover's stroll 'neath starry skies,
Our footprints in the sand.
The gentle waves caress our feet,
We journey, hand in hand.

The glowing moon, our only light,
It shimmers on the sea.
We pause but for a moment,
As you steal a kiss from me.

The winds that gently rustle trees,
The miles of endless shore,
So blessed are these moments,
They will live forever more.

In hearts that tread upon this path,
This walkway in the sand.
The unspoiled beauty of a love,
That travels, hand in hand.

I cradled Kate in my arms, and felt the miracle in her womb press against me. I didn't deserve her. No one did. We kissed, gentle at first, then long and hard. Darkness replaced the final, sinking slit of sun as the wind whispered confirming secrets in our ears. Our thoughts were far from work, war, or family discord. They were but a distant memory in my love-clouded consciousness. All I needed for sustenance was Kate's affection, and she gave it freely and plentiful.

"Gabe, what if after the baby is old enough to understand, we renew our vows? She can be the flower girl."

"You mean the weddin' we never had?"

"Precisely. Niagara Falls was nice, but I always envisioned something else. We'll invite my parents to come, and all our new friends. Maybe even your father?"

"Hold your horses. Let's not get ahead of ourselves."

"All right, then. But isn't it a lovely idea? I'll wear a white gown with little satin bows tied all around the bottom. The bridesmaids, in lavender, and there'll even be a maid of honor."

"Who?"

"How about Millie?" she teased, producing a hearty guffaw from us both. "Only jesting of course, the poor dear. I wonder how she's faring on the open market."

"Oh, I reckon her pap will have her back on the alter before you know it. He always seemed to be the brains behind the thing. Glad I had the wits of my own to notice that angel in lavender come a-strollin' in and save me from my misstep."

"I like to think I had something to do with it..."

"I love you to the bitter end, K-Dub," I summed it up, wrapping my arms around her fragile frame. "Am I squeezin' too tight?"

"No, I'm sure she's fine."

"There you go again with the girl talk." I's secretly hoping for a strapping son to advance the family name.

"She comes to me in my dreams, quite often. Precious, blonde pigtails, says her name is Amelia."

"Amelia. After my mama. Sure it ain't just your heart making a wish?"

"No, seems so real. I can actually touch her, ask her questions. Why, just last night I dreamed we were all picnicking by the pond in Mansfield. Swans were carving a path in the glassy water, littered with fallen leaves. Amelia was quite pleased with herself, and tossed pebbles into a mirror image that broke into concentric circles. As the ripples radiated to the far reaches of the banks, she and I suddenly found ourselves sitting on a branch high atop an elm, looking down. I noticed the patterns in our clothes and the detail of the ribbons in her hair. So vivid, so clear. You were below, crying. Tears of joy, I expect."

I had no idea Kate was having such experiences. "Then it must be," I said. "How 'bout if her middle name is Kate, after the most wonderful woman in the world?"

She paused, listening for an answer in the ether. "The girl says *yes*. Amelia Kate Stone."

The weeks spent at that ivy-covered lover's retreat done us both a world of good. We hiked, slept late, dined on all kinds of scrumptious meals, played in the surf, and talked about everything under the sun and moon. Made love like it were the last days of our lives. I know I's said it plenty, but words don't describe the depths of my love for her. Long as I breathe, I'll never forget them moments we shared on Long Island.

All the way back to Manhattan, I anticipated experiencing Amelia's first breath as a father. Katie convinced me I'd be painting the nursery yellow or pink, instead of blue. Lawd, what a shock if'n she comes out with a winkie, not the other. Honest, t'ain't no matter, girl or boy. I's gonna be a father!

Meantime, so many husbands and fathers was taking they last breaths on the country's battlefields. Gettysburg claimed some 43,000 lives the past week, alone. President Lincoln made a trip there and gave a short but splendid oration. Reminded the wind-whipped crowd why we commenced to fighting this thing in the first place. "Four score and seven years ago," he began. What a speech – short, but potent and haunting. It's the one we'll never forget.

Hard to fathom how God would allow such atrocities to some, and not others. They's folks on both sides of the conflict, reading the same Bible, praying to the same maker. I re-examined this whole good and evil concept. I mean, who were the angels, and who were the demons? Each side saw theyselves with the wings and the other with the pitchforks. Surely, they's some sorry sonsabitches up North, and some kind, loving folk down South. I should know. Man upstairs had hisself a big ole sich-ee-ation with this one. Yes, indeed.

Can't say as why some folks' lives are so drastically different than others – like Edwin and John, for instance. Same womb, same parents, same occupation, and same talents. And yet, vastly opposite outcomes. Maybe it had to do with how they lived in previous lifetimes, if you subscribe to that sort of thinkology. Them Buddhists called it karma; what goes around comes around. Sensible concept, I reckon. No matter, somewhere along the line of lifetimes, Jeremy Gabrick Stone must've done something decent...

CHAPTER SIX

WAR AT THE DOOR

Upon our return, Kate and I instantly felt like we been kicked out of a goose down bed, landing smack dab on a hardwood floor. There was an ominous energy to the town, disconcerting restlessness. I don't know if it was due to the grave loss of men at Gettysburg the week prior, or what, but it was real as rain.

Edwin had requested my presence the next evening to discuss business. We was to meet at O'Flaherty's Pub on 48th Street, on July 12 at 9:00 p.m. Probably be a long night, he said. Kate was fine with my staying out late, but told me she'd likely be absent when I woke the next morning. After her early doctor's appointment midtown, she would pay a visit to the *Daily Tribune* to meet with her new friend, Abby Hopper Gibbons, in hopes they'd print some articles the ladies had penned.

I parted the smoky sea of drunkenness also known as O'Flaherty's, and found my way to a private back room. Red velvet drapes with gold tassels divided the sections. It was here I first encountered the legendary John Wilkes Booth. He and Edwin were pretending to fence with make-believe swords, arguing over what newspapers were dubbing "Draft Week."

"Take that, you blue-balled braggart," John swiped.

"Missed again, you unfortunate hack."

"Draft or no, it's still 20 Yanks to slay one Reb."

"Then 20 it be. Only good Reb is a dead one."

It was like a jousting scene out of Shakespeare.

In effort to replenish the forces needed to win this ghastly war, New York City was gonna enforce a mandatory enlistment. Thing is, they's this deal called conscription, where privileged citizens could pay $300 to make a working class man spill blood in they stead, mostly Irish immigrants. In short, money could buy your way out of the draft if'n you had it. Being we's in an Irish pub, the drunkenly discussions were getting rowdy, and the honky-tonk piano player kept tickling them ivories louder and faster to keep up. Finally the manager, fearing a fight, told him to slow it down and play some soothing ballads to calm the savage beasts. Seemed to help.

"It's suddenly quiet," said John, miming a deathblow with a powerful thrust to Edwin's midriff. "Too quiet. Perhaps I shall go out there and deliberately incite a riot."

"Always craving attention, aren't you?" Edwin answered with a sharp thrust. "Those Celtic drunkards are Yankee, ten to one. They eat Southern sympathizers like sharks crunch minnows."

"That widow-maker Lincoln's only chance is the row upon row of teeth at his disposal. Volume over valor, is it?"

They got the words out between quick, exhaustive breaths.

"Stifle yourself, you quixotic clown," Edwin mimicked a broad swipe at John's knees, who acrobatically leapt several feet in the air, most impressively. "Our fine president will repair the deep chasm, restore peace and equality."

"I shall never share your wretched sentiments, brother. Never!" John diced away with his imaginary saber. Interesting note: Edwin later said Johnny fancied weaponry used in heroic bravery, and collected several pieces from the Mexican War.

The handsomer of the two (if'n I's qualified to judge), John Wilkes boasted a solid, athletic frame, wavy black locks, and a stylish mustache that curled around his lip, halfway to the jawline. His large hazel eyes and long, curly lashes were reminiscent of his pap, whom I later saw in some photographs. I must admit, it was understandable why female patrons swooned. His daring demeanor and impassioned attitude was immediate to me. He spoke in a rhythmic, almost poetic tone. Poised and polished, he was a gentleman of grace and refinement, one might think upon first impression.

"Now then," Edwin was first to pull a chair, "if my rattlepated sibling is quite finished, let us get down to business."

A female server in fishnets and corset delivered a round of cognacs. John Wilkes winked, fondled her buttocks (so much for bein' a gentleman), and acted familiar – carnally, or at the very least, well beyond her capacity as barmaid. Edwin slid his serving to the center of the table. He'd had it with spirits, and requested coffee instead. "With each sip, I'd kill my Mary all over again," he lamented. John grabbed Edwin's glass, adding the contents to his, doubling his dose.

It was stuffy and warm in that rear room. Dark red wallpaper with black, leafy vines first drew my eye. Huge, ornate mirrors and dimly lit wall sconces served as accents. The drapes reeked of smoke, and they's stains on the carpet that I hesitated to guess the origin. Still, the brothers requested the privacy for meetings and relief from admirers.

"Johnny Booth," Edwin plunged in, lighting his polished cherry wood pipe (I preferred the smell to the taste), "this is Gabe Stone, the talented artist I've been telling you about."

"Mr. Stone, a pleasure." He extended a sweaty paw, breath rank with alcohol. From my vantage, I noticed a grotesque wound at the back of his neck.

"Excuse that damned cavernous sinkhole," John gruffed. "Feels like you could drive a fist through it."

"No apology necessary," I said, sitting. I's a tetch nauseated at the sight, truth told. He fetched a sash, and wrapped it twice around the bloody dressings to conceal the eyesore.

"Buy him a bourbon and he'll tell you about the time he fired a bullet in his bum," smirked Edwin, sucking long and hard on the pipe stem.

John returned a sinful sneer. Evidently, John had accidently shot hisself in the thigh with a stage manager's pistol while offering to remove some rust. The brothers were chock-full of jagged quips aimed at establishing pecking order. Edwin was clearly the executor of the family power and finances – a position the younger desperately craved to inherit.

"Do I detect a Southern accent?" John solicited, sipping.

I nodded. "Bayou Teche, Louisiana."

"Ah, native Rebel. I knew I liked you from square one."

"Well, you liked me too much. I'm a New Yorker now," I hastened to clarify.

"So what brings you up here? The good fight..."

"To the dead and dyin', there *is* no good fight."

"Enough prattle," Edwin economized, slapping the table with the palm of his hand. "We obviously ain't see'd eye-to-eye. Politics aside, Johnny, are you not in need of assistance with, uh, other things?" he grappled, less eloquent than usual.

They held a brief conversation in whispers.

"Let me handle this." John spoke through gritted teeth. They shot a mutual glare, then forced smiles between them.

Was I being railroaded here?

"I've invested a modest sum of ten thousand into real estate and petroleum stocks in Boston," John began. "Since I'm preoccupied, mentally and physically," he winced slightly, rotating his shoulders after the ill-advised horseplay, "I would like to offer you a position as my assistant."

What was this? I's supposed to be joining Edwin, not John. Had plans changed? Was Edwin displeased with my talents? No, I says, John Wilkes wouldn't have offered if the elder Booth ain't praised me ever which way. "Well, I…"

"Before you hastily decline," said John, "I'm told you'd be a wonderful addition to my operation. Meticulous, fastidious – I like that. You could create and build scenery, paint backdrops, oversee the actors, help manage my box office, and maybe more."

What was this, P.T. Barnum? Am I one of them suckers?

"There'd be travel, of course," Wilkes continued. "I'll see to it you are comfortably cared for at each venue." He tapped finely manicured nails on the glass goblet.

"That's just the thing," I politely explained, "my wife is expectin'. Not so sure travelin' is in her best interest---"

"I'll pay you handsomely," he cut me off. "Say, $20 a week, plus room and board." He lifted the glass, whirlpooling the contents.

"Make it $50 and we'll talk." I wasn't interested, so I blurted a figure beyond reach. John went wide-eyed. He was a star, making $600 hisself, compared to the jumbo sum of $5,000 Edwin often commanded. No chance he'd entertain such a bloated percentage for a lowly set designer.

"Anyone for blackjack?" he said, taking out some cards and shuffling.

"No, thanks."

"You must be tetched in the head," cried John, taking a gander at his successful brother, who seemingly found it fair.

I'm a rat being batted betwixt alley cats.

"You agree, Edwin?" John's face froze mid-sip. "Are you mad? After an exhale, "Oh, all right, $75. Better be worth it." He narrowed his gaze, putting the cards away.

"Lucrative offer for a man with a growing family," said Edwin, words accompanied by short bursts of smoke. Seems he felt bad about dumping me off, and now was trying to get me a hefty wage with John.

"By the way, where y'all headed?" I probed, calming things.

"Hartford, Boston, Washington..."

"Then points further south," Edwin admonished. "Maybe a run in New Orleans? That's close to home for you, right Gabe?"

"But we's settled in Manhattan," I explained, "Kate loves it here. What about The Winter Garden? You sorta promised me, what was it, $80 a week?" I slipped Edwin a wink. We was finally on the same page.

"Come to think of it, I did," he blew a lazy, wafting smoke ring in support of my story.

"What's the production?" I quizzed the flush-faced Booth.

"Melodrama called *The Marbled Heart.*"

"Made famous by yours truly, a decade ago," Edwin boasted.

Visibly riled, John was more agitated with each passing minute. The competitive banter continued as I pondered the plot. Edwin had indeed decided to partner with brother-in-law and childhood friend, John Sleeper "Sleepy" Clark. They was gonna renovate theaters and mount productions without John's inclusion, or share in the profit. Thing is, Clark insisted on designers of his own, so's I was out. Wilkes would need my services more than Edwin in order to compete. Edwin, being a friend, convinced brother Wilkes to take me on.

"So, here it is," John broke it to me, "$80, not a penny more. Guess I'm feeling generous."

"Well," I smiled smugly, "let me think a spell. Consult my wife."

"Fair enough, but time is of the essence. Provide your answer by end of day, tomorrow. Deal?"

"Deal."

John downed his drink. "Trust me," he leaned in, breath of a bartender who'd been sneaking sips all day, "you don't want to work for that prick, anyhow. Let the Sultan of Snobbery survive without us." He knew just how to cajole, which I respected. So did I, being a royal rascal, myself. This partnership, if there was to be one, would be interesting to say the least.

"How about that card game? I've reconsidered. Another drink?" I was in a celebratin' mood.

"No, I'm good. Now get along home before I go broke, and that lovely wife I heard about closes her legs for the night," John slurred. He'd had his snoot full. Slim chance he'd remember much else.

"Eighty-five, right, Edwin?"

"Heard it with my own two ears."

I wouldn't let on, but I'd pretty much made up my mind to decline the offer. Kate loved our new Manhattan home. I promised her we'd stay put. I had worked with the great Edwin Booth, and would undoubtedly be asked back if I's patient. There would be other offers right here on Broadway. Besides, half the fun was teaming up with Edwin and watching John squirm.

P.S. – I only called him "Wilkes" at times 'cause Edwin said not to. He preferred "Johnny." Must say, though, they's something about Johnny Booth few could resist, me included.

Faint shafts of morning sun found escape routes through the drapes, casting dust-filled beams that stirred me to wakefulness. In the audible distance, I heard unsettling screams and commotion. Was I dreaming? Was there a domestic quarrel next door? Ole Silas McGivney been out drinking and gallivanting all night?

Eyes half-mast, I rolled over to Kate's side of the bed, feeling a cool, abandoned pillow. I's solo, as forewarned. It was late in the morning. The day had dragged itself to 11:00 a.m. according to the watch on my nightstand. In a flash, echoes of gunfire and smashed glass rang out, followed by the smell of fire. I shot up. My thoughts went straight to Kate. Surely, the war ain't made its way to New York City. "Kate!" I called, hoping she was out in the front parlor. No answer. "Kaaate!!" Again, nothing.

I dressed as fast as I could, then bounded out into the crowded streets. A riot was in full force just a few short blocks away. Not our navy-clad militia versus them dreary gray Rebs, but incensed Irishmen, tossing bricks through windows and setting things on fire. Many had paving stones and clubs, and beat the Jesse out of black laborers. Once again, innocent coloreds were catching the brunt of the violence, indirectly blamed. Horrific as any whippings I'd ever witnessed on the plantations.

Wails of agony were heard from the trees, where blacks were beat and set ablaze. One neighbor called it "the war at the front door," as he defended his home on the stoop with a rifle in hand. Police were being attacked, too – they seemed to be the target of much of the aggression. Where were the soldiers? Surely, Mr. Lincoln would send reinforcements immediately. But there was none.

Dodging the mayhem, I saw the Bull's Head Hotel on 44th all aflame. Fire engine sirens pervaded the dense, ashy air. In fact, they's puffs of thick dark cotton billowing from all directions, exacerbating the sultry, oppressive midday temperatures. Them degenerates was screaming and a-swearing something frantic. They smashed glass, looted the shops, and dragged well-known black sympathizers into the streets. What in God's merciful name...?

"Stop!" I commanded, over and over, to no avail. How would I find my Kate in this mess?

"Resist the draft," they bellowed, as somebody announced the *Tribune* building had gone up. I remembered Katie saying she's headed there after her doctor's appointment. The *New York Tribune* was the leading Republican newspaper, but now was a source of contention for incensed citizens opposing the draft.

Upon arrival, I stood across the boulevard as staff sprayed the mob with a shower of automatic rounds from howitzers and Gatling guns. I ducked and forced my way through the throng, praying Kate was somewhere safe. I recognized the panicked expression of a friend and theater colleague named Leslie Miller. He worked hair and makeup for *Hamlet*. "Gabe," he cried.

"Les, I'm desperate for my wife. Please help me."

"I saw Mrs. Stone being whisked off by a small crowd of police towards the 8th District trolley."

"Thank you," I breathed a bit easier. "Are you all right?"

"Yes, but my colored companion, Mr. Percy Gates, was lost in the mob, swallowed in a torrent of gang activity at Gramercy Park. There was cannon fire and everything! I'm just so afraid." He covered his mouth, reduced to sobs. "I was hoping the *Times* or *Tribune* could offer information on casualties."

Leslie had special relations with Mr. Gates, but love is love, I s'pose, and at the moment, my heart sank for him.

"To hell with Abe!" The shouts grew more intense, as even the fireman on hand seemed to sympathize with the gangs. Some of them had been drafted, too. I saw dockworkers and stagehands I knew, helping torch all manner of government and black-sympathetic establishment: dance halls, brothels, boarding houses, and even orphanages. Someone said the mayor's residence had been destroyed.

The sky was a dim, dapple gray; so hazed, I could barely see the tops of buildings. I brushed all evils from my mind and focused on Kate and the baby. It comforted me somewhat to hear she had surrounded herself with police. Their job was to protect and serve, right? Kate was wise and resourceful. She'd find a way to shelter.

Rounding a corner, another horror was upon me. To my left was a turbulent hotbed of activity – a riotous group of Irish working class, like ants on a candy stick, attempted to tip a trolley carrying reserve police. They wielded wooden planks and crowbars, and pounded the passengers over and over. Side to side, they rocked the car violent, tossing bodies out both ends like a dog shaking slobber. Then, with a final Herculean heave, the horses toppled and the wagon flipped on its side to a mix of cheers and horrific screams. I rushed to get close, jumping into the fray, parting the sea of bodies like Moses. Many were immediately crushed in the melee.

As I attempted to offer assistance, I's clubbed malicious in the back of the head, between my shoulder blades, dropping me breathless to the hot, gravely pavement. My tight, blackened lungs was without oxygen as I gasped for breath. I rolled onto my back, groaning. There, under the enormous weight of numerous men and metallic tonnage was a mortally wounded Kate, beaten to a bloody pulp. Crimson streams oozed from her eye sockets, ears, and mouth. In a twisted mess, she looked me straight on with dull, dead eyes, entombed in a frozen, blank stare.

"Oh my God!" I forced words with what little I could muster. "Noooo!!" I felt a fury from deep within. Mustering my faculties, I dragged her lifeless body free and clear to the curb. Our child had obviously perished, as well, Kate's abdomen pressed flat from the crushing force. They's no way a baby could've withstood the assault. I nearly fainted, clinging to my sanity by the slenderest of threads. My heart felt like it was cut out and tossed to the dawgs. May as well have been. I lost everything I held dear in one swift, senseless moment. Seeing stars, I sank to the gutter in a crumbled heap of absolute waste.

"Death to the abolitionists," some shouted in macabre celebration. "To hell with Abe," chanted others. Some wept as they formed makeshift triages to assess the victims. I just blanketed Kate with my body, benign to all sensation. Life had ended, right then and there. God shut his eyes on me. On all of us.

CHAPTER SEVEN

TRAIL OF TEARS AND NEW FRONTIERS

Thursday, July 16, I's released from the hospital, back into a city that suffered the most horrific urban event of the Civil War. Over 100 killed, thousands injured. Federal troops arrived by train, direct from the fields of Gettysburg to help squash the incursion. A rather composed mayor pronounced the "riotous assemblages" had subsided, and "most business was running in its usual channels."

Well, happy to hear we're back to business. My thoughts were grossly sardonic, at the very least. Never mind that everything I cherished in life was ripped from me in an unthinkable act of terrorism. Forget the fact I would never know the child that died in Kate's womb. As long as it was business as usual, I reckon we'd recover. *Blast all you muthafuckers!*

I wandered aimlessly in a catatonic haze. Just blank, like a letter that ain't got no address on it. Eyes were open, but my brain recognized nothing. Jelly legged, I finally found Bleeker, numbly ascended the steps, and entered the vacant second-story apartment. It was dark and silent, bed unmade just as we'd left it. Rotten peach slices and breadcrumbs on the table from the breakfast Kate fixed herself. Her hand-written note read, "Morning, darling, try the fruit – delicious! Home by 2. Love you, K-Dub."

It was the emptiest, most abysmal moment of my life.

Her body, which only days earlier had flitted joyously from room to sunlit room (singing and a-prospecting the birth of our daughter), now lay in a box in the ground at Manhattan's Marble Cemetery. Headstone with just her name, nothing else. Like she wasn't a person with feelings, talents, loved ones, nothing. The memorial service was more than I could take. There was a handful of folks in black and gray attire, moaning and crying on cue, just like y'always expect. I kept pretending Katie was there with me, mourning someone else's misfortune. She would've said, *Praise be it isn't us, Gabe. We're going to grow old together.*

The minister read Bible passages in a workmanlike manner. Little or nothing to do with her or our lives as marrieds'. I placed a letter in her casket that rattled-on repeatedly about how much she meant to me, and how the second I slipped away, I'd come looking for her. I silently prayed for God not to twiddle his thumbs with it, bring us back together soon as possible. Her parents came, which was awkward, but comforting. I was supposed to protect her once they'd handed her over to me. Fine job I'd done. Maybe this was punishment for all my prior wickedness, or maybe this was my line, just born to it.

Mr. Wilmington gave a brief, stoic eulogy, which was appreciated in light of the fact I was mostly unable to speak a word all day long. And that's just what the day was: *long*.

I drew the curtains and collapsed on the bed in utter despair, wallowing in misery. I dreaming of digging a hole next to her and jumping in, burying myself alive. I didn't care to eat, drink, bathe, nor live another minute. Nothing but comatose slumber for weeks.

August 18, 4:30 p.m. The clacker thudded thrice, shaking me from a pleasant dream about Kate. I's in and out of consciousness since six that morning. I ignored it at first, as reality once again slapped me sober. Perhaps they'd mercifully leave me be, but in their persistence, I pried my languid bones from the mattress, traversed the corridor, and cracked the ingress to spy a messenger holding an envelope. The hallway stunk of cabbage, sausage, and onion. After all, it was nearly supper. "I ain't home," I managed to utter.

"You G. Stone?" the messenger asked. I blinked *yes*, though he couldn't see me. "I have a telegram for you."

"Go away," I pleaded, resting my heavy head against the door. "I died in the riot, along with my wife and child. Please go." Not entirely untrue.

"Please sir, I've been paid to ensure delivery. Will you at least accept the letter so I can get back to my job?" I nodded blankly as he slipped it through the gap held only by a thin security chain. The return address said J. B. Wilkes. I tore it open directly.

17 August, 1863

Dear Mr. Stone,

In consideration of the recent atrocities, I extended the time allotted to answer my request, but can wait no longer than noon on Friday, August 21. Offices have been established adjacent to Mr. John T. Ford's new theater in Washington. This will be the starting point for a two-month theatrical tour, ending up back at Ford's for a multi-week run in November, maybe longer. As promised, a weekly sum of $85 shall be paid in exchange for scenic design and execution, talent management, and box office assistance.

On a personal note, Edwin and I send our deepest condolences on the passing of your wife and child, as reported in the casualties list of the Tribune. Edwin says you played a significant role in helping him heal from the loss of his beloved Mary, wishing heartfelt blessings and prayers.

The gravity of the current circumstances has renewed my commitment to entertain the masses, and bring sunshine back to a battered nation.

—J.B. Wilkes

Never got over it, just through it. Days later, I forced myself to move ahead with life. As I came home after a grocery run and a long walk along the Hudson, I felt Kate's spirit in the breeze, urging me to make a change. I went to her clothes closet and took to bent knee, smelling her scent in the fabric. I wept uncontrollably, conjuring the memory of when I'd last seen her in that frock, coat, or hat. I half expected her to come walking right into the room, asking what in the world I's crying for. I could practically hear her necklaces sway against the wood, like they always done when the door would open or shut.

Then, I thought I felt the warmth of her hand resting on my shoulder, and a whisper, telling me she loved me. I methodically packed her things, then my own, and notified the landlord. I would join John Wilkes in Washington City.

Winds whipped tiny tornadoes through the dust and dirt of Tenth Street. The nation's capital was dry and windy, and my nose was constantly full of sand and grit. With Kate's passing, they's too much agony associated with that New York apartment, those streets. I was glad to be somewheres else. Anywhere. Perhaps I'd return one day, but for the time being, I needed a fresh start.

The city was a shambled array of unfinished projects. T'was a city under siege, though no Confederates had yet threatened its environs. Abandoned by loyalists seeking safety to the North, and vacated by the Rebel sympathizers who returned to the South, it was an island without a true identity. Families had packed their wares and bailed. No real mail service or telegrams remained, and markets was scarce and overpriced. It was a disorganized pile, if'n you ask me.

Johnny reported conditions weren't much better in Connecticut, neither, where *The Marbled Heart* was playing to less than full houses, and receiving disappointing notices. "The backdrops were handsome," the critics declared, but Booth was "second-rate," and should not be attempting to recreate the roles Junius and Edwin made famous. I felt bad for Johnny, as the Fords were noticeably lowering their expectations for a successful November run here in Washington. During dress rehearsals, we'd found Booth thoroughly engaging, but apparently the critics were cranky. In fact, we thought of scrapping *Marbled* altogether, and quickly mounting a version of *Richard III* to stir things. He'd had triumphant success with that classic, to the point that even Edwin declared Johnny's performances above his own, and comparable to Junius'. We switched night to night, according to Booth's mood, which only frustrated and infuriated ticket holders expecting to see the other. Should've just stuck with Shakespeare, if I had my way of it.

"Art thou faring well, knave?" Johnny solicited in fluid Elizabethan. "Methinks you requireth a stiff drink."

We strolled the flowered fields around the Smithsonian Institute's red-brick tower. Darkness had all but swallowed the sun.

"I'm down, but not out," I shared. "Just so sad."

"There'll be brighter days ahead," he encouraged. "Just you wait and see, Stone. Brighter days..."

I scoffed, not nearly ready to forget.

As we walked, John seemed acquainted with some of the local element. He received secret winks, nods of acknowledgement, smirks, and tips of the hat from the occasional loiterer or shadowy wallflower. *Who the hell were these people?* Hope he had a weapon with him. (Did I just say that?) "What about you, Wilkesy? You doin' okay?"

"First, don't ever call me that, and why wouldn't I be?"

"Well, your reviews in Connecticut stunk on ice. Don't that pester you?" I was suddenly in the mood to mess with him.

"On the contrary," he said with steely resolve. "I'm overcome with a sense of duty and power."

"What do you mean?"

"When the world has all but beaten me, I become someone else. Thespians gain insight and direction through the power of their characters, their heroes." His whole being became infused with passion. "The vitality and inexhaustible wit of the braggart, Falstaff. The elegant insight of Feste in *Twelfth Night*. Even the pure wickedness of *Othello's* dark Iago. But the role I find most identifiable... Brutus."

"The assassin?"

"None other," his chest puffed, eyes twinkling in the last hint of dusk. "Duty and power," he reiterated, proudly. "See, we stars are special, Stone. We're above the insipid banality of the common man, above his laws, his consciousness. You really ought to try it some time," he sneered, figuring I'd always be his errand boy.

"Funny you should say so," I offered, with method to my madness. "There's times when I'm watching you and Edwin that I get so inspired I want to jump up on stage and join in." I looked over at him, cheeks tugging at a grin. "So, I don't believe you've ever told me – when did you know you wanted to be an actor?"

"To answer that," he lifted his eyes, searching his memory, "you must understand the roles of family inheritance and reverse psychology. You see, my father was an actor, his father was an actor, and so on. It's in the blood, the marrow. And yet, Father took grand measures to see to it we pursued other avenues; avenues less grueling, less damaging to the body and mind."

"Well, you gotta agree, your mind is pretty damaged." I scored a point. "As is your thumb, neck, ass..."

"Touché," he shot me a look. "You really want to know, or not?"

"Go on..."

He cleared his throat. "So, here we were, living in a home that was, frankly, a virtual theater. There were costumes strewn about, mountains of cloaks, armor, wigs, props. Pile upon pile of Playbills, posters, and advertisements cluttered the floor. Shelves, closets, and desks replete with books and scripts, all in different languages, stacked like pancakes for our perusal." He was animated and expressive; even his personal stories were engaging. "We were wide-eyed with wonder," he continued. "Such celebrity, such glamour. It aroused a romantic desire to be just like him. No matter what dad said to the contrary, we were hooked. Though the great Junius constantly touted Edwin's potential, it was mother who told me my piercing, expressive hazel eyes were the exact counterpart to father. Just how far they would take me remained to be seen."

"When did you know you had the chops?" I beckoned, two steps behind, trying to keep up with his quickening pace. "When did you absolutely know you could do it?"

He stopped abrupt, pondering, hands on hips. "Probably when we moved from the farm to North Exeter Street in downtown Baltimore. It was there I ran up against the Bully Boys of Baltimore, the infamous local roustabouts. They were always looking for a fight, hell-bent on causing mayhem for us. I had to protect my brother, whom I daresay was more dazzling in the classroom than the stickball field. With his tightly curled hair and the way he dressed, he was a prime target for trouble."

"What did they do to him?"

"Bullyragging, mostly. Mockery. A few beatings."

"You don't say."

"Yes, but this toughened me, prepared me for the pain and rejection that accompanies the acting trade. It made me good at stage combat, as well, and feats of gymnastics."

"This is all fascinatin', but what I'm really lookin' for is, when did it click? At what exact moment did you flat out *know* you could move people with your abilities?"

"Triple Alley Players," he blurted, "beyond question. That was the basement theater ensemble we formed – myself, Edwin, and Sleepy Clark. We regularly packed the benches full of neighborhood kids. Charged three cents a seat. We acted out bloody battles, sword fights, robberies, and beheadings. You know, the stuff of nursery rhymes, children's tales," he smirked. "As long as it was atrocious, action-packed, and gallant, they were putty in our hands. They all looked on, wide-eyed, starved for more. Quite a sensational little racket we had going. Of course, Edwin kept me under control, delegating the good parts to he and Clark. Even at a young age, Edwin always kept his own ambitions well ahead of mine.

"Anyway, opportunity finally knocked when Edwin accompanied father on tour in Pittsburgh, New York, and Philadelphia. The lucky little shit. In his absence, I wrote a scene for myself whereby a dastardly horse thief stalks his beloved who's been unfaithful. I retched every harbored ounce of anger, hurt, jealously, and rage I'd ever stored in my underappreciated being. The poor gal we'd cast to play my partner, Lucy Chenoweth, screamed and fled for her life through the aisles as I slashed away with a mock dagger. I think there came a moment when we were no longer play-acting. The more she cried in terror (I sensed it from the audience, as well), the more I conceded to the emotion. Finally, a voice bellowed, "Scene" from behind the curtain, and the lamps were mercifully doused. It was tense silence at first, then rafter-rattling claps and cheers. *That* was when I knew." He whipped his head around, abruptly switching topics. "So, then, dinner at the National Hotel? I know a shortcut."

I was frozen for a second, still engrossed in his tale.

The gleam in his eyes told me he'd wished he actually finished her off. I was certainly not going to accompany him down any dark alleys. "Uh, n-no, I'm enjoyin' the walk," I stammered. "I-I'm fine. You go ahead."

"Suit yourself, Stone, but don't lag too long. These are hangouts for hell-raisers, whoremongers, and predatory ruffians." He seemed to take pleasure tormenting and instilling fear.

"Slum here often, do you, Wilkesy?" I countered bravely.

"Sweet, naïve boy." He patted the top of my head, spewing more psychological warfare. With a quick roundhouse, I sent a smart rap to his hand. "Don't ever reform," he patronized. "I need your type around."

"My type?" I bent a brow. "What's that s'posed to mean?"

"Scotch goes good with water, Stone...think about it."

After reading John's disheartening letters from Connecticut, I'd actually sympathized with the louse. Those feelings subsided shortly, as a seemingly sorrowful, frustrated man returned a rejuvenated, malicious trickster. He created nothing but ill will, inciting riots in billiard halls, and throwing props and such at stage management. He took out his loathsome plight on everybody with newfound fervor. That hot-tempered asshole was leaving a wake of deviltry behind him like a skunk leaves a scent, all because of bad reviews. Me and my pal Billy Ferguson, a stagehand, drew straws to see who'd warn Wilkes of Mr. Ford's displeasure. I lost, and ended up shooting billiards with the bastard all night in a pool hall across Tenth.

"Rather tame tonight, huh, Wilkes?"

"Tame, yes," he heaved a long sigh, squeakily chalking the tip of his cue. "I blame the rain and the depressing casualty reports." He completely dismissed the notion it had anything to do with him, sinking shot after shot into leather-laced pockets of the well-worn, red felt table. Booth was a fierce competitor with enormous egocentricity. Each time I's lucky enough to grab a single game, he'd challenge me to best two out of three, then three out of five, and four out of seven. Wouldn't let me leave until he triumphed soundly, then let everyone at work know about it the following night.

I stroked his ego. This was the only way with him. "Johnny, those buffoons wouldn't know real talent if it kicked 'em in the jewels. You're simply amazing out there. Don't fret, my friend."

"What are you getting at?" he wondered in a woebegone way. "Questioning my bankability?" Booth buried the eight ball, then racked quickly to ensure I'd stay a while longer. "Two bags of fan mail per day says my future is secure."

Stinking of brandy again, he resembled an angry raccoon. Big dark circles under his eyes; wet, oily looking locks. Bet I's the only one willing to be near him. Probably his best friend on earth at that moment.

"Well, reviews have been lackluster," I warned. "Ford may not extend the run."

"Oh?" He cracked the cue ball and scattered colored orbs like agitated hornets, dropping three stripes upon initial break. "And what, pray tell, gives you that impression?"

"Ford said so. Ask Ferguson, if'n you like. He and I been lookin' out for you, Johnny. People talk."

"What people?" he brooded, shooting a sinister squint.

"Just...people. Oh, I know you entertain with your gymnastics and jokes and all – the crew gets a kick from it. But the tirades and malicious pranks, coupled with bad reviews are troublesome. Edwin would never...."

He snapped. "Don't you dare compare me to that self-absorbed jackass. I'm not interested in how my brother runs things. Father's little prince!" his voice simmered with rage. "You know, ever since we were boys on the farm, I received the short end of family affections." This was the alcohol talking. *Edwin's a budding star*, Father said. *You aren't suited for the theater. June and Edwin, yes, but not you Johnny. No sir, you'll stay and watch the farm.* Bullshit! That's what it is. Pure and utter bullshit."

He was performing, I could tell. He was like an impassioned Shakespearian soliloquy. Loud voice, flamboyant gestures. "And Edwin, with the smug taunts: *Perhaps one day I'll let you launder my costumes.* And his overblown tales of touring, and San Francisco, and adoring women. He'll never know the hardships and agony of my plight! I've been shot, stabbed (both unintentional and intentional), frostbit, sun-scorched, overworked, and underpaid. I've suffered sleepless nights, unjust reviews, small venues, and audiences that acted more like oil paintings." He unloaded his burdens.

Then his stick slipped and struck the table side, splintering into pieces. He unintentionally sent the cue ball over the lip and under a lady's frock. The patrons burst out in instantaneous applause, both for the speech and the accident. I restrained a laugh, not knowing whether to crack up or cry. His amusingly inebriated monologue ran the gamut. Most walked on eggshells in Booth's presence, but not me. I ain't afraid to be straight with John, considering our brief but eventful history.

"I's under the impression the two of you were on good terms," I told him as I sipped my brandy.

"Edwin's most recent correspondence said the time spent as a family was healin' and pleasant. Went s'far as to say you helped hide and nurse his theater critic friend, wounded Union officer named Badeau, along with his black servant durin' the riots."

"Yes," I'd broken his pattern, "well, that was then. This is now."

"Look, ain't no such thing as advantage or disadvantage."

"Huh?" he groaned, gathering severed stick shards.

"In your house, all is well – whether to buy, whether to sell. That's a little limerick of Kate's."

"What the hell are you talking about?"

"Sakes alive," I says. It was an uphill battle, but I's trying to make a point. "Things ain't necessarily good or bad, they just *is*. Compared to the starvin' actor beggin' for bit parts, John Wilkes Booth is nothin' short of a demigod. And compared to that same strugglin' actor, the soldier dyin' on the battlefield seems less fortunate considerable. See?"

His expression softened as it seemed to sink in.

"On the other hand," I went on, "the millionaire oil investor probably thinks Edwin Booth is a mere wanna-be. Get it? It's all relative."

His eyes sobered. "Stone, you're a strange little sod, but for some damned reason, I like you."

He had no idea.

John downed another shot. His voice was hoarse and fading. "You mean well," he rasped. "My apologies for the behavior."

"What's wrong with your throat?" I asked. "Croup comin' on?"

"No, this durn thing developed on a snowbound trip to St. Louis. Been on and off all year. This rain surely doesn't help."

"Well, take care of yourself. We can't have a mute star. T'ain't drama for the deaf and dumb now, is it?"

"I'll take some hot lemon tea back to my room. Anyhow, truth be told, I lost a fortune in oil stock last month. You happen to be the recipient of my wrath. Again, I'm sorry. Please don't discuss it with my family. That's all I need to hear – Edwin bragging about his growing surplus. They needn't know my misfortunes. You know, Gabe, aside from mother, my dear sister Asia is the only one who truly loves me. I miss her deeply. Letters can't replace her understanding embrace. I've had many women in my life, but none as beautiful a soul as she."

Was that a tear trailin' down?

"I forget now, you have any brothers or sisters?" he asked.

"No," I reminded him. I was seeing a side of Booth that made it difficult to comprehend his legacy. I'd seen Johnny be the most kind, sincere, debonair fella when he had a mind to. Then, in a flash, he'd turn sinister as shit. His obsession seemed less and less for the stage, and more on riches and hatred towards Lincoln's War, as he put it. He was a *whatever I put my mind to* sort of soul, which caused me growing concern.

After several moments of friendly exchange, I lowered my guard. I reminded him that President Lincoln and First Lady would be in attendance the following week, and what an honor it was that our nation's leader chose to patronize his play. I was trying to lift his spirits, but stupidly struck a raw nerve.

"What do I care about ole what's-his-name – *King Abraham Africanus*? The menial rube eats and wipes his ass with the same fingers. That ignoramus is lucky I don't jump the footlights and beat him with the blunt end of a pistol." Deadly earnest now, "Better yet, sneak out at intermission and fill him full of lead in the lobby."

"You'd never get the chance," I begged. "Presidents don't sit among the people, let alone mingle in the lobby." He was just shooting the bull, but my mind and mouth continued right on going as usual. "Dignitaries always sit in the boxes, balcony level. You know that. Only one way in, one way out. You'd be caught for sure, lessin' you leapt out the front."

"Are you quite finished?" I nodded in affirmation. "Thank you." He tugged his collar. "As I was about to say before you rudely started your lecture, he's destroyed my beloved South, and ruined a country formed for the white, not black. I have a mind to kidnap the bastard, and serve him up to President Davis, bound and gagged."

John Wilkes' words was for show, and yet, more disturbing than ever. He threw back shot after shot of breast-burning whiskey. They was lined up seven long, upside down on the edge of the table. His blood-red eyes revealed the rancor of a man that ain't just telling tales, but actually intended to carry out his hateful threats. He told me once that he fantasized as a boy about epic heroics in the face of conflict. Almost seemed to thrive on the drama, he was eaten alive by his own self-importance.

"Only wish I had a life-size Lincoln dummy to pummel, each time my rage arises," he forced his failing voice to relax. "Take target practice," he whispered. "Draw a bull's-eye and blast a hole for every state in the Confederacy."

My imagination stirred. Drunk or not, this dialogue was engrained in my brain. His views were extremely one-sided, unwavering, and diabolical. Here I was, a true patriot, elated at the idea of meeting Lincoln. In fact, I admit I's a little obsessed. John had only death and destruction in mind.

Like I said, the world was full of rascals. The one called John Wilkes Booth was no longer lurking in dark, cold shadows. His intentions were crystal clear, white hot as the summer sun.

Unable to sleep, I lit the kerosene lamp and penned another note to Edwin. The conversation with John was most alarming to me. I began to question further involvement in his operations, suggesting Edwin reconsider taking me back in New York. He was having continued prosperity with his Dramatic Oil Company (that's what they called theyselves). I asked would he rethink the thing? At the very least, I decided not to accompany John on tour, but instead do my designing full-time from the offices on Tenth Street.

I'd made fond friends there: Ferguson, Ford, John Peanuts (the boy who sold snacks in the alley), and Fanny in the front office. I'd fashioned a comfortable home in Washington, too. T'wasn't a grand mansion, but my spacious Funkstown flat afforded me a studio to design, paint, and sculpt. The neighborhood later became known as Foggy Bottom, which tickled a tetch because farts was always so dad-burn funny to me.

I was typically awake all hours working on a sacred, secret project that I would tell you about, but I'd have to kill you. I would shock people with my art, just like that witch-lady said. Mr. Ford had lent me some photographs of Mr. Lincoln, and from that, I created the masterpiece of a lifetime.

CHAPTER EIGHT

JUST PLAIN LINCOLN

"*Of all the countless renditions of my husband (that the artists and photographers have presented), I have yet to agree that any one in particular captures the mysterious layers of his complex character...before this.*" -Mary Todd Lincoln

The First Lady sent a letter addressed to the theater, thanking me for the portrait that Ford forwarded on my behalf. I was flabbergasted and pleased as peaches for the compliment. *Mr. Lincoln and I wish to extend an invitation to visit the Executive Mansion this coming Monday afternoon at five o'clock, as we understand the show will be dark*, she said.

Not just dark – closed, I hasten to admit. No extension. Nonetheless, words couldn't express my excitement. I did not expect to hear back from the Lincolns. Word was out they was not impressed with Booth's performance in *Marbled*, and thus, elected not to visit backstage. Probably best, as I ain't cared to witness the potential fireworks of a face-to-face between philosophical foes.

Five o'clock Monday, punctual as always, I entered the grounds of the great White House and strode up the semi-circle dirt path. No guards, no nothing. In fact, folks was picnicking and loitering right there in the yard. They could've literally tossed corn cobs or apple cores into them tall, open windas, if'n they had the aim, since they was no screens to speak of. (Ain't sure they was such a thing at that time, anyhow.) They's this tarnished bronze statue of Thomas Jefferson, hand over heart, holding the Constitution, but it had turned moldy green from neglect. Looked like it ain't been polished in months, maybe years. An unsupervised lad was striking the legs repeatedly with a rose stem switch. No blame respect.

I made my way up to the front portico beneath 10 capacious columns. Whole surroundings slightly smelled of sewage from the nearby canal. I kept waiting for a guard or something to step out and greet me, but none did, so's I simply opened the front door. The smattering of picnicking hang-abouts (who didn't seem to mind the odor) must've wondered what business little ole me could have possibly had with him. I hardly looked official; wasn't even wearing a coat or nothing because it was quite warm. I just walked right in; so much for security. I got no answer for that...

Once through the threshold, the vestibule opened to a grand hallway. Right off, a solid wave of muckity-mucks and bluecoats passed by like a herd of cattle, finally revealing the gentle giant, standing right there to my twelve o'clock. His back was turned, hands clasped behind, head down. How poorly his black suit fit – snug up top, baggy around the inexpressibles.

After a moment, he turned my way. Abraham Lincoln was a lean, rangy man with narrow shoulders, a prominent nose, sunken cheeks, and melancholy eyes set deep in shadow. His bearded face bore the creases and concerns of a country at war with itself, animated only when he extended gratitude towards me. I was in complete and utter awe.

"Mother informs me I have a five o'clock meeting with Mr. Gabe Stone," said the president. "Might that be you?"

"Yes, sir," I sort of regurgitated. I stepped forward into the light and stared direct into his wrinkled overlay.

"I am delighted to make your acquaintance," he offered, in a high-pitched tone that ill-matched his height and aged appearance. I heard he's 50-something, but he looked 70. Brushing aside his formerly black, unruly hair, he said, "I am a great admirer of talent, and you, son, deliver by the cargo."

"Thank you, sir."

"You're a regular Rembrandt, you know? Where'd you learn to paint like that, Academy?"

"Uh, Minneapolis Poly..." I pulled up short. I couldn't lie to *Honest Abe*. "Actually, I's mostly self-taught, sir."

"First off, let's reserve the *sirs* for medieval knights and cranky old congressman. Secondly, good for you. True knowing comes from within. Speaking of knights, bow, will you?"

Huh?

"Go on, bow. You bend at the waist and all, don't you?"

I obliged. *Where was this goin'?*

"I hereby appoint you Royal Court Artist," he jokingly decreed, touching both my shoulders with his index and middle digits as I stooped low.

"Thanks, your Majesty," I croaked like I'd caught cold, only I ain't. "Sorry, just nervous, I s'pose."

"Nervous? I'm the one who should be nervous in the company of such artistic ability. In the Renaissance era, who were the true leaders? Not the politicians. It was the artisans, the painters, and poets – that's who we revere and remember. They were the ones that made all the difference."

I smiled, thinking how much I liked the man already.

My portrait was placed on a gold stand with an eagle on top, in the Great Hall for all to admire. Though poorly lit, it was strikingly accurate. Needed to be. I learned that another artist (British guy named Matthew Wilson) would be painting Lincoln soon. Abe said he's sure mine would be better. My chest swelled as he told me the painting would remain here until a proper place had been decided. His vote was the State

Dining Room, pending Mary Todd's possible veto. "I'd hang it right now," he said, "but I best clear it with my shorter half; that don't mean she's short on potency, you know."

"I understand."

The mansion (on the outside at least) was reminiscent of some of the finer Southern manors, yet inside, it was deplorably shabby. Dust coated the chandeliers and moldings, the wallpaper and carpets were dank, and crap and clutter covered every desk and shelf. Still, I wished Granddad could see me now. *Never amount to nuthin', huh, ya curmudgeony old crank?* I imagined shaking my fist, unsure whether to look up or down, if you catch my meaning.

"I understand you design scenery at Fords?" Abe said.

"Yes, that's correct."

"Mrs. Lincoln and I frequent that wonderful theater. Ford is a friend."

"Mr. Ford speaks highly of you, as well." I kept fussing with my hands; didn't quite know where to put them. "I must mention, when my late wife and I first arrived in New York, we attended a performance of Laura Keene's musical, *Seven Sisters*, same night as you and Mrs. Lincoln."

"Yes, of course," he nodded. "We loved that one." His expression shifted, and a concerned warmth flooded his eyes. "Now, you'll have to excuse me, but you said late wife? Was it illness, or as a result of the Great Trouble?"

I told him of my tragedy during the draft riots. The president was quiet for a moment. Them gray eyes got more and more glassy. He broke the silence and described the loss of his sons, Eddie, then Willie, just last February. "Our beloved boy slipped off here in the mansion from typhus, possibly dysentery," he informed. Washington was rife with disease, especially in summer. "Death haunts me." He suddenly wilted like the most depressed dandelion in the field. I must say, I figured I'd meet a direct, calculating commander. Scarce expected a genuine human being, vulnerable and openly emotional. And yet, he was confident, reliable, and supremely earnest, all the same.

He pulled me aside, hush-toned like he's telling tales out of class. "Speakin' man to man, I also lost a love before I met my Mary. Died right before the wedding. I s'pose I never fully recovered. Man to man, now," he cocked an eyebrow – sincere, trusting.

"Guess every heart breaks alike," I surmised, "slave, plain Joe like me, or president of the most powerful nation on earth."

"Reckon God keers for us all the same, son," he said, exposing prairie roots. He laid slender, weathered fingers on my shoulder. I admit to nervousness at first, but quickly felt welcome. In no time, he'd opened up like a long lost friend. I dare say, almost like an equal. "It is well-documented that I'm no orthodox churchgoer," Abe admitted, taking a seat on some red carpeted steps. "It nearly cost me many an election. Religion tends to do more dividing than unifying, but I do believe a heavenly realm awaits," he straightened his bowtie, "where your wife and child, and my dear ones eagerly anticipate a reunion." He squinted, looking away solemnly. "My end will befall me long before yours. Perhaps soon, I believe."

"What do you mean, Mr. President?"

"Please, just plain Lincoln will do."

"All right, Mr. Lincoln," I complied. Ain't seemed quite right addressing the leader of the world in such a common way. We was virtual strangers, but I admit, the moment we met, I felt we's kindred spirits.

"If you have a minute, would you like to follow me?"

"Sure," I said. What was I gonna tell him, *Nope, gotta go home and fix my fence?*

Couple of guards with big long swords were standing nearby the whole time as a precaution, listening in, or trying to anyhow. Lincoln excused them with a reassuring nod.

Abe creaked and listed as he labored along, all flat-footed, walking like a rickety tower of unbalanced bricks. His head tilted slightly towards his left shoulder. I followed him down the cavernous corridor into an ellipse-shaped room of blue. He shut the door behind and sauntered to a round velvet sofa with a plant growing out the middle. "Like the mansion?" he asked. He took a seat and spanked the cushion for me to join, raising a dust-plume.

"Oh, yes." I hesitated for a moment. "Well, honestly, it is a tad dreary and hungry for some style. This blue room is nice enough, I s'pose, 'cept for the flies and mosquitas." The back windows were half-open to catch a breeze, letting bugs come and go as they pleased.

"Yes, the blue and red rooms are my favorite spots in this damned blast place." *Well, I'll be! Lincoln cursed?*

"The First Lady asked for a deficiency appropriation to spruce it up, but how can I expect people to pay taxes for such a thing as decorating when our soldiers can't even afford blankets?"

"I like your thinkin'…Lincoln." As if he ain't heard that one a million times. Nonetheless, he managed a slight smile.

"And I like you. Can't put my finger on it," he removed some spectacles and tapped his pointer digit to his lips, "but I do."

"You talk different than you write," I said. "Simpler."

"Yes, so I'm told. In public and on paper, the statesman appears. Reckon even ole Lincoln can sound eloquent if given the time to properly prepare his thoughts."

He checked his watch again during a few seconds of silence.

Now this is more like it, I says to myself, taking a solid gander around the room. The furniture was blue satin with gold damask. Giant golden cornices anchored either side of the French windows that provided picturesque views of the grounds. The pièce de résistance was the enormous two-tiered gasolier with 20 glowing glass bulbs. "Needs a mural on the ceilin'." I came right out with it. "Bet that'd be a pain in the rump to paint, though. Too bad Michelangelo ain't alive no more. He'd do it right proper."

"Yes, he sure would," he admitted, then thought a second. "Maybe I can convince the missus to let you cook something up."

"Me? Oh, I don't…"

"Sure, why not?" he furrowed his brow, tilting his head. "You're a Renaissance man, remember? Why don't you paint the Kentucky landscape, or Springfield? Make the flies and skeeters feel more at home," he laughed to hisself. Then he took a look towards the partition. "If the ceiling's too tough to get at, maybe this wall here could use your talents? 'Course, it would be fitting to feature some sort of Washington scape, or Philadelphia, maybe Boston Harbor. You know, historically pertinent."

"Oh, well…I'm not so sure I's capable," I said. "It's one thing to paint on canvas in your own studio, you know, a controlled environment where you can make mistakes, spill on the floor and whatnot. I'd be way too shaky to paint right here on the mansion wall; too a-feared I'd muck it up considerable."

"Muck it up? Nah, not you, Rembrandt."

I immediately reconsidered. Probably fetch a heap of money if'n I'd agreed to it. Mary Todd would find the funds.

"Perhaps you sell yourself short. It's just a wall."

"Alrighty then, I'm willin' to study on it."

"Good. I'll start chopping away at Mother, but it won't take but a few swings. My Molly loves your work as much as I do." Molly seemed to be his pet name for Mary Todd.

It was so strange being a guest in the Executive Mansion. It didn't seem like a president's house – much too informal. It felt more like a moldy ole museum that got blowed up by a bomb or something. I mean, if the kitchen was half as dirty as the rest, I'd be afeared to stay for supper. "Mr. Lincoln, I may be outta line, but who cooks and cleans 'round here?"

Name's Miss Mary Ann Cuthbert. Why, are you hungry?"

"No, just curious." Then I got to wondering about the water closets. "What if a visitor needed to take a leak? Or a b.m.? She tend to them places, too? Keep 'em sanitized and such?" I forget why I asked them direct personal questions, but I did. Sometimes my brain just started going haywire all on its own.

He smiled and revealed yellow, slightly misaligned, stained choppers – all his (not made of wood like you sometimes hear). "Well, which is it?" Lincoln inquired. "Hungry or constipated? There's a clean crapper down the corridor…"

"Neither. Just askin's all."

"Oh, well, if you're just asking, this is a government office, true, but a home, too." He buried his hands in his pockets. "This place belongs to the people, especially the downstairs. Upper private quarters, little different story. It's a mess up there. You oughta see how my monkeys treat it when I ain't around." He shook his head. "Long story short, you need something, nature comes a-calling, don't hesitate."

"Thanks, nice to know."

"You remind me of my eldest, Robert. Direct, but sincere and thoughtful. He is joining Grant's army. We worry so about his safety, but the Lieutenant General assures me he'll be kept safe from harm, best possible. He graduated Harvard, you know."

"No, I didn't know," I sheepishly admitted. "Don't that make him eligible for somethin' nobler than gettin' his ass blowed up on a battlefield?" *Blast, my big mouth.*

"I suppose," Lincoln smirked, "but Robby has his heart set on it. Hard to separate a man and his convictions, despite his mother's and my protestations. To him, ain't nothing nobler than serving your country's military." He looked away and straightened a crooked picture frame. "Jeff Davis couldn't convince you to join, huh?"

"Come again?"

"Jefferson Davis, insurgent bigwig...couldn't convince you to enlist?"

Was this a joke? A trap? He thought I's Confederate! It must be my durn accent. Was I fixing to be surrounded and taken off in cuffs? What if my intentions *was* criminal? I waltzed right in like I owned the place, after all. Seemed as if any commoner had access with very little fuss. "Oh, no, Mr. Pres...I mean, Lincoln." I got all panicky, half-expecting Feds to jump out from behind a curtain. "I-I assure you, I side with the slave. I's practically colored, myself, seeing how I'm from New Orleans. By way of St. Louis, anyway. I bolted North soon as I could. A country that denies absolute equality to the negro ain't my country."

"Steady, son," he raised a hand, narrowing his gaze and picking my brain. "You suggest absolute equality? Nigg..." he corrected hisself, "black same as white, in every way?"

"Yup. Hundred percent. Don't you?"

He took a calculated pause. "No. Political suicide," he said, guarded. "I allow freedom and opportunity must be granted to all law-abiding citizens. However, I still maintain there's an enormous chasm between slavery and absolute equality. Whites are superior, no doubt." He paced a spell in a worrisome way. "It's this damn slavery that's the thing; if slavery ain't morally and constitutionally wrong, nothing is. We should round 'em all up, ship 'em back to Liberia." He mumbled low, obviously perplexed and shaken. "End this godforsaken mess, once and for all."

I heard him say this, clear as day. This had to be a test. Shocking as it sounds, I refused to label Lincoln a man who favored whites. Even *he* was politically forced into saying it, that's how crazy things were. The war pained him more than most know. This is what I believe in my heart, anyhow.

His youngest boy, Tad, come a-running in at this point and broke the mood a bit. By the way Lincoln acted with him, I could tell Tad was his pride and joy. After a brief introduction and exchange of whispers, Tad runned off again.

"Mr. Lincoln," I spoke up with everbit of courage and conviction I had in me, "may I say somethin' on the slave matter?"

"Yes, of course."

"I been as close to it as anybody. I knowed the negro as not only slave, but as friend and family. You wipe away all the bullshit and what you got there is everbit equal to the white man as day equals night. You got to know it. Screw the stipulation *under the law*, I'm talkin' the heart and soul. God showed me truth time and again, and he'll show you if'n you let 'em."

After a moment of reflection, he said, "Thank you, son. Not to worry, God works as we speak." He was visibly calmer now. "We're working to keep slavery from spreading west, or continuing at all. I've considered penning an Amendment to free blacks entirely."

"Really? Good. You'd be doin' right by it."

"Getting it passed is another matter." With hands behind his back, he approached a towering gold leaf mirror, filling it with a hollow gaze. "What do you fear, Mr. Stone?" he asked, staring at his own reflection.

"Please, call me Gabe."

"Very well, Gabe." He looked directly at me through the mirror, rotating slowly. "In that case, you may call me Abe. Abe and Gabe," his demeanor lightened considerable. "Let's form an act, and tour Europe." He managed the crumbs of a chuckle.

"Ventriloquism is popular nowadays," I chimed. "Reckon I should be the dummy, outta respect for the office."

"No, no talking dummies – Shakespeare!" Lincoln was greatly energized now. *"Two Gentleman of Verona.* Can't you just picture my knobby knees and berries shoved in them tights?" Our bellies busted uncontrollable for a long spell. We choked and gagged and coughed with delight. 'Tis a rare thing when your president makes reference to his own pills. "I beg your pardon," he finally sobered, "I posed a serious question, then coarsely jested. My apologies. Just so blamed cleansing to laugh like this. We should all do it more often."

I kept coughing, not even remembering the question.

"What do you fear, Gabe? That was my inquiry."

"Right," I said. I took a deep breath, then another. "Oh, I don't know, dyin' with my music still inside me. Never seein' my Katie again. You?"

"Assassination." He removed his glasses and pinched the bridge of his nose. Things got serious in a snap. "I pretend to Mary and her confident, Lizzie Keckley, that the threats are empty and unfounded, but that's only because Mary has already lost two sons. She wouldn't survive another such heartache. I, myself, am at peace with any eventuality. It is the family I fear for."

I wanted to tell him about Booth's threatening discourse, but didn't dare. "Mr. Lincoln, sir, may I change my answer?"

"Why, of course."

"Nothin'. I fear nothin'."

"And why not?"

"Because there has to be more than this. You said that you believe in a beyond, where souls go to await reunion. Well, I believe the same. If death is the corridor back to love and the ultimate source, I'll gladly take it. I just don't think you nor I are quite done here any time soon."

"Right you are, my friend. You make a fine point." His eyes twinkled with renewed interest. "In that case, Gabe, may I change my answer as well?"

"You can do whatever ya want, you're the president."

"I fear the end of this great nation. If folks could only climb inside my heart and mind, if only I were seen by all as my maker sees me. Ever since my election, I've received threats of all manner. I've even switched routes into Washington under a veil of secrecy, cancelled appearances, and traveled in disguise to avert disaster."

"What kind of disguise? Wig? Glasses?" I loved a clever camouflage.

"No, just a plaid-rimmed Scotsman's beret and full-length trench coat. I reckon I already got the mole and funny nose."

I loved his dry sense a humor. "Well that ain't usin' your imagination much. One stiff wind, the hat flies away, and everyone knows it's you right off. I'll help you do better. What about guards? Can't they protect you?"

"Gabe, if a man's conviction is to kill, there is little to be done. I know this. My service is limited, and my tenure shall undoubtedly be cut short at the hands of an assassin."

I was chilled by his startling prediction. "Is this a gut feelin', or is there intelligence to suggest it?"

"Depends on your definition of *intelligence*. I have a packet full of more than 80 direct death threats, and spirit messengers that forewarn. I looked in the mirror after I won the election, and saw two faces looking back: one true, and the other old and wrinkled, fated for disaster. Already got the wrinkles, just waiting for the latter. And yet, I find solace knowing my demise somehow fulfills God's fate for his people." Abe's expression relaxed. He was strangely at peace with the thing.

"C'mon now, don't say that. I get them spiritual messages, too, in my dreams. But ya know, I always feel I can change 'em. Well, at least sometimes. It's a curiosity, fate and free will. Which one do you allow it is?"

"I allow it's fate." He scratched his whiskers.

"I allow it's both. I equate it to bein' on a steamer, headed down the Mississippi. You get on in Memphis, knowin' you's headin' for New Orleans, and nuthin' to do about it. That's fate. But while you're on board, you got the free will to spend the trip doin' whatever ya please. Playin' cards, drinkin', dancin', and suchlike. Make sense?"

He was staring off into space, yet somehow gleamed with understanding. "How do you manage to know me so well, Gabe? In my heart, in the eyes of your portrait, it's like you've exposed my soul through brush and paint."

"Oh, I don't know," I admitted. "Reckon we were on a collision course to meet, we three."

"Three?"

"Yes. There's this voodoo witch that gave me a psychic..." I nearly spilled it.

"No, go on," he nodded. "I, myself have entrusted mediums to help guide me, and reconnect with loved ones. Mary has 'em here often. On occasion, it is somewhat of a carnival, I admit. And yet, other times, they're inexplicably accurate and valuable. I am somehow resigned to the fact I must die so the nation might live."

Just then, I hatched the scheme to end all schemes, like I's appointed by a higher power. It was what them Japan people call *satori* – instant awakening in one stupendous bolt! When I think about it, I get all gooseflesh. It would involve many people, and take time to formulate, but I was hell-bent on making it happen. It would be my life's opus, setting this entire circus in motion.

"Apologies, Gabe." He dug out his fancy watch fob again, then dropped it back into his vest. "Let's continue this discussion another time. Soon, I promise."

"Splendid. I accept."

"I'm afraid my duties return me to early evening meetings." Abe studied me, smiling. "Please, let us be sure to continue our communications in the near future. I feel I've found a loyal companion and ally in you."

"Same here. Ya know, my pap and granddad raised me, and loved me in their own way, I guess. But they never took the time to listen or consider my side of it. You did that today, and you the durn President of the United States! Thank you."

"No, thank you, Rembrandt. You've indeed learned me as much as I learned you." He winked at me. "Come back next Monday, and bring your brushes and paints. You got a wall to beautify."

"Deal."

Sounds like horse crap, but ole Lincoln and I became bosom pals, honest Injun. He was sort of the great uncle I never had. He said I's just the sign he'd prayed for, too, admitting time and again to asking God for a beacon – a thought, person, or event to somehow pierce the dark depressing cloud that hung over him for years on end. At the end of the day, best way to define it was this: Lincoln showed a whole lotta parts of hisself to a whole mess of folks, but I reckon he saved a special unseen side for me, and me alone. I can only comment on the bit I seen, the things we discussed, and the things we experienced as friends.

I did end up painting a mural right there on the White House wall, only in a private dining room, instead. He said no depiction of Springfield ever done it more proud, and it would force him to keep the room cleaner, too. My being around for the month gave us loads of time to talk. In truth, them deep conversations I just described might've taken place much later in our fellowship. Exact recollections were unclear, dad-gum. Nonetheless, we exchanged thoughts and ideas, unguarded, unedited, and at times, downright undignified. Go ahead and scoff, but you can put it in your pipe and smoke it for all I care. I know my telling you so don't make it so, but it *was* so, and that's why I'm a-sharing it with y'all. No more to say on the subject.

We met once a week, sometimes more, at that large white mansion on Pennsylvania Avenue. We'd get to laughing, occasionally crying, and always voicing things ain't fit for print.

CHAPTER NINE

OVER-PRONOUNCED H'S

I stared at a weathered tintype of Kate and me, the only one in existence. It was a sepia tone treasure that graced the dressing table, posed for on our wedding day, set in a fancy gold frame. It would be the thing I'd grab if'n there was a fire. We were supposed to be celebrating our second anniversary, and the baby would've been a bona fide toddler by now. A lone tear trickled down and stuck to the tip of my chin. I always figured we'd build a simple cottage on a shady plot somewhere – Jersey or Connecticut maybe, Children in the yard, Ma and me on a porch swing with a glass of lemonade.

God had other ideas.

I made me a nice little home near Georgetown, though. My daily routine consisted of a hike on foot to Ford's in the mornings, where I worked as in-house senior designer. Sounded strange: *senior*. I's just 22, or was it 23? I forget. No matter. Then, I'd take a trek to Union Square to check the progress on the Capitol dome, return down the great mall in back of Lincoln's house, and make my way down to Foggy Bottom at the shores of the Potomac to watch the fireflies come out. Full day, for sure.

Frequently, dark clouds would shroud the city right quick. Great lightning storms drenched me like a drowned rat before I could take cover. Then came the humidity and awful stench. The storms created puddles that served as breeding grounds for disease. The District suffered from unpaved, muddy roads, god-awful garbage collection, and swarms of bugs and mosquitos. I reckon that's how come the Lincoln boy got so sick.

When I had spare time, I volunteered at the hospital in Georgetown, one of many new facilities built to house the ill and injured soldiers. Overflow got sent to the Patent Office, and sometimes even the Capitol building. Believe it or not, I worked right alongside notable novelist, Louisa May Alcott. Perhaps she had a hand in encouraging me to pen this here memoir. Likely not, but I'd go ahead and say she did. Made for a spicier letter when I corresponded with Edwin and John.

On a sidenote, the city was expanding rapid, straining the water supply. A new aqueduct was being built to store ten thousand gallons of fresh water a day. That would surely provide relief to the tens of thousands of suffering citizens and soldiers. I's happy about that. All I got to say for now...

Needing to reach out in the worst way, I scribed a letter to my old friend Mary Randolph at Nottoway. Somebody must have forwarded it, as she'd gone down to nest in New Orleans. I told her of my plight, and how I'd lost the family I loved so dear in the draft riots. She wrote back promptly, offering much support and warm condolences. Mary just lost family, herself. Her older brother, Algernon, was kilt at the battle of Vicksburg in May.

Damn, when will this nightmare be over?

Mary was fascinated, however, at the news that I's working with the Booths. *Here we was, talking about them like dewy-eyed admirers, and just look at you now,* she wrote. I wouldn't dare say all it took was bouncing on an old mattress, and conjuring it in my mind. She'd think I'd swallowed a jug of loony juice. Maybe some luck and skill weighed in, too. *Perhaps I shall visit you someday after a performance, shake hands with the first family of the American stage?"* I chortled. They was just regular folk to me, them Booths. Both magnificent and miserable, and I'd come to know them well. Maybe she'd get the chance, the next time John toured through New Orleans. I think he's headed there soon, but I'd have to check the itinerary.

Mary's world had turned topsy-turvy, too. Her father took Moses and the slaves to Texas to plant cotton, like Pap had done. Maybe it was safer there. Texas was huge, like a country to itself. Not a bad place to hide until the dust settled.

Mr. Randolph left the ladies behind to maintain Nottoway. Mary shared the harrowing tale of being blasted by a federal gunboat on the Mississippi, only to be spared by a Union shipman who'd once been graciously entertained at the home and urged a cease-fire. She spoke of an actual cannon ball being lodged high up in the wood siding. Lawd have mercy! Southern hospitality had saved that magnificent place. Made me miss home and simpler times.

Years afterwards, I caught a case of the *lonesomes*. Though no one could ever replace my Kate, I wrote Mary to inquire about her marital status. Couldn't hurt, could it? She was the only other gal I truly fancied. Just my luck, she'd wed a prominent New Orleans lawyer. Guess the portrait proved successful after all. They tied the knot right there in that wonderful white ballroom. Horace Upton, I think she said his name was. Fortunate man. They had six youngins, did I mention that? What a blessing.

Life had surely marched forward. I could tell because I'd begun losing hair (except in my nose and ears), losing sleep, and losing my boyish physique. On the plus side, I ain't crying near as much, if at all. They's a bitter sweetness to the realization that time had passed. I thought of my Kate on a daily basis, but not minute-by-minute no more, or even hourly. Wherever Katie and Amelia were, they's safe and well. The notion soothed.

Now bear with me, but the only way to give you the sense of it is to write it as it sounded. By and by, my dialect improved (or worsened, depending on whom you ask). I worked real hard to sound like a Yank. If I was going to be one, may as well sound like one. I slipped here and there, but that doesn't matter (see, used to say *don't matter*, or *ain't no matter*). I gained it back later on, but for the time being, I hid it well.

I continued communicating with John Wilkes and Edwin with regularity. Edwin was wooing crowds as both actor and producer. The Winter Garden and Walnut Street Theaters were flourishing. His and Sleepy's monopoly extended to Philadelphia and Boston, and would be expanding again soon, I'm sure. The finely furnished Gramercy townhouse that Edwin purchased was a testament to his ongoing success. He could be seen taking handsome carriages through the parks and pathways of New York with his little daughter, Edwina, and was frequently accosted by throngs of adoring fans. John, however, continued to tour – including the deep South (I'd have to tell Mary) – to help fund his struggling Petrolia Oil ventures. Edwin said John was obsessed with money, and Wilkes was so envious of his brother's success that he lied about the status of his unproductive wells. It was all a convenient smokescreen for more sinister activities, we'd learn, as Edwin caught wind that J.B. was recruited by the Confederacy to dethrone Lincoln. "That tyrant wants to be king," John would declare, with an up-to-no-good gleam in his eye. He always called Abe *that tyrant*. Most troubling. I hope the president fashioned some better disguises. I'd have to look into it, and soon.

Journaling the devastation and destruction in New Orleans, Wilkes once wrote, "If Secession was wrong at first, it has been made right by the inhumane treatment by the North, as seen through the window of this train. I hasten to tell you that the tyrant Lincoln will pay for his actions, if not in bonds, in blood, once this terrible war is ended."

My heart was heavy as an anvil, I must say. For one, I still loved that sinful South even more than Johnny did. Lincoln would be their best friend come a reuniting phase. He simply had to win a second term. Also weighing on my heart was my concern for Abe's safety. His fears of assassination seemed well-founded. If Wilkes was ever to harm or kill Lincoln, he'd surely hang, or die in the process. Any way you slice it, I lose a friend. Wilkes' letter went on to say that he couldn't stand to see his beloved Confederacy this way, and might be heading to Boston for a month-long theater engagement. Then he'd perform a one-nighter with his brothers in New York, and come home to the Washington/Baltimore area for a single show on March 18, right here at Ford's.

His last appearance.

Edwin and I reconnected, as he was in the capital for a rare, out-of–town engagement at the New National Theater. One frigid afternoon, we met for lunch between sold-out performances of his play, called *The Iron Chest*.

"At long last, it's the great Gabrick Stone."

"How long has it been, Edwin?" I asked, brushing sleet from my shoulders, eyeing the selection of delectables as we made our way inside.

"Too long, friend." He swiped a wedge of Veneto Asiago cheese and took a deep whiff. "All work, no fun as of late," he said, placed it back on the shelf, and did the same with a block of Camembert. "So, what do you recommend here? I'm famished."

"Everything," I informed, as I reviewed the elaborate sausage selection, undecidedly. "Love the meats, but I'm partial to the pasta. Ask for angel hair and add some grilled shrimp scampi. Ooh, but the eggplant's good, too," I got a craving. "You really can't go wrong."

Florentine Café was a favorite local eatery on nearby Constitution Street. To reach the restaurant, you first had to pass through an Italian market up front. The market was mouthwatering, with racks of fresh breads, bottles of wine, cooking oils, and snacks, like crackers, cheeses, cured meats, and peppers. There were giant sugar-hogshead barrels of salted fish, and a glass compartment of baked goods. It was always hard to say no to the calzones, Italian meat pies, and cinnamon sugar twists.

"Bonjourno," the counter-boy called to each passerby and patron, whether he was busy helping a customer or not. Made you feel at home, like family.

Inside the eatery's main section, the place was dominated by empty wine bottles hanging from the ceiling in wicker baskets, along with strings of dried chili peppers for ambiance. On the back wall, a painted mural featured Venice with gondolas floating along on a warm summer's day. A violinist sat atop a raised platform, serenading guests in his native tongue. The Florentine made for a fantastic escape from the inclement conditions.

"Fabulous place, is it not?" I said, removing a heavy wool coat. "If nothing else, it's 30 degrees warmer in here. Cold as a corpse outside."

"Mmm, yes," Edwin agreed, staring out the frosty aperture.

"Winters on the Potomac are quite the experience, indeed."

"Oh, indubitably, old chap" he joked, talking like a Brit.

"Why are you laughing and speaking all funny?"

"Nay. 'Tis you who sounds so different, so...*proper*. Lost your twangy accent?"

"Nope, I've found *yours*," I countered.

Edwin pulled his chair from the table and draped his fur-lined overcoat across the backrest. "It's not a criticism, friend. I wear accents like scarves, you know. I've been known to dole out dialects so convincingly, the locals ask me for directions. There's an entire art to it." He sat, inching the chair to the table. "Currently mastering Australian. G'day mate, I live in the lan' down unda'. See, sometimes I, myself, don't truly know where I'm from." He raised a brow, smirking.

Truth told, I never fully dropped the twang, or drawl, whichever it was. I was a bit of a chameleon when it came to talking. I could do English, Irish, and Canadian. I just recall during this time, I tried real hard to sound more Northerly.

The place was sprinkled with the navy blue of Union soldiers, which always made me feel more

secure. Washingtonians constantly feared Rebel insurgence. Bridges and passes were so tightly guarded,
they were a hassle to freely cross.

"What can I get you, Mr. Booth?" asked the waiter,
all rattlebrained and giddy. He didn't even give me the
slightest consideration – not even a *good day gentlemen,*
or *what can I get you gentlemen?* Just, *bang!* – right to
Edwin. It was either a testament to the actor's notoriety
or the waiter's preferences, if you catch my meaning.

"What can you recommend in a red wine?" Edwin
asked.

"Try the Nebbiolo," the young man said. "It's costly, due to the recent insect devastation in Italy, but well
worth it."

"That will be fine."

"And you, sir?" he asked, pen to pad, not even looking my way.

"Just water, thanks."

"Don't be shy," said Edwin. "It's on me."

"Well, in that case, I'll have the same."

"Very good, and were you ready to order?" Again,
eyes fixed on Edwin.

"Garlic shrimp angel hair in a light marinara," the
famed thespian blurted. "Don't skimp on the garlic."

"Excellent choice," the server jotted. "Scallions and
parmesan?"

"Both, please." Edwin lowered his tone, cupped his
hand next to his mouth, and said, "I'll be sure to over-
pronounce my H's in the face of fellow actors tonight.
They'll appreciate that."

The waiter restrained a laugh, overhearing our private exchange.

"By the way, will you be attending?" Edwin asked.

"I can't, sorry. Much work to do."

"I'd love to," the waiter whispered under his breath. Edwin and I both heard it.

"He meant me," I rolled my eyes.

An irked Edwin cleared his throat, looking away. "I need a scotch. Bring scotch first, then wine with the meal."

"Certainly, and you?" He addressed me out the corner of his eye.

"No to the scotch, yes to the shrimp pasta, extra cilantro.

"Very good." He vanished to the kitchen.

"Sorry for that. Happens with great frequency. It's just the price I pay" He snapped his napkin, and placed it gently in his lap. "So, Ford has you busy, eh?"

"Always."

"Nice to hear. Not too swamped, I hope. I may have an assignment for you in New York."

"Assignment? Really? Do tell."

"Later. Business is bad for the digestion."

"I'll risk it, tell me."

"Later. Let's just enjoy our meal."

The café sat 55, but there were easily 70 or more clinking plates and glasses. The typically cozy confines buzzed with energy and conversation. I tried to eavesdrop; most of it was military prattle. After 15 minutes, two bowls of steaming noodles were set before us, piled high with fresh New England catch. A mouthwatering and memorable bill of fare. Edwin insisted on paying for the whole kit and caboodle, which made it taste even better. Not that I was a complete charity case, but let's face it, Booth was raking in thousands a week. He was probably just looking for ways to spend it.

"How about the latest from the battlefront?" I began, twisting a forkful. "Sounds like we're no better off than we were a year ago. Current stalemate is like McClellan at Richmond all over again." I had just heard some soldiers say this, and hoped he knew what that meant.

"Sadly, our collective efforts have not made the expected strides ," said Booth, stabbing a shrimp, waving his fork in the air. "Lincoln will lose reelection if he doesn't do something drastic. The 13th Amendment is the key issue."

"All I know is, ole Abe's a fighter. He'll see it to a second term, you watch. He's a shoe-in. Told me so, himself." He hadn't, but there's my irreducible rascal side again.

"Oh, you've met with the president?"

"Yes," I told him, proudly. "I done...uh, *did* this painting of him, and now it hangs right there in the State Dining Room." Another half-truth, since Mary Todd hadn't yet approved Abe's suggestion.

"The president is a character, is he not?" Edwin dipped a sesame seed breadstick in his scotch.

"Sure is."

"We've exchanged many pleasantries over the years. Don't know if he's a fan, or just thankful I saved his son, Robert, from being runneth over by a speeding train."

I spit a shrimp shell into my napkin, and thought, *you don't have to boast. Wilkes ain't even here.* "Incredible.

So, not to change the subject or ruin your digestion, but have you talked to Johnny much?"

"No. I'm quite blue about it. We had words. It's a long story, and I won't bore you, but it was severe."

"If you wish to keep matters private, I understand, but I have news of my own about an exchange I had with him."

"Disconcerting?" he asked. I nodded and wiped sauce from my chin. "Well, I'll go first. We engaged in a terrible shouting match during his recent visit to my home in the city. I banished him from the site, right then and there. Mother was aghast! It came on the heels of a disastrous train ride from Philadelphia. Johnny nearly choked Sleepy Clark to death for insulting Jefferson Davis."

"What the hell is wrong with him?" I begged.

"Your guess is as good as mine. I saw such hate in his eyes, Stone. It frightened and appalled me. He has grown ever tiresome with his defense of Confederate conspirators, and apathy towards ongoing attacks on Manhattan – this, the very city we witnessed ablaze at the hands of marauders during the draft riots." He set his fork down, sharply. "I don't even recognize him anymore."

"Do you think he's wrong in the brain?"

"Well, who knows? In his defense, it could be temporary derangement due to illness. He's plagued with persistent high fever and skin infections. Doctors say it's Streptococcus. The entire stay, he suffered nausea, headaches, and chills. He mostly slept the hours away, weeks on end. You couldn't have awakened him with canon fire."

"Yes, he was ill when we last spoke, too. His voice was severely hoarse and he looked feverish. Then came the cough, like a sea lion with bronchitis."

"I would have said walrus, but yes."

"Speaking of fever..." I dabbed my napkin in water, then patted my forehead between bites of cajun shrimp pasta. Even though it had begun to snow, I was burning up.

"Friend, why not follow me back to the theater directly? These walls (and waiters) have ears. We can discuss things further in my dressing room. I'd hate to spoil this lovely lunch with unsettling talk of my wayward brother. The young one with the bad attitude, not June, who by the way, is due back from San Francisco any day."

I picked pepper from my teeth. "I'd love to meet him."

The eldest Booth was asked to join Edward and John on Broadway, in a one-night gala engagement. June, not unlike John, sorely needed income. He'd had mild success trodding the boards out West, but he never reached the acclaim or notoriety of his brothers. Not even close. Edwin had made the biggest name for himself. The middle Booth was at the height of his financial prowess, and dressed richly in European fabrics and fashions. Edwin described how his enterprises were thriving, and how his theaters turned huge profits. He'd soon hire teams of designers and carpenters for the 1864 fall season.

Booth flashed a ten note (twice too much for the bill), tucked it under a saltshaker, and from halfway out the door, told the waiter to keep the change.

When we reached his handsomely furnished dressing room (a bear skin rug, floor-to-ceiling mirror,
leather sofa, and potted plants), I was coaxed to accept
an invite to join him back in Manhattan and help design for the highly anticipated benefit performance of
Julius Caesar. A shameless self-promoter, Edwin widely advertised the showing. One-sheet posters hung on
every wall, smaller bills were affixed to each bench
and lamppost. *The Great Edwin Booth*, they boasted in
big bold type, with June and John Wilkes in noticeably smaller lettering. Think that sat well? It would be
the spectacle of a lifetime, to take place at the Winter
Garden, starring all three Booths at once, on the same
stage. Proceeds would go entirely toward erecting a
statue of William Shakespeare in Central Park, only he
hadn't told June and John yet. This would anger them
no doubt. In a letter I received, Wilkes said they were
tricked into participating.

19 August, 1864

Greetings Gabe,

*Hard to keep my whereabouts straight, I know.
Traveling as usual. Baltimore, Montreal, New
York, and Boston. I have fallen under the spell
of a young lady named Isabel Sumner, 10
years my junior. Who does that remind you of?
My efforts to win her heart are ongoing, so I*

apologize for my absence of late. We exchanged photographs, and I went so far as to present an engraved gold ring. I'll keep you posted.

Edwin has asked June and me to join him in New York for a gala performance of Julius Caesar, but each time the subject of fees arises, he is oddly silent on the matter. I smelleth a trick. Hope you are well.

-JWB

Much to my dismay, I was unable to work on the *Julius Caesar* project, after all. The Fords kept me occupied with assignments here at home. Probably best in the long run, as I was able to make great advances on my own ambitions. I heard it was a rousing triumph, though. John was right – the boys received nothing for their involvement. This further complicated already strained relations. I was surprised and somewhat disappointed in Edwin. That didn't happen often, but I was. Families should look out for one another. Then again, who was I to talk?

Edwin said the *Caesar* benefit was grand, but not without its own unusually dramatic occurrence. A fire broke out at the hotel next door to the Winter Garden, right in the middle of the show. Brigades crashed through the doors during the latter part of the first act, causing widespread panic and confusion. Some feared it was a Confederate arsonist group, as other hotels in town had erupted in flame right about the same time. Nothing was ever proven, and nothing was ever as catastrophic as the riots. Ironically, when senseless acts such as these were perpetrated against innocent citizens and properties, both John and I were fond of saying, "Where's my country?" We just had entirely different ideas of what that meant.

Perhaps most troubling, Edwin also confided that John secretly spoke of plans to kidnap Lincoln. He and his cohorts would make Abe a prisoner of war in Richmond, in exchange for the release of Confederate captives. Some of Edwin's friends were implored to join John's group in the dastardly scheme, but eventually refused recruitment. The conspiracy went as deep as Vice President Andrew Johnson, they said. Johnson was a Southern sympathizer and resident of Tennessee. It was shocking and difficult to believe, but that was the story. With Lincoln's elimination, Johnson would ascend to the office of president, ensure proper treatment during reconstruction, and allow all land to return to original Southern ownership. Was I a traitor for not reporting it, straight away? God, I hope not.

A part of Edwin refused to believe that Johnny was capable of such an act, but I wasn't willing to take the chance. The jig was up, as was my time to prepare for the inevitable.

CHAPTER TEN

CAUSE FOR CELEBRATION

The rain of November 8, 1864, should've been a cleansing and celebratory shower. Abe soundly defeated McClellan for re-election, due in large part to the fall of Atlanta at the hands of Sherman's menacing march. Lincoln asked me to take a walk with him before a celebratory fried oyster feast in the East Room. He often liked to bounce stuff off me prior to tossing it to the inmates. A *fool's filter*, so to speak.

"Congratulations, sir." We shook. "Four more years."

"I'll do my level best to make it that long."

"Now, stop. You will. It's in the bag. You've got military momentum, family, friends, and all those two-faced back-slappers and boot-lickers in there that you call your Cabinet." That raised a slight smile. "What about God? He surely has an eye on it. You're not alone, you know. We're never alone."

"You're right. I guess this is the light at the end of the tunnel, eh, Gabe?" Lincoln kept a firm, two-handed grip on a black umbrella with an eagle's head carved in the handle – to remind him who he was. "I must say, I don't know what I would've done if I'd been removed prematurely from this mess. I couldn't let some Johnny-come-lately like McClellan steal my thunder, take credit for ending this trouble. Don't know how Molly would've fared either. She loves it here, playing queen to her court."

I didn't dare tell him Mary Todd's joy was over the fact she'd shopped herself into a mountain of debt, and his $25,000 salary was the only way to dig to daylight. Eavesdropping strikes again.

"You seem oddly underjoyed," I said. We clomped through puddles and followed the footpath around the war department adjacent to the White House. We made a competition out of who could crunch the most snails, but with those size 14 feet, Lincoln won handily: 28 to 12.

"This calls for celebration," I patted his back.

"Because I smashed more snails with my miserably aching feet?" He was obviously making a joke.

"No, you ninny, on account of the triumphant butt-kicking. You're *Landslide Lincoln*, you know that?" I playfully shook his shoulder as he stopped to acknowledge my gesture. "That's what folks should call you: Landslide Lincoln."

"Right you are." He allowed himself a sigh of satisfaction. "Quit bein' so smart or they're liable to rescind their vote and put you in the palace, in my stead."

"The position would suit me," I kidded. "Been around you long enough to at least fake it fairly well. *Do this, do that. Fetch me this, where's my that?* See? I got it down pat."

"You know, you talk differently. Where's that drawl I've become so fond of?"

"Hibernating for the winter."

"Well, wake it up, I miss it."

"What about you, Mr. Eloquent Orator?"

"Never you mind. Don't ever be ashamed of who you are, or where you come from. I've never seen a body lose his natural accent so blame fast. I only drop the hick-speak in letters and public addresses, so people can relate and feel more secure they're being governed by a competent leader."

"I know, I told you that."

"Oh, right, that was you, wasn't it?" He dropped his chin, voice trailing off. "I'll address the masses on March 4. Will you read the speech, make sure it's fitting and proper?" He wiped his upper lip with the cloth. I think he'd developed a slight sniffle.

"Well, sure, but I doubt you need me to."

"Ain't said need, said *want*." He looked up like he saw something but weren't telling. Raindrops caught the light, descending in the most interesting perspective – like you were racing through the stars or something, with terrific speed. We stood and watched for a moment, in silence.

"Are you all right?" I asked. "This is a wonderful night. We all want you to be happy."

"I don't know, Gabe. I'm just so blue all the time; can't seem to shake it. I'm worried about getting the amendment passed. Being with friends helps, but I'm afraid if I don't avoid this emotional swamp, I'll never arrive to the promised land, never truly be glad again."

"I understand," I told him. "I do. So many dead, so much yet to face." I had a thought. "But if there was a reason to smile on a daily basis, what would it be?"

"I should be counseling *you*. Still, I don't know."

"Of course you don't, but if you did know, what would it be?"

He paused for a spell. "My horse, Old Bob, he makes me happy. And my dog, Jip."

"Okay, what else? How about some humans, maybe?"

"Taddy, Robby, Mary, my good friends Lamon and Seward..."

"Ahem."

"Oh, and of course you. That goes without saying."

"See, it's the relationships in life. Not positions of power, nor wealth, conquests or accumulations."

"True, never did keer much for those other things. But think of all the relationships torn to shreds over the trouble I've caused."

"Yes, but on the sunny side, think of all them colored families you'll preserve once they's set free for permanent." And just like losing hiccups you forgot you even had, I dropped my Northern talk and slipped back to a comfortable twang.

"You know, son, if there is a positive, I believe I've reached higher moral ground heading into the next four years."

"More information, please." I labored to keep up. I needed at least two of my steps to one of his, even with a flat-footed gait.

"This Emancipation Proclamation – if the black man is willing to give his life to serve the Union, surely he's entitled to make a life for himself within her borders. Same as you, me, and every other son of Uncle Sam. Declaration of Independence states, "All men are created equal." What part of *All* is exclusionary, am I right?"

"Right."

"Be it because of race, creed, or law. It's no longer a constitutional issue, it's about human decency."

"That's what I've been sayin'. God finally got to you."

"Mmm, yes," he nodded. "Molly was right about my dream of being on that fast-moving sea vessel. It was all about passing the 13th Amendment. We've long had the resources to put this insurgence to bed, just lacked the will to do it. God tells me to end it with whatever means necessary. This war being punishment for the eons of sin and slavery that must not continue."

Fireworks blasted and crackled their innards over the jubilant city. Muffled cheers filled the mall along the western elevation. There was a stretch of silence, both of us satisfied to be in each other's company. It had been a while.

"Let's play Reveal-a-Nugget," I suggested.

"What is that?" He hesitated a step, then continued.

"Reveal-a-Nugget...tell a secret, something unknown about the other fella. Some dark skeleton from the past."

"All right, I'll go first," the president said. "I'm what, 30 years your senior? More nuggets, for sure. I used to co-own a saloon in Springfield called "Berry and Lincoln." I tended bar."

"Well, I'll be! Fix me another, Mr. Presi...(hiccup)... Mr. Presi...(belch)...dent." I acted like a drunkard. "So, what happened to it?"

"I sold it when my partner became an alcoholic, right about the same time I'd sworn off the stuff. Two men, headed in opposite directions." He nodded. "All right, now you go."

"Well, just so many to choose from." I scratched my head, studying on it a spell. "Got one. On my weddin' day to this one gal, I runned off and married someone else."

"You win," Abe flatly announced.

"No wait, there's more. I suffer from brain trauma. Got speared in the melon by a buck, got headaches and memory loss to show for it."

"Really?" He stopped in his tracks. "Maybe that's why we're so compatible. I, myself got kicked in the head by a horse!"

We shared one of our million giggles together. When we rounded the corner, we heard music and merriment from inside the mansion. "Shouldn't the missus be out here with you, stead of me, takin' a ro- mantic stroll with her husband?"

"Naw," he shrugged. "Mary's more at home play- ing hostess. She loves the gossip and pretension. Let her have her moment. I'm not much into fancy fare." Several strides of silence. "We're a couple of mis- fits, ain't we, Gabe? Me, the two-term hayseed, gone

160

dignified leader of the free world. You, the Southern boy abolitionist." He sobered to the circumstances. "By the way, how's it going with the Grand Plan? I'm sure my incumbency will only add fuel to certain fires."

"It's going very well, but I need your help with a few particulars."

"Whatever you need, just ask."

"Thanks. Still a couple more touches till I's ready for ya."

"There's the bumpkin I remember," he cried. "See, you forgot how to talk for a while."

"And you forgot why you been put here, Mr. President."

We pressed ahead to the White House lawn. The muddy grass was wetting our shoes and britches, but we'd stayed fairly dry, shin-up. "Shall we?" Abe looked cloudward, then back at me, winkin'.

"Indubitably," I answered. On the count of three, we dropped our umbrellas, letting the cloudburst pelt our faces, catching drops in our O-shaped orifices.

"Better than any champagne, I reckon."

"Sure is," he agreed, as a steady rain targeted our tongues. "May these drops stand for kisses from the angels of our better nature," Lincoln proclaimed.

We were soon soaked, just beyond the protective cover of the portico, while guests enjoyed the warmth and well-deserved revelry indoors.

CHAPTER ELEVEN

HAIRY SITUATION

It was Saint Valentine's Day, 1865. I was to meet Lincoln in the late morning, as he broke from meetings to get his hair and beard trimmed. Handmade hearts created by local schoolchildren were strung throughout the White House halls. As a frequent guest, aides and security knew me, and easily granted me access beyond the ground glass screen that separated the family quarters from public sections of the home.

Typically, we used a private family room for our weekly BS sessions, but today we met in his second-story office (he called it the "shop"), next to the Cabinet room. To prepare for a dinner date, a barber had been summoned and set up a makeshift salon in Abe's office. He placed a cloth on the floor to catch the discarded trimmings, as Abe reclined in a ragged leather chair pushed back from his scarred, impossibly cluttered desk.

"Good day, Rembrandt," he greeted me placidly, not wanting that poor, unfortunate barber to slip and nick his neck.

"Good day to you, sir." I stood to the side, patting his left forearm that draped over an armrest. "You know, commanders-in-chief can afford better office furniture."

"You don't like my chair?" His eyes stayed fixed forward. "A great many wished they were sitting in it. I've sometimes wished some of them were instead of me, if I had my druthers."

I giggled and said, "You're in fine form for early in the day."

"Well, it may be early to you, but my days commence before dawn. And in regards to my wit, the Postmaster General made the same comment as you did. My reply was identical, but that was late afternoon, so don't waste your praise."

He was Honest Abe, after all.

I patiently waited for the final whisker to fall, whilst the two revealed Valentine's plans. The barber (Ike, I think) had theater tickets; Lincoln was to dine with close friend William Seward (whom he always called Governor) and his wife. I, unfortunately, was solitario. I'd abandoned my spark so long ago, I's unsure it'd ever reignite. Abe said he'd pull some strings and find me a fine girl. He meant it, too. "If a woman as fair as my Molly finds me suitable – and let's face

facts, I ain't pretty – there is surely an angel somewhere, waiting for you. In fact, I know an adventur-
ess not far from here, goes by the name Lulu. Tell her
Abe sent you." He elbowed my ribcage and let out a
playful holler.

There was never a man with a softer heart and more
honest purpose than Abraham Lincoln.

The president had been called from the room for a
few minutes, needing to tend to a matter downstairs.
Ike cleaned his implements and was fixing to fold the
droppings into the blanket and make his exit.

"Wait," I said, ever the opportunist. I pulled a
cloth from my pocket. "I don't think nobody'll mind."
I scooped a sizeable pile (which turned my stomach,
as I detested touching wet hair shavings, famous or
not) and placed 'em in a pouch, secured by strings.
"Barnum's Museum has Pocahontas hair. Presidential locks got to be at least as valuable," I speculated,
brushing stray strands that clung to my palm. Nothing
more was spoke of it.

Abe returned and apologized for the interrup-
tion. Ike had since gone. An urgent military matter
required Abe's immediate attention, so our meeting
was postponed until another time. There was much I
didn't understand (or care to) about the duties of the
president. He was constantly bombarded by congress-
men, senators, lobbyists, constituents, and secretar-
ies of this, that, and the other. You can have it if you
ask me. Never-ending briefings; hours spent poring

over memos, proposals, and correspondence; and not to mention the White House was almost continually filled with miscellaneous government people, busily handling issues and affairs. Then, there was always a line of citizens and family members, all demanding his attention. No wonder the home (and its chief resident) appeared haggard.

Most late afternoons, folks would wander in and out virtually unannounced, and some even slept in the halls. Like Lincoln said, if somebody truly wanted to cause a crime, there was little could be done to prevent it. I suppose the possible perpetrators simply weren't aware of the opportunity. A few did enter and vandalize drapes and furniture and such, but that was about it.

Lincoln often spoke of Mary Todd's family – the tribe of trouble, he called them. Half were Southern sympathizers and formerly wealthy slave owners, constantly asking to trade concessions. Talk about your conflict of interest. "Hard enough trying to please the wife, now I'm being leveraged for favors by the next of kin." He was forced to find government jobs and whatnot the cousins. "I'm always most relieved to see your friendly face, Gabe. Never lose a wink of sleep wondering if you've overstepped your welcome."

"I just feel sorry for ya," I'd tell him.

"Whatever for?"

"For havin' to put up with this here scalawag for a whole nuther term."

My kerosene lamps worked overtime that night, as they had for many months. My studio was my laboratory. I, the mad scientist, had one eye on my monster, and the other on the proverbial sand in the hourglass. Knowing Wilkes so well, I'd compiled a sizeable notebook of information, tendencies, and whereabouts. I concocted page after page of notes and instructions, diagramming the *who, what, where, when, and how's.* Like a writer or director of a chilling drama, my one-night production was set for April 14, running simultaneously to the benefit showing of *Our American Cousin,* starring Miss Laura Keene. (Ironically, she was the star of the show I saw on the night I first came to New York. Lincoln was there that night as well, only the idea of actually calling him a friend would've seemed insane at the time.)

While the world celebrated, exchanging love letters with their sweethearts, I painstakingly prepared my own chain letter of love. You see, the world was like infinite lines of dominos: one falls, and it spreads like wildfire, affecting all else. Simply put, change one event, and the repercussions are felt like waves across the far reaches of the sea. That was my mission, to change the course of events.

The headaches had returned, as did bouts of forgetfulness. I chalked it up to the long hours I put in on the Grand Plan. Life was art to me, and I would shock the world with mine, just as the witchy lady predicted. Like Abe said, who does history revere from the Renaissance? The artists. We live in a visual world, and creative minds can bring the invisible to reality. Artists help capture and shape perceptions with our paintings, photographs, and (in the case of P.T. Barnum and other magicians and flimflammers) misdirection.

You getting any of this, or is it more incessant jibber-jabber? I'll assume the latter and give it a rest...

Lincoln and I spent many days together poring over the details of our profound project. I knew for a fact John Wilkes was spending similar amounts of time in Montreal and other secret locations, working counter to our efforts. It was a chess match that I...we... mustn't lose. You're probably asking yourself, "Why not use your relationship with John, and just ask him point blank about his plans? Kidnapping? Murder?" Frankly, he knows that Edwin and I are Union, so do you really think he'd divulge? Not on your life, mister. Besides, I ain't so sure he knew just what he intended yet. He had secrets even his beloved mother and sister, Asia, ain't suspected.

In the weeks ahead, the triumphs of Lieutenant General Grant and General Sherman pushed us closer to ultimate victory. The tides had turned, and General Lee was ready to waive the white flag. Lincoln's legacy was secure. March 4 arrived, and Lincoln was about to give his second inaugural address. I stood on the steps behind him, alongside security advisor Ward Hill Lamon, Mary, and her seamstress friend, Liz Keckley, in the East Portico of the (now domed) Capitol building.

Volumes upon volumes been written as to the different politics and players. Far too many for me to tell, or even understand. Again, that's for schoolbooks to say. I will simply speak my truth, as I experienced it, and let it alone.

Weeks of relentless rain caused Pennsylvania Avenue to muck up something miserable, so folks stood anxious in the soup and slop as Abe spoke to thousands on the mushy street. Have a listen:

"At this second appearing to take the oath of the Presidential office, there is less occasion for an extended address than there was at the first. On the occasion corresponding to this four years ago, one eighth of the whole population were colored slaves, not distributed generally over the Union, but localized in the southern part of it. All knew that this interest was somehow the cause of the war."

Least, those are the parts I remember. He went on to say that neither side expected this trouble to continue as it had, and God would see fit to end it as soon as possible, as the Lord was the final judge. Abe ended by saying, "With malice towards none, with charity for all…"

He'd delivered a beauty of a message, as evidenced by the resounding applause and whistles. They's such cheers and tears, especially from Ms. Keckley and the colossal black faction. We felt satisfied from where we stood, but one man in particular was outraged. This angered man yelled, "that means nigger citizenship," and that he's a-gonna run Lincoln through for sure. You guessed it – t'was Johnny Booth. Only we ain't knowed it at the time. You know, come to think of it, maybe Booth said it after Abe's impromptu speech the night of the Confederate surrender. Aw blast, I forget. Anyhow, we heard they's a photo of the two of them (Abe and Booth) snapped right there as Lincoln was orating. Believed to be the only picture of the two together. More on that later...

On March 18, Johnny gave his final performance at Ford's Theater, here in Washington. Critics praised him, which pleased me 'cause I'd seen Booth at his best and worst, and liked him much more when he was cheerful. He played the role of Pescara in *The Apostate*, one of his father's favorites. He was mesmerizing; brawling and a-thrashing about with intense energy as if he knew he was taking his final bow. The last line in the show was something to the effect that he knew he was hellbound, but death and damnation was worth ultimate victory.

Scary how life imitated art and vice versa.

I bear hugged Booth after the curtain fell, sensing this could be the final friendly exchange we would ever have. Any exchange, for that matter. I asked him, "What's next for you, J.B.?"

He replied, "Whatever it is, it will be decisive and great." What a sad, sorry sonofagun. He had youth, brains, talent, looks, wealth, and family heritage. I had gotten to know them boys, experienced a riot and subsequent loss of my wife and child, worked as their employee, and consoled John through challenging times.

I even nursed his emotional wounds and manicured that infamous moustache when his thumb was acting up. All that was left was to undo the dad-burn deviltry he was tangled up in. No short order.

I had one shot, as did he, and I had to make it count.

CHAPTER TWELVE

SETTING THE STAGE

To say Ford's Theater was less than full on April 13 would have been a gross understatement. Something phenomenal was taking place outside at sundown, and it seemed most of the District's eighty thousand or more were taking to the streets. On an average Washington evening, the place dripped with an eerie darkness – nary a gas lamp, streetlight, nor candle. In wartime, resources were scarce, and utilities costly. But not on that night. Less than a week prior, Morse code had come from Union headquarters, announcing an end to the worst conflict in American history. Nearly one in three adult men had given their lives. Lee had finally surrendered at Appomattox. The news sparked like lightning along endless branches of cable wires.

When the civic bells bonged seven, the city erupted like a volcano: fireworks, lights and lamps, bonfires, and cheers and screams of utter jubilance. Every home and business lit wax tapers, gas jets, or oil lamps. It was bright as the noonday sun. People flooded the avenues and city sidewalks, hugging and a- kissing, howling to the heavens. There were flags and banners of red, white, and blue. People wept openly and shook hands with complete strangers. Our world was safe again. We, at last, were the United States of America.

I stood out front on Tenth with John Peanuts, watching the thing unfold. We shook hands and embraced. Each and every American had been profoundly affected by the last four years.

I took a moment to turn my back and weep. Tears streamed down my cheeks uncontrollable. The cause of so much bloodshed, so much pain and loss – including that of my own wife and child – had mercifully ended. Every cruelty, whipping, lynching, torture, and amputation, was somehow avenged. Maybe God had finally opened his eyes for us.

"I'm surprised we ain't closed tonight," Peanuts said, not noticing I'd been bawling in the side alley behind him. "Grover done shut his doors over on E." He was referring to our biggest rival, Grover's National Theater, a Lincoln family favorite. I suppose the noise and illumination was too much to justify the expense of holding a performance. Laura Keene, however, was not the kind to cancel an engagement. She'd sold her theater on Broadway and took to the road. There were

guaranteed ticket sales well in advance of this unex-
pected celebration. Though more than half the house
was vacant, she would not disappoint by closing down.
Tonight, she would star in a play called *Peggy the Ac-
tress*; tomorrow, the much anticipated *Our American
Cousin*.

As part of the Grand Plan, Mr. Ford and I arranged to have the Lincolns in attendance for Keene's
Cousin. They were initially supposed to see *Aladdin's
Magic Lamp* over at Grover's, but I switched it. I think
Tad was upset, so's he eventually went alone with a
guardian. General Grant and his wife were scheduled
to accompany the Lincolns, but that'd be a fly in the
ointment, so's other plans were made last minute.
Mrs. Grant was all too pleased to skip. I take it she
wasn't too fond of Mary Todd. "Too theatrical, dramatic," she said, attributes that worked well for us as
things played out.

After the April 13 show, Ferguson, Jimmy Ford,
and I stayed late to dress out the Presidential Box, or
at least made plans to do so. Between three and six the
next day, we were to drape American flags over the
rails, place a large framed portrait of George Washington in front of the facing to show respect for the office.
There were thick, red velvet curtains flanking the opening, that could be drawn to give Lincoln some privacy,
and canary-yellow eyelet drapes as accents. Mr. Ford
borrowed a pair of stately *ole glories* for each side of the
opening, and a blue Treasury Guard flag in the middle

where a temporary pine partition usually divided the space into separate sections.

Harry Ford brought out the rocker from his bedroom. A comfortable seat for Abe. He also found a chair and settee for the First Lady and guests. Every item staged exact, not to be moved an inch during the event. This was critical. Now all I needed was the cast of players.

Checking my pocket watch, it was after midnight by the time we exited the theater on that indescribable evening of splendid illumination. April 14 had arrived. I was exhausted, so I caught a ride home, only to return again the next morning: the day I had planned for months.

To my surprise, I spotted Miss Keene and a few others driving through the streets, as people still strolled and roamed in a festive mood. We exchanged waves and went our separate ways.

It had been a night no words could fully describe.

CHAPTER THIRTEEN

MUSTACHE VS. BEARD

On nights like this, I allow the moon shivered to shine. By day, the skies were clear, but come sundown, the moon and stars stayed hidden the whole blasted time. Who could blame them?

It was April 14, 1865.

I awoke with the sourest of stomachs and drew a hot bath to calm my nerves. Ain't helped, as I vomited in the very washtub I's sitting in. Mostly bile, but I felt instantly relieved. Then I dressed and boiled an egg on toasted bread for breakfast, a habit I adopted from Abe.

Whilst shaving at the basin, I slit my nose, which bled like a bugger all morning (Ain't nuthin' to the blood I saw that fateful day). I brushed away acidic, distasteful breath, and like a nagging toothache that just won't go away, replayed the Grand Plan in my head incessantly. I bounced on my mattress like a metronome until I's good and tired. And sweaty. Bathed again, but this time, no barf. And with a strong cup of coffee, I was off to Ford's.

I thought of Abe, who relayed he's having a most enjoyable breakfast with Robert, then off to meetings. It was reported he's in an unusually chipper mood. I returned a note suggesting he take the afternoon off, maybe take a relaxing carriage ride with Mary before coming to the show. They would dearly need the time together. A long absence awaited; too long, as history books will tell you.

Lincoln spoke briefly of a dream he'd just had, in which he was witness to yet another funeral in the White House...*his*! That raised chill bumps. I felt more responsible than ever for his survival and well-being. Blazes, not just his, but the whole durn country. As for John Wilkes Booth, I knew he made a habit of collecting his mail each day at the theater, usually around eleven o'clock. To my relief, he was predictable as advertised.

"Hello, Johnny, quite a spectacle last night, huh?" He refused eye contact, thumbing through a stack of cards, catalogs, and a particularly long letter from a friend.

"Hmmm...yes," he remained fixed on his reading, "the illumination. Bright and splendid, indeed. Might makes right after all, I suppose." His voice was low, monotone – not the demeanor of a man filled with rage and obsessed with revenge. Maybe Abe was in for a normal, enjoyable night of theater, after all.

"Any developments in the love life?" I stoked the dialogue.

"No. It's over with Miss Hale, and now I've frightened off Miss Sumner, as well."

"Sorry to hear. Perhaps buying rings is a curse?"

"Perhaps. I had breakfast with two lovelies this morning, though. Got biblical with both of them in my room."

"Two at once?" I gasped. "That's gettin' back on the horse! Might you and the gals be in attendance tonight?" I planted the seed. "Your pals Lincoln and Grant will be here. We'll seat Lee in the box with 'em," I played shit disturber.

Booth froze, then turned, menacingly. "Lee would never have himself paraded around like conquered Romans...but yes, I'm coming," he grinned, lying through his pearlies. I knew for a fact he'd planned to see *Aladdin* over at Grover's. "I love Laura's work, you know that. *American Cousin* is a favorite. So funny." I could see the wheels spinning in that bastard's brain. "What's the line in the second scene, act three, that always brings the house down?" he asked breezily.

"You mean when Trenchard calls her a 'sockdologizing old man-trap?'"

"That's the one," he forced a thin smile. "Is Harry Hawk equal to the part?"

"Oh, yes. Busted the crew up proper in rehearsal today."

"Fine, then. I'll be there. Drinks afterwards?"

"Sure."

At exactly 6:04 p.m., Wilkes trotted up on a borrowed bay mare, and stabled her behind the theater. I had a perfect view from the shack behind Taltavul's Bar. He entered the Baptist Alley stage door, and immediately took the stairs to an area beneath the stage. I followed, barefoot, as not to alert him. He went in and out a couple trap doors. I followed. Then, out a side door to the west alley running alongside the saloon.

He re-entered the theater from Tenth, entered the lobby, then turned left, up to the dress circle. He snuck all the way around the audience, left to right, then prowled with an arrogant authority into the President's Box vestibule. A door separated the balcony from a short hallway. He shut it behind himself, disappearing for nearly 45 minutes. *What the hell was he doin' in there, plantin' explosives?*

I watched him exit while I hid behind wooden folding chairs. He finally scurried away in the shadows like a sinister, sly fox. When he was gone, I entered the vestibule and noticed he'd concocted some kind of lock for the door, so's nobody could enter. Looked like he chipped the plaster and wood shavings with a knife, grooving a hole big enough to house a pine pole from a music stand. The rod was resting on the floor next to a sprinkling of dusty plaster. I'd let it alone so's he ain't knowed somebody saw it.

Can't rightly say where he went after that. He probably joined the group that helped plan this thing (I long suspected he ain't acted alone). They'd surely get shitfaced and work up the courage to commit this heinous act. But how?

It was nine o'clock on the dot when Wilkes returned. Darkness had settled over the city, and the
performance was well under way. The president arrived 15 minutes tardy, to a show-stopping round of
cheers. He and Mary Todd paused to acknowledge the
people as the band played "Hail to the Chief." Some
officer named Rathbone (and his fiancée, Clara Harris) accompanied in Grant's stead. Folks was probably
down about it, hoping to catch glimpse of the man that
whooped Lee, but that was fine. It was Lincoln that
John was after, first and foremost. Although I bet if'n
you asked Booth, he'd have drooled at the chance to
kill two ducks with one Derringer round.

In any event, after much hoopla, Abe finally motioned
for the actors to resume. Whole house had a cranked up
feel from then on. I was crouched stage right, near Laura
and Ferguson, where I had a perfect view of the box. The
backdoor squeaked as a stagehand named Ned Spangler let Johnny in. Spangler was a mutual friend and a
fine carpenter who regularly helped build sets. He even
helped build the Booth family home in Bel Air.

I ain't too panicked at this point, knowing John
would wait for that big roar in act three to do the
deed. Whatever means he was taking, there weren't
explosives. I inspected the cubicle thoroughly that afternoon, and he ain't been back since. I's sure he'd try
and shoot him. Knifings are messy, too risky. Takes too
much time, and leaves too big of an opportunity for
things to go awry. No sir, my money was on a bullet in
the back of the head. What a coward.

Sporting a black slouch hat, dark coat, and tall tan
riding boots, John slithered away just as he'd done

earlier on: down the stairs, below deck, and out into the alley. This time, he cut through Taltavul's; I knew he was too cowardly to commit murder clearheaded. This gave me time to beat him to the box and await his arrival.

As things played out, he downed a bottle of forty-rod whiskey and water, blowing smoke with the bar-keep, but he acted all rushed-like. Finally emerging onto Tenth – just past the halfway mark in the show – Booth turned to enter the theater through the front. Buck (John Buckingham, a doorman) recognized him and let him into the lobby. Wilkes asked for the time. "Take a look, there's a clock inside," Buck reminded him, never even asking for his ticket.

Booth traversed the foyer and ascended the stairs to the dress circle mezzanine. A plethora of standing-room-only patrons leaned against the wall, whispering to one another as he passed. Guess they recognized him. Did I mention the house was absolutely packed?

Roars of laughter erupted, followed by applause. Seems one character asked another if they felt a draft, when an opportunistic actor seized the moment, and referred up to Lincoln. "Why no. There *is* no more draft. Right, Mr. President?"

Big, big guffaw.

Booth watched from there for a spell; he was the only person in the whole joint ill-amused by the clever exchange. You got to know, to this point, his plan had gone unimpeded. The critical juncture was dead ahead.

He continued across the circle. *Oh shit*, he must've thought to himself, as a uniformed officer named McGowan blocked the door. Was he last minute, added security? No. McGowan inexplicably tilted his chair to let John pass, laughing heartily at the dialogue down on stage. Booth paused a second time, removed a calling card, scribbling something, and handed it to a reluctant usher – the final checkpoint. He was allowed to enter. What it said, I haven't a clue. Here's a hypothetical: *Let me in, I'm going to kill the president.* A card with the Booth name alone likely did the job.

At that instant, Billy Ferguson and Miss Keene signaled me offstage right: three thumps to the heart, then an index finger to heaven (my dear Griffin's contribution). Able to see him enter, this was instrumental in the timing.

Like I says, whatever Booth was doing is probably in all the texts and annals. I ain't seen these particulars with my own eyes. At this point, I was fully engaged in my own matters. My heart was a-trembling with fear and anticipation as I saw the light being blocked through a burr-hole in the door. Some speculate that Booth drilled it, but I ain't so sure. Seems I recall seeing it there before. In any event, it worked perfect, as he could see Abe's head rising several inches above the seat. The Grand Plan was now in place, that's all you need to know.

I took up my position behind the pine partition that usually split the box in two, now leaned against the wall. On stage, Harry Hawk (as Trenchard) offered a rebuttal to the old bitty Mountchessington's prior insults. "Don't know the manner of good society, eh? Well I guess I know enough to turn you inside out, old gal – you sockdologizing old man-trap."

The audience roared, as expected. My muscles tightened, and I felt a sudden wave of nausea. *Brace up, here comes.*

The door swung open. There's John Booth, his ole self, eyes aflame, muzzle cocked. Before I could blink, he raised a Philadelphia Derringer pistol and fired point blank into the mess of unruly hair! For a split second (as if frozen in time), he was my ole pal Johnny standing there. He was the fella with the scar on his neck, what shot hisself in the ass, loved his mama, and wished the world would accept him like they had Edwin and Junius. But from that instant, he became the devil incarnate, darkest villain Uncle Sam had ever known. A cramp of fear seized my stomach.

A gelatinous substance oozed from his target, as Lincoln's head fell forward, ominously inert. Mary Todd's shrill scream rang out, echoing off walls, as she held the body upright.

Damn, that was fast – too fuckin' fast!

Whilst I was practically paralyzed with fear, Major Rathbone instinctively reached for the gun. Wilkes fought him off forcefully, pulling a dagger, and slicing Rathbone under his arm. The officer yelped, bleeding profusely. The box was lit only by a small, dim chandelier over the president's rocker. Between the darkness and the chaos, it was all a big blur.

Next thing I knowed, Wilkes shouted, "Freedom," and leapt overboard, hooking his spur on a flag. I heard a resounding *thud* as he hit the stage some 10 or 12 feet below. Though I ain't seen it, folks said he landed awkward, rolling his ankle, and cracking the fibula three inches above the joint. Once front and center, John presented the dagger to the upper balcony and shouted, "Sic semper tyrannis! The South is avenged!" He always loved the Virginia state motto, the plagiarizer.

As he hobbled hurriedly off stage and into the shadows, the crowd was confused, stunned, and silent. Probably figured it was part of the play, since it took such a theatrical turn. One lone voice shouted, "Our president's been shot," as a puff of smoke billowed from the box. I think it was Clara Harris who hollered, I forget.

Then, absolute chaos.

"He did it. The evil bastard actually did it!" I cried, with my best display of fear and outrage. A pale Mary Todd cowered in the corner with the others, slack-jawed, eyeing me grimly. Her doughy cheeks were white like flour. Clara tended to Rathbone, who was obviously in some serious pain.

Talk about efficient, Booth hadn't wasted a single second. Whole thing happened before I could count *eight Mississippi.*

CHAPTER FOURTEEN

SHOCKED BY MY ART

Within seconds, horrified, angry cries erupted from all areas of the audience. A few folks climbed on stage and chased the would-be assassin. Across the theater, patrons shouted, "Kill the man," "Catch the bastard," and, "Our president is dead." Some threw chairs, others wept. Most pushed and shoved their way to the exits.

It was a complete madhouse.

Miss Keene appeared by the footlights, imploring calm. I, on the other hand, had less than a minute to work my magic. The vestibule door was being kicked and pounded. I reckon Booth's makeshift lock served me well.

187

While poor Rathbone clutched his arm, gushing blood, the others sat on the settee, shaking and a-trembling. Now listen very, *very* close, because here comes the corker: I approached the rocker and carefully lifted my masterpiece---the head and torso of an absolutely identical likeness of Abraham Lincoln, made entirely of wax, horsehair, and human whiskers. It was as good as Madame Tussaud on her best day, if I do say so myself. An unscathed Lincoln emerged from behind the wallpapered partition. "Is it safe to come out?" He was crouched down, heart pounding like Booth had been successful in his bid, holding an eight-ounce beaker of pig's blood in his left hand. I helped him pour a generous dribbling over his upper neck and left shoulder to match the entrance wound on the wax head.

I'd throwed in all the fancy touches, my most potent asset.

Now let me take the opportunity to accurately describe this counterfeit Abe, this perfect work of art. Launt Thompson, our famous sculptor friend, helped me carve the president's bust from clay. Once we felt we had a stunning likeness, we made a mold (head and shoulders only) and filled it with a waxy resin. I'd done some full-value portraits – you'll recall one was presented to Abe and hung in the State Dining Room. I'd painted his face (moles, blemishes, worry lines, and all) as truthfully as possible before adding black horsehair, strand by stinking strand (took months), cut and styled. Then came the beard. I used his own clippings from that memorable Valentine trim. Once satisfied with the image, I fixed the head to a pole from a body maquette stuffed with hay and straw, like them rudimentary dummies I done in my youth. I ain't skipped a trick! Nothing is wasted, I tell you. Not a moment, or thought, nor random conversation with a stranger. Even blame horse tails and barber droppings; I used it all. Hot damn, if I ain't King Rascal!

In effort to match realism as best I could, I'd filled a bladder with blood and brain matter from a cow, and placed it just inside the rear of his head (or parietal part, if'n you hanker to get phrenologic). The tiny bullet ball had pierced it, releasing the contents onto the chair and carpet, as planned. Poor Dr. Leale (a young medic who heroically raced to the box) later said the wound would have likely sealed itself, not oozed out like my mannequin had. Oh, well. I's an artist, not no forensics expert.

I felt bad for soiling Ford's property needlessly, but not too bad. I mean, holy shit, I just saved the president! Lincoln quickly took the place of the mannequin, which I'd concealed behind the partition. He laid face-up on the floor as I quickly filled Leale in on the details. Another doctor soon arrived, an army surgeon named Charlie Taft. He was updated right quick, as well. Immediately, a third theatergoer named Sanders scaled the outside of the box. Three's a crowd, but whatcha gonna do? Just meant more hush funds and government threats. Cost of doing business, I s'pose.

With a complete cast of characters, what I called Act Two was on. Mary Todd wailed with reckless abandon, like we rehearsed. "My husband's blood! My dear husband's blood." Which of course, it ain't. Some poor hog donated that. The surgeons leaned over Lincoln, cutting his collar and slitting his shirt neck to elbow with a penknife. Laura Keene had since arrived to join the drama. She sidled up alongside Abe, staining her white flowered dress with pig's blood in the process.

"Sorry," I inserted with an undetectable whisper.

"For what?" Laura kept in character. "Our president is slain."

With Leale leading the way, Lincoln lay stiff as a stilt, eyes shut, carried by a conglomerate of doctors and soldiers like ants hauling a twig twice their size. We snaked our way around the balcony circle, slaloming between overturned chairs, tipped lights, crumpled programs, and other discarded articles. It was as if a circus tent caught fire and everyone fled for they very lives, animals and clowns included.

Per my advice, we flipped the body feet-first to descend the lobby stairs. A crowd of shocked, solemn onlookers had assembled in the muddy earthen street, gasping and a-sniffling as the fallen president was directed to the boarding house across Tenth. That's where we performed what I call Act Three.

Once Abe was in the clear, I retreated back to the box, now eerily vacant and horribly soiled with deep crimson. Being Good Friday and all, it made me think of the blood of Christ, spilled for his cause. I know this ain't quite the same, but in a small way, it was: supreme sacrifice for the greater good, rife with conspiracy and controversy. But enough already.

I noticed Abe's favorite beaver-pelt top hat on the floor, and decided to try it on for size. It was much too large for my pint-sized thinker, and slipped laughably down over my eyes. John's pistol lay next to it, still warm to the touch. The gun was small – the type a lady might carry in her handbag for protection. *Was that the best gun he could find?* Nothing but a reflection of Booth's cowardice, in my estimation. Did the trick, I reckon. Made me think the murder might have been a last minute decision, after all. Out of context, I'd have ribbed him considerable for it. Ironic how such a dainty instrument could do such destruction, both physical and emotional. The Bowie knife he drew was much more imposing.

Short of tricking him like so, the only chance to stop a man with a knife and gun, was to have two guns, but what good would that have done? Lincoln's safety was top priority. I pocketed the tiny firearm for posterity's sake. I think it got lost or stolen, but for a time, I had it.

"Gabe, all clear," Ferguson called. I hoisted the waxy hero down to Billy, who'd made certain the house was free from stragglers. He carefully placed the half-a-statue in a large prop case; after all, that's what it was, a prop – albeit a bloody brilliant, unbelievably accurate one! We shrouded it with a crinkled, paint-splattered tarp for good measure.

I still have the padlock we used to secure that treasure trunk until waxy Abe was needed again the next morning. The lock had three rows of rotating numbers that released a metal hook from the clip. Johnny Booth hisself gave the lock to me as a gift from England for my 23rd Birthday! I swear it's true. Ain't that a kick in the can?

I think the only one who slept a wink was Lincoln, snores and all. He'd been paraded past the crowd of horrified onlookers, and into a four-story brick boarding house across the street from Ford's. The owner, a feller named Peterson, was instructed by us *Grand Planners* to take his family out of town to make room for Abe and the entourage during the death scene. A sudden council convened and debriefed until daylight under strict lock and key. Some ten or so dark-coats crammed into a tiny back bedroom. The space was no bigger than three tall men lying head-to-toe, maybe two men wide. They filled every square inch with nervousness. I know it's been depicted in paintings that there were many more on hand. I guess everybody wanted membership to the *I was there when Lincoln died* club, but there weren't no more than ten, tops.

Abe wanted to stretch, but he's so tall his feet hung over the edge. "This is about the most inelegant blame deathbed imaginable," he complained, so we slid his legs sideways for comfort. Ain't helped much, but what can you do?

Mrs. Lincoln, having been given months to digest the scheme, was still severely distraught over its eventuality. Her husband would have to say goodbye soon, sent on a westbound train to California. Not only would they remain separated for the next five years, but she and her sons had to pretend their precious papa was truly gone. Seemed cruel, I knowed, but it had to be this way. Least he's alive. This detail was imperative to family (and national) security.

Mary Todd wept and paced, confronting me numerous times during the evening, begging to let her and Tad go with him. Pleading for more time, her unrestrained outbursts got so bad that she had to be forcefully removed. Pressing matters needed to be discussed before Abe's dawn departure, including the all-important switcheroo back to wax for the funeral viewings.

The First Lady insisted on seeing Lincoln nonstop, against strict orders. Much was required of him, and he needed rest before his taxing trip to San Francisco. Mary Todd was getting so loud, we feared she might alert the curious group gathered outside. Lincoln tried his best to calmly reason with the hysterical woman, but it appeared she was on the verge of a nervous breakdown. "Ain't it enough he's spared?" She shook, blubbered, and fainted like a wilted flower as if she's the one dropped dead. "What about Tad? He needs his Papa!" She cried uncontrollable. My heart was a melon-sized mass in the back of my throat. I can only imagine Abe's. But we had hashed and rehashed this thing numerous times prior: Johnson's four-year term, plus one, we all agreed. Then, a joyous reunion with family and a subsequent relocation to Vancouver Island, Canada. It sounded like a solid plan. I guess it ain't truly hit Mary until now, the actual moment of separation. She made such a fuss, Stanton finally made her leave. This could pose big problems down the path. If I ain't mistaken, the White House psychologist, Dr. Huckabee, was sent to intercede, and right quick, confound.

At some point, I think around one-thirty or so, an urgent message arrived. Code words "T.L. Road" let us know it was okay to let the man in. That was secret code for *Thank Lincoln Road*: the path to his safety and survival. There had been an attempt on the life of Secretary of State Seward, too. Maybe even the Vice President, but we weren't sure of that yet. Seward was viciously stabbed in his sleep, but still alive. Abe was livid. Someone else had been shot in Seward's home, as well. No definitive word on the condition of either man. It seemed a conspiracy was in fact, in place.

Damn it, I thought, growing pissier and sadder by the second, *shoulda collected more information from Booth. Shoulda seen if there were others I could've saved.* I felt bad enough for Rathbone, who sat with his wife, bleeding and in great pain, before being took off for treatment. My anger at John grew riper as each ripple radiated.

Mary Todd's short-fused temper arose as she kicked and flailed, clinging to Abe's ankles. She knowed time was a-ticking. He kissed her forehead, held her tight, and promised to send word as soon as possible. Blue-suited officers took his arms and urged him back to the bed as there come another knock on the door. Again, "T.L. Road." A prop trunk was briskly wheeled down the narrow hallway, past two parlors on the left, and into the back bedroom.

My masterpiece had arrived. Time to shine.

The gathering of dignitaries said their goodbyes to the president, who had since been bathed and shaved clean. We dyed his hair reddish-brown and slicked it back with an oily gel. He wore a set of bifocals, thick as wine bottles. Actually think it called more attention than it concealed, but hey, ain't looked like Lincoln, that's for sure. Abe wore padding around his waist to add girth, and a heavy trappers coat with a fur-lined collar.

"Now there's a proper disguise!" I remarked. "You might as well be the King of Siam. Nobody, but *nobody* woulda knowed it's you."

"Gabe, I cannot thank you enough for everything. I will miss you, my dear friend. This is not the end of the line for us. Just a sabbatical. I always wanted to cross the Rockies, see San Francisco. We'll meet up some day, have a laugh."

"Don't get cocky out there," I begged. "Hide. Booth is still at large. He hates your ever-lovin' guts, and blames you for the war." I hugged his pillows, releasing tears on his fur. That ain't sound right, does it? But you get the picture.

"What were my in memoriam words?" asked Abe, looking back on a blood-soaked pillow. "Gotta have some famous words said as I slipped away into the hereafter."

"You were brain-dead," I reminded him. "You couldn't speak."

"Don't be daft. Not me, not *my* last words. What I mean is, someone makes a comment as I die."

"Oh, okay. How about, 'Now he belongs to the angels?'"

"Wait, even better, 'Now he belongs to the ages.'"

"Perfect. To whom shall we attribute the...tribute?"

"Give it to Ed Stanton; he's worked hard for it."

So, together, with the benefit of my inside knowledge and extraordinary artistic skill, we'd dodged death and bamboozled a nation. T'was the most sensational dupe in American, maybe even world history! Lincoln left a detailed set of reconstruction plans – policies that favored the South like it were his own precious homeland. In a way, that's how he'd always seen it. Whether or not them instructions was followed was out of our control.

Around 4:45 a.m., a black carriage emerged from the fog, and unceremoniously escorted him into the abyss. He'd snuck into this godforsaken town and was sneaking back out again. I would deeply miss the man; not the mythical Lincoln, the saint birthed the moment he "died." Not the Great Emancipator that freed the slaves and saved the nation. But the real man, in his flawed, humble humanity. Wart, berries, and all.

To give me room to work, them chuckleheads conducted business in a separate chamber. Not exactly sure about the details of their discussion, but I reckon it dealt with the transfer of power and the delivery of the dreadful news of the death of a president. Maybe they were strategizing the capture of John Wilkes, as well. Not rightly sure. I just heard a lot of mumbling and the occasional argument. S'pose the first order of business was to pay off them pigeons caught in the crossfire. Many knew more than they should. Each received one thousand dollars cash, in exchange for their eternal silence. I'm sure the threat of execution loomed large, as well. That notion doubly hit home come July 7, when they hanged the conspirators from the penitentiary's rather public gallows.

I popped the lock and removed the statue. The full body would be attached by a pole. This served as visual confirmation of a cadaver. People needed proof. Long as no one dug their nails into it, you couldn't tell the difference at 10 paces. Not on your life. In fact, during the viewing in the State Room (and subsequent whistle stops to Springfield and beyond), thousands filed by, including family, close friends, and unaware officials and dignitaries. All said he never looked more like his old self. Healthy, at peace.

Wiping sweaty palms, I attended to final details: closing eyelids, fixing the nicks and scrapes, and re-applying blood and matter. I also generously poured extra blood on the bed for realism. Gruesome sight, I must say, staged or not. What amazing lengths went towards saving him, but this was the only way. What a testament to the man: our love and gratitude for rescuing the country from complete physical annihilation, and moral degradation.

"Only in death can come life," the voodoo queen had uttered, lo, them many years back. This was it. This was what she had seen: a war between the states, Kate and Amelia's deaths, the assassination of a president, bloodshed, tears, and torment to millions. Bet she ain't bargained on it when I handed over a measly quarter.

CHAPTER FIFTEEN

AFTERMATH

While Lincoln was chugging steadily westward, the nation mourned. His loss was even felt in the South, where Booth's act was widely condemned. Oh, a great many probably cheered, but in general, they's deep regret because they'd ultimately lost their greatest ally. And you know something, they had.

My thoughts soon shifted to John Wilkes. *Where had he gone?* Surely not north to Edwin's New York townhouse, nor to any other big city where his face would be recognized. He'd either be detained or killed, and likely soon. He was hiding in the woods of Maryland or Virginia, no doubt. This was his backyard.

On April 20, Secretary of War Stanton posted a bounty poster offering $100,000 reward for his capture. Actually, half for John, half divided equally for John Surratt and David Harold (chief accomplices, names I had not heard before). I must admit, that kind of loot would be life changing. Knowing Booth the way I did, I had as good a chance as any to get near him with minimal fuss, make a capture, and collect the cash. But no. I justified my inaction by telling myself that Abe was safe, and Booth was at one time a friend, and was sly enough to find his way out of the country. Was it right, letting him escape without even trying? Probably not. But hell, ain't like I's harboring a criminal in my closet. I had no idea where the scoundrel was hiding. Plus, he easily could live a life incognito, like Lincoln. Doing his thing. They got playhouses in Chile and Peru, ain't they?

Ten days (or thereabout) after the big hoax at Ford's, word came across the wires that Booth had been found in an old tobacco barn in Virginia, shot dead. My first instinct was that this was a mistake. Or a lie. John Wilkes was way too clever to be caught so easily. He would find a way to somehow evade detection. He was the most thorough sneak I'd ever known. He was a skilled actor, trained and experienced in makeup, costumes, and disguises. But alas, who's to argue? When the American government tells you something, it's got to be true...right?

I was, in spite of everything, saddened by the news. Edwin asked if I would be on hand to support the family at the official identification, as relatives and close friends needed to confirm the body was indeed their own John Wilkes Booth.

I, of course, agreed.

Late April, 1865. With a packed travel bag at the foot of my bed, Edwin sent urgent word not to board the morning train.

No such identification ever occurred.

No questions asked.

In the five weeks following the president's departure, a constantly black-clad (and mostly lost) Mary Todd Lincoln was barely stable enough to roam outside the White House. She kept strictly to the upper level with Tad and Ms. Keckley, far away from Johnson and his band of *know-nothings*. Massive theft plagued the unsupervised ground floor, and she was the prime suspect. "In total disregard for my grief," she declared, "they had the audacity to accuse me of stealing government property! What nerve."

I felt bad for her, as she was devoid of any semblance of support. She'd only received two letters of correspondence thus far from Abe (alias Angus Langley of Louisville, Kentucky). He had arrived safely in San Francisco, and was living in an army compound called The Presidio at the mouth of the bay.

Mrs. Lincoln was a shattered mess, no longer steely, but frail and confused. This was only the first month of the mandatory five-year separation. A huge security risk, she'd soon be removed from Washington

City in secret. On May 23, while national attention was focused on the Grand Review of the Union Armies (victory parade, for short), they shipped her and Tad off to Illinois for safekeeping. She refused to return to Springfield, though, and who could blame her. Seeing the town where she once lived happily with Abe and the boys was too much to take.

Restless, she decided to tour Europe: the trip Lincoln had promised her once his second term concluded. She went to Italy, Germany, and England, acting all royal-like, as reported in eyewitness accounts. She grew more unstable as each year passed (especially after Tad's short life ended), so Robert brought her back to the States and tried her for insanity in the courts. Can you imagine? His own mama! For shame. She was convicted shortly after the evidence was read, and was placed in Bellevue Place Asylum in Batavia, Illinois, for nearly six months. The courts said that considering her incontrollable grief, her head injury (she was once throwed from a carriage and struck her cranium on a rock – that makes three of us), wild spending habits, and extreme set of phobias, she ain't fit to care for herself.

Although ultimately found to be sane, she called her family "monsters of humanity," and disappeared. She even missed the five-year anniversary date, never to be reunited with her husband again. Maybe she *was* crackers! History says she's exiled to France, liberally spending Abe's $85,000 estate. Quel dommage.

This nearly killed Lincoln for real. He'd got hisself all dressed up, fistful of flowers, heart full of hope, but she never arrived. He sent government search parties, detectives and so on, but she was not even on the continent. Finally, officials found her in London, but she acted like she'd had a lobotomy, saying, "I don't know what you are talking about. My husband is dead. Back off or I'll alert the papers." This, of course, was to be avoided at all costs, so the search party returned without her. We surmised she'd grieved like Abe had been assassinated, just to make it through. She convinced herself of a lie so she could move on. Then came the mental illness. Our decision to stage his death had all but caused hers. For this, I's truly heartbroken. I asked Lincoln if I could come visit, help him heal, but he declined. He wasn't up for visitors. I understood.

I guess ugly repercussions were inevitable, and there was a handful. Every decision had its consequences. After the event on April 14 at Ford's, they was never able to open doors for business again. I was riddled with guilt. My mischief had cost the Ford family dearly. Their prized possession was now nothing but an empty shrine to Lincoln, thus ending dozens of jobs, including my tenure as in-house designer.

First thought was to contact Edwin, see if he would take me under his wing as discussed earlier on, but my letters went unanswered for some time. I's unsure whether it was because the family was grieving, or he was busy with business, or angry at me for providing information that led to John's capture – which, of course, I did not.

Nonetheless, I decided to switch professions and try my hand at acting. Maybe John had it right when he told me actors could escape themselves, live vicariously through their characters. Maybe pretending to be someone else for a while was just what the doctor ordered. Reckon I'd taken the art thing to the maximum, anyhow. I'd studied actors extensively (some of the best, like Edwin and John Wilkes). I could do this. I moved back to Manhattan, where I spent the next four Broadway seasons as a supporting character actor. I reckon producers already knowed me in my artistic capacity, so maybe they'd cast me in their plays, as well.

Land, don't you know it worked! I's often extra judgmental of the scenic designs, being that it ain't my job no more – but hey, I can't do it all, though I'd have liked to.

These were some of my happiest post-Kate days. I only wished she could see me now. For all I knowed, she could.

This next part's recorded on June 6, 1867, 3:08 a.m. I's dreaming the hours away. Nothing special, been dreaming my whole life. Most dreams, as you know, are sorta fuzzy and nonsensical, but as I laid there in a proper snooze, I dare say what I experienced was not that, but rather, reality.

I found myself at the Wilmington farm in Mansfield, Ohio, atop a grassy hillside. I admired the vast green meadow, sprinkled with the most luminous yellow flowers imaginable. Like they had lamps inside them – that's how bright they was!

I noticed the red barn below, and the glassy pond, partially shaded by elms. I started to descend the slope, gaining speed as my shins bent the tall reeds.

I nearly stumbled over myself from forward momentum. For an instant, I couldn't feel my legs at all, but rather, floated down briskly, ending up at the banks of the still, dark water.

I heard laughter, so I wheeled around. A darling girl with corn silk pigtails and a pinafore approached. "Daddy?"

"Amelia," I cried. She darted to me and leapt into my arms. Just knew it was her. We spun in circles, her calico gown a-billowing in the breeze. "Where's your mama, short stuff?"

"Here I am," said Kate. She appeared to my left, sharp and clear as could be. I reached for her, and hugged her tight as a drum skin.

Her gown was mustard seed yellow, with little red flowers and a white lace collar. I paid close attention to the detail to prove I ain't projecting it in my head. "You've done a beautiful thing, saving Lincoln," Kate said. The words went right into me, like a thought. "That was the best sculpture ever! Realistic as rhinestones."

"Real fine, Daddy!" Amelia tugged at me. She had the bluest eyes, faint freckles, and a beauty mark to the right side of her mouth – just like Kate. She was polite. Pretty as a picture. Square one, we had a surreal, perfect love.

I noticed the chickens, ducks, and pigs in the yard. Always had them. They lazily fed on their favorite vittles. I leard the sounds of chomping and pecking as they stopped intermittently to converse with their own species, in their own language. My awareness was heightened. I saw every color, every fabric pattern, and even the textures of their frocks and hair. Both gal's tresses smelled sweet, like apples. On the farm, Kate always liked to add apple juice to her soap bars. Key distinction.

Just then, I heard a door creek from the main house adjacent to the handsome red and white barn. Closed with a conclusive jolt. Down the wooden steps strode a beautiful woman wearing a baby-blue hoop skirt, Southern style. Lace collar and parasol, too. Her chestnut brown hair was pulled up in a bun. She had a matching fan that she's waving to cool herself, and she kept wiping the back of her neck like she's bothered by the humidity. Out of habit, maybe? It don't feel all that humid.

"Grandmamma," Amelia called out in her bright, little girl soprano, buzzing over like a mosquito to lamplight.

"That ain't your mother." I turned to Katie, a bit befuddled. "I know your mother."

"Not mine...*yours*."

On second look, sure enough, it was the woman I had seen at my bedside when I's a boy. She looked lovingly at me, as only a mother can. Her eyes were mine, exactly, as was the cleft in her chin. "I have always loved you, guided you, protected you. I'm so proud of you, baby boy. Just you keep going, your work is incomplete."

"What do you mean?" I asked.

For a few beats, no one spoke.

"The man you saved, the president? His killer is not here on this side of the veil. He walks the earth plane."

"Booth is alive?"

"Yes."

"I knew it, dad-blame!" *Can ya cuss in heaven?*

"You will get messages and a golden opportunity," she continued. "Listen to the voice, and follow."

I spun around to tell Kate, but she and my precious little Amelia were gone. Then back to Mother. She, too, had vanished. The three women I loved most in life (and death, I s'pose) had pulled their energy back and dissolved.

Wait, was I dead, too?

Saddened, I wiped tears from my cheeks with the back of my hand. Suddenly, a brisk blast of wind whipped up, scattering the air with twisting swirls of dried leaves. Variant shades of gold, orange, brown, and red. Beautiful. It reminded me of Thanksgiving harvest time. I felt them hit my face, causing me to stir and scratch my chin, nose, and forehead. Instantly, I opened my eyes to a face full of lacey eyelet drapes, tickling me as a midnight breeze penetrated my bed-chamber window. I was awake. My brain was rattling something fierce, and my ears felt full – like when you're clogged from congestion. Only, I ain't the least bit sick or allergic.

What in the blue-blazes just happened?

The following afternoon, I fought off a fuzzy head and nagging headache, and mustered the gumption to knock on Edwin Booth's door over in Gramercy. I lifted the fancy knocker with the brass lion head backplate, and let her drop with a decisive clank. Then again,

twice more. That, I remember. He answered from behind an intricate leaded glass ingress etched with the
initials E.B. Or wait...maybe not. Might've only been
a creative idea I never pursued discussing with him.
Confound this murky memory.

No matter.

"Yes, who is calling?" a familiar voice inquired.

"Edwin, it's me, Gabe. Gabe Stone." The door
opened slowly. His face was noticeably aged. Hair was
long, gray at the temples. The stress on the family must
have been immense. It was in the eyes. He wore brown
slacks, and a purple, diamond-stitched smoking jacket
with black velvet trim at the wrists and collar. Slippers
on his feet. Without hesitation, we hugged genuine,
having survived immense sorrows as virtual brothers
and friends. I'd missed the man more than I realized.

"What brings you to New York, J. Gabrick Stone?"

"I've been back in the city for some time, now."

"And neglected to call on us? Tisk-tisk."

"Sorry. You ain't answered my posts. Thought you
was cross or somethin'."

"Heavens, no. Why would I be? Mother gets the
mail most days. I receive many letters from admirers,
so if she doesn't recognize the name, she tosses them
in a dresser drawer. I'll need to add on to the house if
this keeps up." he smiled crooked. "You know, I try
and go through affairs myself every so often, but with
the many recent months of sorrow, well... I meant no
offense, my good man."

"None taken."

I really must get over the habit of thinking I'd
done something wrong. Guess it's on account of Pap

constantly blaming me for everything since I's knee-high to a gnat.

"So, then...still designing?" Booth asked, leaning with one hand braced against the doorframe, holding a pipe in the other. "Haven't seen your name attached to any productions for a while."

"No, I'm an actor now."

"An actor, you say? Do tell." We were still on the stoop. "Please, where are my manners? Come on in!"

His home was much too dark for my taste, but lavish. Smelled of faint, sweet tobacco and leather. Only the finest fabrics, furniture, fixtures, and whatnot. Top notch as always. We sat in the front parlor and talked for hours. The room was a tasteful shrine to his theatrical legacy. The walls were covered with photos of Dad, Junius, and the brothers, in various productions; framed posters and playbills; and mounted props, like swords, shields, and masks. Mannequins with lavish, Elizabethan costumes guarded his treasures, beckoning to be admired. It was worthy of an admission ticket. This clearly was not an occupation to the Booths, but a way of life, a philosophy, a spirit.

Shortly after Lincoln's "death," Edwin announced his retirement. It seemed inconceivable to him (in light of the family's shame) to continue on in the public eye. Furthermore, several distasteful articles resurfaced about his mother's long-ago affair with Junius Brutus Booth, and the siring of their illegitimate children. It was even suggested that this may have warped the mind of John Wilkes. It was a scandalous, insensitive story that should have long since been laid to rest. With a heavy heart and a wounded name, Edwin planned to fade into the sunset. This was disturbing and unimaginable for me, and I wasn't about to let him wither like an old apple core on a hot summer's day, just because John had made such a mess of things. The rascal in me emerged again.

"I still think you ain't correctly seein' it through," I told him, as I dined with Edwin and his lovely mother, Mary Ann Holmes. She looked sunken and somewhat skeletal from the scrutiny of having birthed America's most tarnal villain. "Any publicity is good publicity," says I. "I mean, Edwin, who gives two shits what folks say? You're an American icon. What Johnny done was his affair, not yours...and likewise, nor yours, neither" I fixed my fork towards Ms. Mary Ann.

"I don't know," Booth said. "The hatred we face, the oppressive memory of what my brother has done carries heavy burdens to my welcome grave."

"Listen to you, tellin' yersself such a story. What if you turned it around in your favor, instead? Just to exacerbate the thing? How 'bout you not only make a comeback, but produce a revival of *Our American Cousin* at the Winter Garden. Make Sleeper Clark the star!"

"Dark notions, Stone. *American Cousin* is Laura Keene's property. She'll hate me even more than she already does."

"Keene's property? Legally?"

"Well, no, but sentimentally, for certain. And Sleepy is barely released from Old Capitol Prison on suspicion of conspiring against Lincoln. Now he is to star in the very play that killed a president?

"Bully, right?" Oh, boy, was I stirring the pot. There were times in my life when I was just such an irrepressible stinker. Don't know why, just was.

He thunk on it for a minute, then spread hisself a smile from coast to coast. "Bully, bold...brilliant!" He removed a cigar from a small box and cut the tip. "Stone?" he offered me one.

"No, thanks."

"Oh, that's right," he said with a mouthful, striking a flame and lighting the roll in a circular motion. "Friend, if I haven't yet said it," he dragged and blew, "you've always been the perfect blend of cantankerous and compliant."

This was definitely my cantankerous side.

"You should resurface as an actor, too." My deviltry continued. "Why not *Hamlet*? That's your triumph. Run the sucker into the ground. Five hundred performances, more than any show in your history. Repair the damage John done twofold."

"I shall alert our partner Julia Ward Howe immediately," he said, picking tobacco flakes from his tongue. A black porter served these small, round beef fillets, topped with mushrooms and smothered in a rich brown sauce. Sakes alive, ain't even need no knife to cut them. They's scalloped cheese taters, too, and asparagus tips dipped in butter and egg-white crème. How he kept hisself trim, I'll never know. I had a nice bloat to my own gut a-going. Started to look like an upside-down question mark.

"Edwin," I whispered at some point in the discussion, "was there ever any physical confirmation of John's body?" (Don't worry, I had sensitivities. I waited until Ms. Mary Ann had vacated.) "I mean, I heard stories of Johnny being dumped in the river. And yet I seen the Booth grave marker at the Naval Yard. You ever spy him for yourself?"

"No," he admitted with renewed vigor. "One afternoon, we met with the family dentist, who said he'd examined the skull and felt the teeth were a match. But between you and me, he swore the cadaver had red hair and freckles. Johnny was jet-black, as you know. Gave me pause."

"Can't you demand to have him exhumed?"

"We inquired," he whispered. "Official word from the government was, 'No, not interested.' I can show you the letter dated May 4, 1865, from Edwin Stanton, Secretary of War."

"Not necessary," I said, insisting he sit. "I trust you. But, why on earth would they not be interested? They's such speculation and emotion surrounding it. Wouldn't you think they'd want to put the matter to rest in the public eye? Show everyone the proof?"

"They say it already *is* at rest. A fella called Colonel Baker had Johnny's diary, family photos, a pin, belt, and watch. He said they were recovered on the body."

"Well, that proves nothin'. Wilkes coulda dropped 'em durin' the escape. Somebody else coulda picked 'em up?"

"I concur. Conspiracies abound. I lie awake nights, wondering if a letter will arrive one day from Johnny, saying he's alive. Then my rational mind takes over again."

"I hate when that happens."

"We're wasting our time trying to bring back the dead, Gabe. Dear Father Abraham is martyred, too. I say rest in peace, my brothers, we've all suffered enough. I'll never understand or condone what's occurred, but rest in peace."

Edwin lit his pipe as we played a gentlemanly game of cards in the glow of the lamps. Gin rummy, I recall. He ain't as competitive and underhanded as John, although he could be if'n he took a mind to it. Still cleaned my clock, but fair and square. I s'pose I ended up paying for that nice meal I just devoured. The wealthy got that way for a reason, don't ya know. *Gotta quit makin' bets with them Booths.*

We talked about old times over powdered sugar lemon bars and rich Columbian coffee. Speculated some on the Freedmen's Bureau, oil futures, stocks, and Reconstruction. Didn't concern me, politics and finance and the like, but I's a good listener. I think that's how come Edwin liked me so. I tucked the whole durn Wilkes scenario in my back pocket. They's so much that remained a mystery. I reckon I finally let it alone after a while. If'n you hold on to things, they fester like a scab you ain't let heal. Like a poison that starts with a small snake bite. Just two little fang marks, but it ends up coursing through your body, finally doing you in.

CHAPTER SIXTEEN

THE TELEGRAM, OCTOBER 1873

Time marched on. Nearly a decade had passed since the American Reconstruction era began, and President Johnson had granted amnesty to everybody who participated in the rebellion. Quite controversial on the Hill. Not sure if he'd followed Lincoln's lead, or what? (Ole Angus Langley couldn't be reached for comment.) Believe it or not, even the likes of Robert E. Lee was eventually pardoned, but not in his lifetime.

Such forgiveness and grace incensed them radical Republicans in the Senate. "Durn rebel lovin' pansypuss." They blasted Johnson something awful. "Surely the scoundrels should hang," barked the Union purists.

"And what of the freed slaves? Mix right in to society? Give 'em land, jobs? Votes?" What a mess of bull manure it was in the wake.

Yes'um, lines were being drawn left and right. Johnson's liberal tolerances seemed insane and irreversible to many Americans. Shouldn't there be any post-war punishment? What happened to the spoils of victory? Seemed we's still being governed by the same bunch of sad sacks that turned traitor in the first place. Abe's letters made no mention or knowledge of it, just talked of cliffside nature walks, glorious bay views, and writing. Lots and lots of writing. Oh, and Chinaman's food. He loved it. Wished I's there to share some of them mushu porks and egg foo youngs.

I yearned to go out and see Abe, but I reckon I's still gun-shy from my last inquiry, when he said he ain't ready for company. I'd just wait a while, let him do the inviting. Being out West sure sounded nice, though. Away from the all the arguments and brouhahas going on back here. Yessir, a downright mess, the disquietude in the Southeast. They tried to impeach Mr. Johnson, but I ain't recollect whether or not it went through. I think they's one vote short or something. Check your school books if you hanker for the facts.

Nevertheless, our new president was Ulysses S. Grant, Abe's commanding general. Reckon the Yanks felt better once he's running things. The paper spoke of a large presence of federal troops in Dixie; keeping the peace and squelching Ku Klux Klanners that's tormenting the blacks. I declare, the North may've won the war, but the South seemed to be winning Reconstruction.

That's all for now on that. Gives a body a headache.

As for me, I'd sort of stopped doing the acting thing on account of my inability to think straight, remember lines, and such. Some of them show business stuck-ups said I's a simpleton and a moron, but I just figured the way to build the tallest building was to knock the others down. Lincoln told me that. It simply slid off my back like a greased monkey. Oh, they's nice folks in theater, too, don't get me wrong, but then they's certainly the ego-mongers. S'pose the constant scrutiny about they lifestyle, and backstabbing competition, made them so. Like I said, humans can act in the durndest ways to each other.

My whole life took a turn one windswept morning, fall of '73, as I enjoyed buttered biscuits with orange marmalade – so good you long to lick the butter drips from your wrists, and jam from your sticky fingers. There come a knock, a telegram had arrived from a lawyer down in the tiny town of Granbury, Texas, special delivery. Looked all business-like and official, marked certified. *Was I in some sort of legal fix?*

This attorney type feller named F.L. Bates, Esquire, informed me I was owed a large lump of cash from a gold reserve held in the name of Amelia S. Stone. That's my mama!

Anyway, Pap had died, and Uncle Cal resisted handing over my share. Bates was assigned by the court to help me get it, as I's legally due. Just the miracle I needed to survive this god-awful economy. I packed up and headed West. Pap had taken the slaves to these parts for cotton production in '62. I decided to swing by New Orleans along the way, then Tyler, and on to Dallas.

I's mighty curious about what my old home looked like.

Just as Wilkes had said, our beloved Louisiana was war-torn, to put it mildly. Many buildings been shelled, homes desecrated, and fields raked bare by the ravages of battle. So very, very disheartening. I traveled by buggy to New Iberia to take a gander. Encouraged at first, I seen the beautiful brick residence called Shadows on the Teche still standing proud. It was all shuttered up and looked a tad weary, but she was still standing. Heard Mrs. Mary Weeks (the owner) had passed in 1863 while the place was being used for Union officer's quarters. The home looked splendidly intact in my estimation. Can't say as much for my dear Cypress Manor, now settled with the ghosts of yesteryear. Roof been blowed right off her, columns exposed they brick infrastructure, wood from the veranda was missing most of the planks, and the outer walls was swallowed by climbing ivy and bushes. Paint wasn't even white no more – mostly a mossy grayish green.

In its neglected state, souvenir hunters had swiped what was left of the fireplaces, moldings, floors, and whatnot. When I think of what it once was, my eyes fill with moisture. Granddad had gone to great trouble and expense to create a home of luxury, and dare I say, intimidation. Nary a detail overlooked. Even the drapes was imported from France, pooled in piles on the floor to show we had the excess wages. I recall he hired this artist to come paint our wood fireplace mantles to look like marble. Called it *faux-marbre*. That's French for *just as real to the eye, but costs more*! That'd impress them. Why not burn hundred dollar bills in a real marble fireplace? I sat and watched as that craftsman toiled away, painting the intricate veins and splatters, then slapped on about a million coats of high gloss sheen. Served me good later on, as I duplicated the technique for my theater sets. In the end, what a waste. Place was nothing but ruins – a meager monument to childhood memories. Odd, but even after all these years, when I dream of being at home, I dream of Cypress Manor.

Cutting through the tangled thicket, I finally found the front door, or rather, where the door used to be. The central hall was a confused mess of plaster, peeled paint, ripped up floor panels, gurneys, and torn clothes (blood-brown stains and all). Land, they's even chandeliers ripped from the ceilings, broken glass, and petrified reptile poop. Hope them crocks ain't ordering in for supper vittles. I's likely a bit boney for their liking.

I checked out the entire first floor; not a square foot that ain't been plundered. Would've broken down into tears, if it weren't for the bad memories, too. It was once all so beautiful.

Carefully stepping over the clutter, I climbed rickety stairs to the second floor, then left, down the hall to my bedroom. Second door on the right. First look, they's empty bottles, rusty surgical tools, dead rat skeletons, and some strange writings on the wall: mostly names and dates (probably men that died up here, if'n I's to guess). I quaked in anticipation of some Confederate spook suddenly appearing, thirsty for revenge on a Yankee boy. I's safe, I s'pose, being both blue *and* gray.

Every creek and thump set my heart to pounding. Probably just the wind slamming shutters against the siding, don't you know? Lincoln's shorter half told me once she'd seen a real bona fide ghost (her dear, deceased Willie) walking around, appearing at the foot of her bed. So, if Willie, why not a phantom soldier ghost? *I won't risk it*, I says to myself. It'd be dark soon. Wasn't until I lifted a sheet and woke a coiled canebrake rattler that I bolted like a locomotive, like I done the night I see'd them real-life voodoo spooks.

As I scampered down the steps, I hit that blasted reptile head-on: a gator perched right there on the landing, mouth wide open with razor sharp choppers. I's trapped. He stretched his jaws and growled, thinking I's a big fat snack or something. So's I took the tried and true route out my window and down the trellis, now fortified with thick conifer limbs for a steadier time of it.

Reckon I'd seen enough of Teche. On to Texas.

Granbury Gazette headlines: "Good Ordinary Cotton Sells at 12 ½ Cents Per Pound, 1,000 Bales a Week!" says one column. "Opera House Hosts Protracted Meeting of Methodists. Many New Conversions," boasts another. (Baptists ain't got but a small presence on page four.) "New Marketplace Erected On East Side of Square." Hell, even the local horses, mules, and hogs was looking happier according to the local babbler. Life in Texas was all about revival and dominion by the looks of it.

I arrived by coach on Monday morning in my finest attire: tie, vest, watch bob, even spit-polished boots. Headed straight to Mr. Bates at the Hood County Courthouse on Houston Street. His permanent office wasn't in the one-horse frontier town of Granbury, but rather, over a hundred miles southeast in Tyler. Just a couple of chairs, a desk, a modest bookshelf with some law reviews, and a two-cup pitcher of coffee awaited me. Bates ain't even there. Must be close, though, because his cup was lukewarm and his leather tote been draped on the seatback.

I waited a while, reading the newspaper from stem to stern, when the biggest, fattest blame cockroach come a-crawling by my right boot. Lifted my heel and gave it a sickening squish. The shell crunched under the weight of my heel, guts oozing out two inches around the perimeter. I'd use the newspaper to wipe it up. *Hmm, let's see, page 1 or 4...Methodists or Baptists?*

"Please forgive my tardiness," Bates entered in a snit, just as I's detained with the other matter.

"Not at all," I stood, shaking the fella's paw, all the while scraping roachy remains under his desk with my heel, out of sight. Couldn't leave a mess. After all, he's gonna make me rich.

"I am usually quite punctual," he said, apologetic-like. *Relax, ain't been more than a few minutes.* He began with the usual pleasantries. "Now, then, thank you for making the long trip. What do you do in New York?"

"Well, actin' lastly. But I's an artist by trade." *When can we get on to the gold I's owed?*

"An actor?" he said, taking official dictation. This made me a pinch uncomfortable, as I tended to stretch

221

things. Who wants every word on public record? "I recently represented a man who claims to have been an actor."

"What's his name? Maybe I know him."

"Uh," he hesitated, "St. Helen. John St. Helen."

"It don't ring a bell."

"No, I guess not. He's local. That's all I can say. Attorney-client privilege." Seemed unnecessarily secretive. Guy must've been in for armed robbery, maybe murder, I mused.

"You handle big cases, then? Not just wills and suchlike?"

"Mostly small civil suits."

"Oh. Is that what it was with that actor? He's owed money by producers or somethin'?" I played Nosey Ned.

"Well, no," he thumbed through a thick stack, "suppose I can mention it now that the trial is over." Bates suppressed a belch, but kept scribing away, making small-talk with me simultaneous. How a body can write, think multiple thoughts, beat a heart, grow hair, digestbreakfast, make a baby, and carry on a conversation all at once was beyond my comprehension. Just thinking out loud again.

"He was relieved of all responsibility," Bates went on. "Had nothing to do with being an actor. He bought a smoke and liquor shop from a man who never bothered to get a proper license. The original owner didn't disclose it in the transfer, so Mr. St. Helen was brought up on charges of operating without a license."

"Got off clean, then? Good for him."

"Any arrests, yourself?" He stuck to the script.

"Uh, no. Probably done plenty to warrant it, though!" I cackled a crumb.

"Ever been married?"

"Yes. She's deceased." Still ain't used to saying it. Put a damper on further frivolity.

"Diseases or afflictions?"

"Yes, reoccurin' brain trauma. Headaches, dizziness, occasional memory loss."

"Any medications?"

"Nope. Just aspirin."

"Siblings?"

"None."

He's full of questions about me, Pap, Granddad, and Uncle Cal. S'pose it's standard formality. Explained it shouldn't take long, just a quick in and out. Just some paperwork, positive identification. You know, to make it official to the judge.

Bates was middle-aged, and had graying hair and a caterpillar mustache. Offered me some water, then refilled his own glass, careful not to spill on the will and testament Mama had left.

"Is that her handwritin'?" I asked.

"Yes, I believe it is. The signature, at least." Still not raising his head. "Were you two close?"

"No, sir. She died birthin' me."

"Oh, I beg your pardon. Of course. Must've loved you, though. Leaving over $100,000 in gold, upon your 21st birthday or death of the father, whichever comes first."

"A hundred grand!" I cried. "You mean to tell me for the last 11 years, I got a fortune in shiny gold bars sittin' in some safe, waitin' on me, and Pap ain't even said so?"

"That's right. Perhaps he had no way to reach you?"

"Perhaps he ain't want to. How did you find me?"

"It took some doing. The 1860 U.S. census puts you with a Wilmington family in Mansfield, Ohio. Then to New York, Washington City, and back to New York. 5406 8th St., number 3C, correct?"

I gave a nod. *Dad-gum, if anonymity ain't hard to come by these days.*

"Good thing we keep track," said Bates, dotting i's, crossin' t's.

"I allow I's set for life," I marveled. "Live free and easy, travel, or just sit on a swing and rot if I took the notion. Choice is all mine."

He didn't respond. Maybe out of envy. Then he said, "Mmmhmm...thanks to your mama."

You know something? She took better care of me with this one thoughtful gesture than Pap ever did. Brought a tear thinking her hand had actually touched that very paper.

Just then, I recollected her exact words in the dream visit. "Golden opportunity!" Spooky stuff, that was, like voodoo. The coincidences kept piling up after that. Out the window, I noticed a most imposing structure. Looked like a large theater. "They put on plays here?"

"Oh yes, that's the world-renowned Granbury Opera House. Beautiful inside. Big balcony, bar in the lobby. You interested in brushing off your cobwebs? Got a one-man show you're itching to pitch? I know the owner."

"No, although I'm experienced scenic designer. Love to see the stage setup. I worked at Ford's famous theater in Washington for a spell, among others."

"Fords, you say?" This gave him pause.

"Yessir. I's there the night the president was shot."

He dropped his pen, removed his spectacles. "Fascinating."

I suddenly had his full attention.

"Anything good showin'?" I asked.

"Uh, no. Don't think so. There's a local troupe that mounts productions, but in the way of big touring acts, you best check with the box office. A few weeks back, Sarah Bernhardt gave a stunning performance of Voltaire on her way to Cuba."

"Ain't she the Princess of Poland or somethin'?"

"No, she's French."

"Oh, right."

"But Madame Helena Modjeska – that's who I think you were thinking of – is slated to make a future appearance."

"Bully." I's fixing to name-drop to make up for my ignorance. "Ya know, now that you mention it, I remember my good friend Edwin Booth sayin' he stopped through here a few times."

You'd have thunk I said that I knowed Jesus of Nazareth.

"Come again?" Bates froze, looking white as a spirit. *What'd I say?* "Edwin Booth – you know him?"

"Sure do."

"And his brother, John Wilkes?"

"Yup."

That done it. Bates hurriedly shut the door, then drew the shade and loosened his tie, sweat brewing above his brow. "If I reveal a secret, against my better judgment, I dare say, do you promise to Providence you will never repeat a word of it? Not a word!" He sat caddywhompus on his desk, leaning close, all up in my cowcatcher.

"Sure," I gulped. "That attorney-client bond goes both ways, ain't it?"

"Yes, I suppose it does." He backed off a little. "Very well then, the man I told you about earlier, the actor..."

"St. Helen?"

"That's the one." Bates raced around the backside of the desk and plopped back down with a bounce. "Well, months ago, he became very ill. Doctors said he was terminal – severe lung and bronchial malady. The clergyman was ready to read him his last rights, only he recovered. On what he thought was his deathbed, he confessed in confidence that he was none other than...(one more look out the window for good measure)...*John Wilkes Booth*, assassin of Abraham Lincoln!"

Well, dip me in wee-wee!

"He gave the most intimate details about his childhood and family. Named all the brothers, sisters, actor father, European mother, and grandparents. He talked about his tours and failed oil well ventures. It was most impressive."

"He could have researched that. Hell, I know just about everything there is to know about him."

"Yes, but listen, he went on to describe at length his plot to kidnap the president. And how, after the war looked all but lost to him and his beloved Confederacy, Vice President Andrew Johnson persuaded him to carry out an assassination, instead. I know it seems implausible. I remained a skeptic throughout his account, but these weren't vague, sketchy details;

there were things he could not have fabricated, things he knew that chilled me to the bone."

"Like?"

"Like the escape route, for one. Meticulous detail. He said he was given passage across the bridge out of Washington City with the code word, "T.B. Road." Very specific."

T.B. Road! Identical to T.L. Road. Ain't no way in hell this was mere coincidence. At that instant, even my goose flesh done had goose flesh! VP Johnson must've borrowed our secret cipher. Stood for "Thank Lincoln," or "Thank Booth," in this case. Highly confidential, matter of national security!

"What else?" Every hair stood erect.

"Well, he told of the circumstances, intricacies of certain discussions with accomplices Herald and Surratt. He knew every date, location, and conversation. Either he lived it, or he earned a doctorate in *Boothology*."

Bates gave many other tidbits that soundly supported the story, but them code words alone was all I needed to hear. I had to find this man.

"Look, if it is Booth, you'd know for certain, yes?"

"Oh, beyond a shadda' of a doubt."

"You know, there's a standing bounty of one hundred thousand if we can prove it and bring him in. Fifty-fifty split? I'm ready to retire, Mr. Stone. Land, am I ready!"

With my latest windfall, I ain't as interested in the reward as he was, but I reckon I's game, nonetheless.

"You know, I always did smell a rat. What about the dead body they dragged from the barn and the articles found on his person? The diary, the photos of the family? You know about all that, right?"

"Certainly," he said. "I'm a seasoned Memphis lawyer. It's my job to know the nitty-gritty. Booth (if that *was* him), told me the poor dead guy was named Ruddy. He agreed to carry the items for him. John handed them over and hid in a wagon under a haul of furniture. Booth meant to get them back, but raced off and hid when Union soldiers came near. Ruddy was mistakenly shot and burned in that tobacco hut, not John Wilkes. He looked similar, but with dark red hair."

Yes! Red hair! Just as Edwin's dentist remarked. "Did St. Helen have any scars? Back of the neck? Left leg?"

"I didn't see his neck, but did witness an indentation above his left ankle where he could have cracked his bone jumping from Lincoln's box. The man often walks with a cane."

"What about an eyebrow scar? Did you see one? Johnny got cut over the right eye in a stage fight."

"Yes, he pointed it out to me, purposely. I tell you, Mr. Stone, this St. Helen may glory in deceiving others to the idea, but why? His discovery would lead to certain incarceration, if not execution. The gentleman bore a striking resemblance, and his mannerisms, theatrical ease, and knowledge of Shakespeare were undeniable. I'm inclined to believe that relief of the burdens he carries is relief enough to risk it. In fact, he told me it was his dying wish to tell the world he was sorry. He only wanted to display loyalty to the South, not commit murder."

"Well, I don't know about that. I, myself, witnessed his hatred towards Abe."

"You refer to the president with familiarity. Did you know him, as well?" I think he meant it as a joke.

"Yes. In fact, I saved his…" I stopped myself. *Don't let on, y'idiot!*

"Riveting. A friend to both the lion *and* the lamb! I must hear more about it later. Of course, there's always a modicum of doubt when you deal in such weighty matters."

"Where is St. Helen now?"

"Here, in town. Works at the Opera House. He entertains on the stage once in a while, and sells liquor in the lobby."

"Can I meet him?"

"Yes."

"When?"

"This evening. I regret to admit I've lied to you, sir. St. Helen is performing his act, *We Three, the Faces of William Shakespeare*, this very night. Meet me at the stage door at ten o'clock sharp, and bring a pistol."

"Pistol? Sir, if it's him, he may surprise me with a bear hug and an invite for drinks."

CHAPTER SEVENTEEN

TO BE OR NOT TO BE

Granbury was no lightweight theater community. Every seat filled to see the small town celebrity, John St. Helen, orate excerpts from Shakespeare. This would expose a fraud, beyond all doubt. I was lucky to snag a lone seat in the back of the orchestra section, R-17 – the one Booth always sat in – behind a lady with a feather in her hat that stuck up a foot if it was an inch. Bates was in the balcony with the owner, Mr. Clive Dawkins. Clive was a small, fastidious little fella with red boots, bad breath, and a bacon strip comb-over.

The theater was a delight. It featured a large deck and proscenium, upper balcony, and a mezzanine that wrapped all way around the house, supported by white wood columns for style. Gas lamps lit the walls every ten feet or so. They's plenty of seats, around three to five hundred, plus standing room on the side galleries. A real modern establishment for rural Texas. As the lights lowered, all I seen was that damn feather silhouette, so's I stood up and shuffled sideways to the end of the row, and watched from the aisle. Couldn't get no closer.

The lamps dimmed, and a large wooden flat lowered, center stage, with writing on it. "When shall we three meet again? In thunder, lightning, or in rain?" That's John's favorite line from *Macbeth*. Couldn't help but correlate it to the mystical triangle of Booth, Lincoln, and myself.

Was this a sign?

The set piece raised, and lo and behold, there he was. Confound it, if that don't look like John Wilkes Booth from where I's standing! If it ain't, Madame Tussaud's made him a wax face direct from the death mask.

This gentleman, whoever he was (if not John hisself), was a natural born rhetorician, an orator of the highest order. His recitations trickled off the tongue with effortless ease and elocution. I squinted and studied, but could not find a slip or unattended detail proving otherwise. I felt invigorated by his command of the language, his presence, and his ability to drag you willingly along with each word and emotion. My heart thumped and my throat tightened. Couldn't wait to tell Edwin his brother lives!

But as the evening progressed, my mind got to pondering. Here's the rub: why wouldn't John Wilkes disguise himself? I expected I'd have to fit his appearance and voice into the image I remembered from long ago. I never imagined I'd see such a mighty good match, straight away! Booth was a star, a widely recognized one, at that. Both famous and infamous for his dastardly actions. That was my dilemma. I mean, if these Texan rubes ain't seen the truth of it, they's dumb as dirt. If they did suspect he's Booth, ain't they all accomplices to a horrific crime, punishable by hanging? And what of the bounty that never got claimed? Can you rightly tell me there ain't one single soul that couldn't use that kind of cash? Two and two ain't equal five in my recollection.

Come intermission, the lobby was a-buzz, me included. This was either John Wilkes Booth, assassin of Abraham Lincoln (and the whole damn town was proud of it), or he had the best tribute performance going. I was beside myself with anticipation of our backstage meeting.

Is? Ain't? Is? Ain't? My mind flipped and flopped all night long, like a catfish on a dry dock.

Quarter past ten o'clock, the curtain fell to a standing ovation. Flowers pelted his feet, and "bravos" bounced off every wall and rafter. Mr. Ford would've been quick to extend, no arguing. Maybe it was the great Booth, after all.

I met Bates, as scheduled, and we entered the stage door.

"See what I mean? It's him, is it not?"

"Hold your horses," I said. "Wait till we's face-to-face. I'll tap my heart three times and point upwards if it's him."

"Then pull your pistol. We'll casually escort him to the prop room and summon the authorities. Police are right across the street."

Ain't got no pistol. Don't need one.

Bates was well acquainted with St. Helen. They were more recent friends than John and me, so's I let the lawyer do the up-front talking.

Dressing room door was shut. Bates politely knocked – *shave and a haircut*. A paper star was stuck on the door, initials J.S.H. sketched in bold block letters, shaded and artistic-like. I must admit, Wilkes often drew a fancy J.B.W. on the cover of his scripts, exact same style.

"Mr. St. Helen? (They agreed he would henceforth be known as such, not John Wilkes Booth.) "John? It's me, Finis Bates. May I come in?" He's all polite, unassuming. I reckon he meant to say, "End of the line, you Lincoln-killin' bastard."

After a moment the man inside uttered, "Just a second."

We entered anyhow, to find him hunched over a basin, removing makeup with soap and hot water. Wore a towel, nothing else. The mirror was fogged, so my eyes remained unsure. Then he covered his entire head with the terry cloth, wiping vigorously, exposing his bare white ass, which I's entirely unfamiliar with, thank you very much.

"I brought a friend, hope you don't mind," said Bates.

"'Course not," the actor replied, patting his cheeks (his face cheeks, that is). He rewrapped the towel, breathed deep, and threw out a vigorous shake. The guy even smelled like Booth, same cologne.

I searched his face. It was...*not* him.

"You are so familiar to me." he said, with a furrowed brow. "Gabe? Gabe Stone?"

I nearly fainted dead away on the spot! He knew me?

"Gabe, it's me, your old pal Wilkesy – don't ever repeat that," he laughed. We hugged that brazen bear hug I'd mentioned. I reached to feel for a scar on his bare upper back. Land sakes, there it was! Only this ain't Johnny. I tell you true, I never forget a face. Very, very close, but no cigar.

Bates raised his brows, eyes a-popping like corn from a kettle. Tried to give him the *nope, not him* look, but he's watching the exchange with dollar-sign lenses. Could you blame him?

"You two know each other, then?" Bates asked. I think he'd hoped my brain injury finally got the best of me.

Maybe it had?

"Sure," St. Helen said without hesitation. "He's a family friend. Brilliant artist and designer, worked on staff at Ford's – 1863 through 1865, was it not? Edwin introduced us at O'Flaherty's Tavern in New York," he continued, "night before that terrible draft riot of July 1863." He lain a hand my shoulder, shaking his head. (Same long, manicured fingers, same damaged thumb.) "I still include your dear departed wife in my nightly prayers. Kate, right? God rest her soul."

Bates shot me the confused look of a Jewish pope.

Am I plumb loco? How in tarnation could he remember such stunning details? Maybe I was a few cards short of a full deck. Damn this blast broken brain! It just don't figure. How could I be so imbecilic? I began recounting my own personal facts and figures to assure me of my sanity. You know: name, birthdate, state, parish, so on and so forth. I'd have bet my entire bequeathal it weren't him. And yet...

He had the nick over the right eyebrow, the familiar dark hair and mustache. Even the voice was admirable. But the shape of the eyes were a tetch off, and he was too jowly and square at the jawline. Course, 12 years had passed, but I's pretty sure. He'd pass for a twin, maybe. You know how twins have differences that family and friends recognize? *Sober up, Stone. He just ain't Johnny Booth.*

"Mr. Bates, would you mind if Mr. St. Helen and I have a word alone for old time's sake?"

"No, go right ahead." His eyes inflated again, big as balloons, before he closed the door behind with a click.

"So...congratulations, John. It was quite a performance." I played along for a spell to see where she goes. "Haven't lost the magic touch, I see."

"Thank you, dear old friend," he said, turning his back on me, seeking shadow. He filled his makeup case with round, flesh-tone cakes, sponges, and such, then buried his nose in a colorful array of flowers he'd received from a female admirer. He knelt to scoop pencil shavings from the rug. Anything to keep busy, concealed. Not the behavior you'd expect when two long-lost friends reunite, especially after one of them murdered the president in cold blood.

"So, Johnny, why you fussin' with the floor? Moonlightin' on the clean-up crew?"

"Oh, it's no trouble. You know how tidy I keep things."

I tried to trick him as he dressed. "Hey, remember when we was in Charlotte (we was never in Charlotte), and you went back to your room with that chesty strumpet, come to find she's a *He-Nancy* in drag? Did we have a howl over that, or what?"

"No, I don't recall. Remind me." He buttoned his slacks, then took a shirt from a costume rack. "I do remember you advising me not to purchase engraved gold rings for gals I barely know. Or how there's no such thing as advantage. Still miffed over that one?"

It was a psychological chess match. Who would make the other slip under pressure?

"Okay, look," I couldn't take it no more, "who *are* you?"

"What do you mean, Stone?" He tied a tie. " I'm J.B. Wil..."

"You know what I mean. Who are you, *really*?"

No response. Then he whispered, "All right, look, let's meet tomorrow at four, next door at Gordon's Grocery and Saloon. I'm afraid I'm running late to meet a lady friend for drinks. My standing ovation should be worth a screw or two." The Booth of old. "See, the same Johnny you always knew. The wolf. Lover of a good brandy. Scotch is better with water, right?" He winked. Checkmate.

He had all the lines down pat. It was almost *too* good.

"Before you stands the man who captured countless wins at the billiard table, shattering cue sticks in the process," he recited. "The quixotic clown." He threw a bag over his shoulder, fencing with a make-be-lieve sword. "The very same soul that paid you twice what you're worth when Edwin rejected you in that pub, the night before your dearest died. Yes, it's me," he echoed all dramatic-like down the hall, "the real John...Wilkes...Booth."

CHAPTER EIGHTEEN

THE FOLLOWING DAY

I had been sitting and waiting on a pad-poor barstool since around three o'clock or so, for a four o'clock appointment. I waited, and waited...and waited. It was now nearly five. The drinks were going to my head – not good, considering my need for a clear-minded meeting.

The place was filling up fast with thirsty cowboys and wily looking women. Thankfully, the barmaids were pretty and personable, and the decor was interestingly eclectic. They had everything from mounted longhorn steer heads, to fancily framed rattlesnake tails and boxing posters. The ceiling was white tin tile. The glass shelves were fully stacked with a carnival of colored bottles, glowing as the slanting sun caught them just right.

Had themselves every convenience, including a piano player, shoeshiner, and grocery aisles. They's even a striped pole with an arrow pointing to the barber in a back room. Sort of a one-stop watering hole of sorts. I think St. Helen had worked here, as I seen some photos of him tacked to a cork message board. Looked like them actor cards the Booths done up during their reign. Seemed to be the popular thing to produce these little photos with personal information on back. Actors would sign them and give them out to admirers, sort of like the bubblegum baseball cards of the later 1880s.

I had met with Bates earlier that afternoon, and he promised not to interfere. St. Helen had something to say, I take it. Something secret – not for publication nor anyone else's ears. When 5:15 p.m. rolled around, I stood from the stool with two thoughts: "Damn my ass hurts," and, "He ain't a-comin'."

Tossing the bartender a tip, I headed towards the egress. St. Helen suddenly poked his head indoors, motioning for me to join him out on the street. He wore thigh-high riding boots and an officer's hat; very John Wilkes. Tapped his heart three times, pointed skyward, and tilted his head for me to follow. (That's right, I'd once showed Edwin and John my secret, superstitious gesture.) Damn, he had both Johnny and me down to a science.

We walked through the center of town and down an alley. Nary a soul out on a sluggish Sunday evening. Then we ambled along a narrow open path with tall cattails and pampas grass on either side, over a small bridge to a jetty. Granbury was split by a beautiful, multi-channel lake that snaked through town. We found an elevated pier with a six-rung ladder. We sat on the weathered wooden planks, silent at first. Finally, he broke the stillness.

"Thank you for waiting," he said. "I was busy preparing. Three or four tequila shots finally convinced me to come."

"Preparin'? For what? What is this all about?" I gruffed, tired of the charade. "Look, let's cut the crap, I knew John Wilkes Booth well. You could get yourself killed carryin' on this kinda sideshow act."

"With all due respect, sir, I know Booth, myself. I *am* Booth."

This wasn't the answer I'd hoped for.

"What is it you wish to know?" he smiled wryly. "If this were a trial, I'd have the evidence to prove it."

"I guess I need to know if John Wilkes Booth survived his escape. Is he alive?"

"A qualified *yes*."

"How do you know?"

"I'm sitting here, aren't I? Go ahead, feel," he offered an arm. "I'm solid enough. I know things only Booth and Stone could possibly know."

"Goddamn it," I blasted. "No more skullduggery. I want the truth!" Frustrated, I sprung to my feet. I took a flat rock I'd collected, and fired it sidearm like a slingshot out over the water. Eight skips, scattering wood ducks in all directions.

"Please, old friend, sit," he said. "If what I am about to say does not prove Booth is still alive, I'll go straight back to my room and drink wine laced with strychnine.

241

You may do the pouring honors. That should solve the mystery for sure."

"Okay, okay," I stayed a-standing for a few moments, hands on hips, admiring my boots. With hesitation, I finally sat and dangled my legs over the edge. "Go ahead, I'm listenin'."

"On the morning of April 14, 1865 – the day I killed the president – I met two beautiful, impressionable actresses for breakfast. Black coffee, two poached eggs, and wheat toast with butter. We went back to my room and had a ménage à trois for dessert. Always yearned to try it, so I took the plunge, fearing this could be my last opportunity." Here, he broke into poetic digression. "Oh, how I loveth sex, and loatheth still the great equalizer, the destroyer of men." I won't bore you with the rest. It went on for a while. Again, just so very Johnny Booth.

"Though time and again I displayed my hatred for Lincoln," he beckoned, "I only intended to kidnap and prove that my cause was just. I didn't aim to murder the man. With that said, David Herold and I barely made it back from Surrattsville that cloudy dawn, when we were detained at the bridge blockhouse by officers. Unbeknownst to us, there were plots that threatened Lincoln's life, and we were not properly credentialed to enter the district. We hesitated to reveal our identity, in case the plots in question included ours. After a while, we were allowed to pass, as it was confirmed that Lee had surrendered to Grant at Appomattox. The guards advised we go directly to the Kirkwood Hotel, where we'd met before with Vice President Johnson. This was his home. When we arrived, Johnson was harried. He said conditions had changed, and the war was all but over. It would do no good to ransom Lincoln for Rebel prisoners. He must be killed, and quick.

"'Will you falter at this supreme moment?' Johnson threw down the gauntlet. 'Are you too meek to carry out the task?'

"You know me; this stirred my call to duty.

"'But surely, I risk my life,' I implored. Even if I escaped the scene, the East Potomac Bridge to Virginia would be blocked. Herold and I had just been arrested, attempting to pass. No doubt, once word arrived the president is killed, we'd be nabbed. Johnson assured me he'd arrange for our safe passage. Said to use the code *T.B. Road*, to gain access. He'd already arranged for General Grant's sudden departure. It was earlier planned for Grant and his wife to accompany the Lincolns to Ford's, but that made the assassination all the more complex.

"With our instructions in hand, we left: me to my harem, Herold to his room. His job was to help Lewis Powell kill Secretary of State Seward.

"Around eleven o'clock the following morning, I came to check my mail at Ford's. I was under the assumption the Lincolns were guests over at Grover's National. Grover, himself told me he'd prepared the Presidential Box for the night. Then I saw you, and if I'm correct, you divulged Lincoln would be attending *American Cousin*, instead."

"Yes, that's right." I nodded, impressed as all get out.

"So, I asked what line got the loudest laugh, and prepared my dastardly deed to coincide, hopefully concealing the gunfire. I tracked a confusing trail to the bowels below deck, up to the box, and fashioned a lock from inside. Then, back to the Kirkwood for further preparations."

"This is mostly a matter of record, Mr. St. Helen," says I, putting a fly in the ointment. "Straight from the trial transcripts. Better be more specific."

"I returned to Ford's around 9:00 p.m.," he said, unruffled, "with a rented bay mare. I was let in by my friend, Mr. Edward Spangler, your carpenter and colleague, and retraced the path I'd laid earlier, under the stage and out to the alley. I nervously tossed back a few at Taltavul's, then conned my way into the lobby by asking for the time. Once upstairs in the dress circle, I took position and locked the door with the bar-brace I fashioned from an old music stand. Through a convenient hole in the door, I could see Lincoln's black hair, six inches above the seatback. At last, he was mine. Just as I heard the infamous line, 'sockdologizing old man-trap,' I entered. Huge laugh as I fired point-blank into the president's head and immediately leapt to the stage below. In my haste, my spur snagged some bunting. I landed awkwardly, cracking my ankle. Limping to the footlights, I addressed the crowd in Latin, then hobbled quickly, stage right. I fled on horseback down a dark alley, without hindrance.

"An unsuccessful Herold was 10 minutes behind.

"Once across the bridge, we went directly to the home of a doctor friend, Samuel Mudd. He removed my riding boot and splinted my aching leg. We slept there that first fitful night, then snuck to see a Southern sympathizer named Cox. He was apprehensive to let us in his home. Instead, he suggested we hide in a nearby pine forest with an overseer named Ruddy, who was my same size and look, except redheaded. Ruddy said some Confederate soldiers were camped near Bowling Green and would come by to escort us to safety for a sum of $300. He then left us in the care of Mr. Jones, Cox's half-brother.

"Ruddy returned a day later, and helped us cross the Potomac by ferry to Port Royal. I was in tremendous pain by now. This old nigra came along with horses and a cart. Didn't recognize me, I s'pose. He just seemed to be following instructions. Told me to lie down, hide under the straw, then he covered me with furniture and blankets. I handed Ruddy some letters, a diary, and a few photos. Oh, and my special pin, given to me by an actor friend. I worried they might fall from my pockets in transport.

"Suddenly, that nigra snapped the reins. Evidently, he spotted Union soldiers on the approach. The wagon sped off into the woods, leaving Ruddy holding the items.

"By the time we wheeled to Garrett's farm – the next supposed stop on my escape route – the tobacca barn was on fire, and a man was shouting, 'It's Booth, we got Booth!' I was brought a fresh horse and galloped west undetected, not stopping until the following afternoon."

"Impressive," I said, "short a few items back at Ford's you failed to mention." I let him have his say.

"Next morning, I was given breakfast, impersonating a Confederate soldier. The kindly woman told me I was in Warfield, Kentucky. Once I reached the

Mississippi, a week or so later, I ventured southwest to a crossing called Catfish Point. Through Arkansas and into Nebraska territory, a transport man hired me to run his rig to Salt Lake City, then San Francisco, where I met up with my brother, June. What a sight he was. I never hugged a man harder in my whole life. I was, at last, safe and secure. I made him swear not to tell anyone he'd seen me, not even the family. I was frightened, unsure of whom to trust. It was just too soon. I needed time to think." He sucked in a mighty breath, then expelled slowly. "There's some things I may have left out, but that was the heart of it."

I wiped my brow. Bates was right: the man could not have concocted such a tale so freely, so matter of fact.

"How did you end up here in Texas?"

"Well, from California, I easily slipped down into Mexico, where I eventually caught trouble trying to impersonate a monk. They don't take kindly to imposters. What did I know about celibacy? Guess I didn't do my homework. I'd portrayed Shakespeare's finest, but monk, unfortunately, was not on my resume."

This broke me up a bit. "Then what?"

"Up through San Antonio towards Austin, before finally deciding to drop anchor here in Granbury. I love it here. And that, as they say, is that."

The sky was but a thin band of pink, lavender, and orange over the western horizon. I'd spent nearly two and a half hours listening to a seemingly sane gentleman tell a harrowing tale with calm assuredness and accuracy. He spoke in vivid detail of a childhood on a Maryland farm with two brothers and six sisters.

Called them each by name, and even said his sister, Asia, was his favorite, bar none. He described his relationship with his father, Junius Brutus Booth, the great Shakespearian star, as strained, at best. He outlined his pap's ongoing affair with an underage European girl named Mary Ann Holmes, Edwin and John's mother, of course. I'll hand it to him: when he talked about his mama, he was tender as a fresh fillet. He bemoaned the family's religious indifference, and how that (in addition to being a theatrical bunch) negatively impacted their status within the community. "Wound up in a number of fistfights," he told me. "Toughened me for the long haul ahead."

It was all quite overwhelming, to be honest.

Clumsily, my leg bumped the ladder, knocking it to the sand some 10 feet below. Seems we was stranded atop the pier. Booth (I's somehow resigned to it) looked down with mild interest and concern. He had unassailably aced the test. Earned his doctorate.

I finally gave in. "I'm satisfied that Booth survived. You not only described matters with a high degree of sensitivity, but with a postmortem nature. Details that clearly occurred after your alleged capture and demise. All I can say is we, the jury, find the defendant... not guilty of impersonatin' a no-good louse. Nice to see ya again, ole friend." Hell, if it waddles like a duck, and quacks like a duck...

He'd somehow talked hisself into being somebody he ain't. I, for one, applauded his efforts. He deserved it. The guy looked exhausted (whoever he was) but deeply peaceful, like he'd fulfilled his life's mission and released his burdens.

"Couple quick questions, for clarification?" I asked.

"Sure. Anything."

"Before you entered the president's vestibule, you were stopped by an usher. What was it you handed him?"

He reached in his vest pocket, and retrieved one of them little cards with Booth's picture on it. *Land sakes – the genuine article!* It was the same exact calling card I'd seen long ago, with a posed photo of John in his twenties, all faded and bent. Fat chance he'd have that rare collectible if it ain't him. My head started to hurt.

"You wrote something down, handed it over. What was it?"

"T.B. Road."

"The usher was in on it, too?"

"Don't know, must have been. VP Johnson just said to use that code whenever I was in jeopardy."

"And when you said you shot Lincoln and immediately leapt over the edge, why omit the part about fightin' off Rathbone with a dagger? He's severely injured, but that could've been *you*. Surely this was a key component to your testimony?"

"Oh, uh, yes, of course." He looked down in disappointment, then across the placid lake, like an actor who'd just skipped an important line. "I'm suddenly feeling ill," he said. "That's all for now, if you don't mind."

"Is it influenza? You look a little gray."

"No. Perhaps my lunch didn't agree with me."

I hurled myself off the edge, plummeting without hesitation. It was further than it looked. "Jump. Do your patented flip," I encouraged. "Sand's soft, you'll be okay."

"Uh, no," he insisted. "Hand me the ladder."

"Why?" *What was he waitin' for?* "C'mon! Dizzyin' 12-foot leaps are among your signature tricks."

"Please, I'm afraid of heights."

"Since when?"

"Just hand me the ladder, and kindly help me down. *Please.*"

Streetlamps lit the path as we walked beneath the tall trees that had earlier thrown oblong shadows across the sand. The man who called himself Wilkes wore a waistcoat, as if he knew it would be a long, chilly night. And riding boots, as if he had someplace to be.

"I like you, Stone," he started. "It's a pleasure to finally meet a man I'd only studied about." We went from shadow to shadow, resorting to whispers as we passed pedestrians along the way. "I wanted to be an actor for as long as I can remember. It hasn't been easy. If you wish to act and do something else, don't be an actor."

"I know," I said. "I tried my hand at it in New York. Wicked way to earn a livin'."

"Yes. It cost me my family and my home in Galveston."

"So, you are *not* John Wilkes Booth?"

"No," he slumped in ruination. It was like watching a balloon deflate. Then looked up, resigned. "However, we share a similar passion to perform, a need to escape the bonds of distressing personal circumstances by becoming our roles."

"Oh, my land," I realized. " Johnny said the same thing to me once. Talked about gaining insight and direction through the various characters he portrayed."

"Exactly!" He livened. "Booth gave me that gift. Like John, acting isn't what I do, it's who I *am*. See here, one day I was working barback in the lobby, setting up for an eight o'clock performance. This man walked in and helped himself to the brandy behind the counter. Didn't even bother to grab a glass, just reached over, unscrewed the top, and chugged. Before I could confront him, he continued through the doors to the empty auditorium. I followed. He found a seat, took hearty swigs, and stared at the unlit stage. Seemed troubled, profoundly sad. I asked the fella what was troublin' him. He looked at me with plaintive, dispirited eyes. I knew him right away – it was none other than John Wilkes Booth, Lincoln's killer. Most people wouldn't have had a clue: he'd shaved the mustache, slicked his hair back. But I'd know that face anywhere, and he could tell I recognized him. An actor myself, I was a big admirer, before the assassination, that is. Instinctively, I turned to run. He hollered, "Stop! I won't harm you, let me explain." So I did. There was sadness in his eyes. Not rage, or ill intent, but doleful desperation.

"We galloped to the very spot you and I just spent the afternoon: Pearl Point. By the way, John jumped off the pier, same as you."

"I knew he couldn't resist – cane, bad leg, and all."

"Oh, it was plenty healed by then."

"Please, continue," I begged.

"I told him how much I'd respected him, save the one terribly unfortunate decision, of course. I'm no assassin, and you know, at heart, I believe he wasn't either. I confessed I'd had a rough time making a living in show business. Lost everything, became a bartender, waited tables and whatnot. He seemed to sympathize. He made me a proposal: thirty thousand dollars in exchange for my sworn secrecy. Said he kept it in a hidden foreign account. What's more, Booth suggested I emulate his identity. He didn't need it anymore, since he was supposed to be dead. If I was willing to risk some potential criticism, I could take over where he'd left off: his look, his style, and his delivery. He'd teach me everything. I figured he meant about acting, until he said, "Being me on my worst day is more exciting than being you on your best."

"I know, he mentioned the same to me, the braggart."

"Yes, well, a light went on in my head. I asked him to share it all; I needed to get in his mind in order to produce the desired results. He agreed, and said, "Success is a formula, a proven method. If it happened once, it would happen again – like baking a cake using the exact same recipe."

"Dad-burn, Johnny may have been a demon, but he was a damn clever one," I admitted. "So, let me get this straight, you shed your own personal identity and jumped into his mind, so you might experience the success you never had as lowly John St. Helen?"

"Yes. We spent endless hours discussing details of his short but amazing and tumultuous life. I wrote it all down, word for word. Slowly, in my own cognition, it went beyond the performing and became my life. I memorized the notes, ingesting them to the point of exhaustion, including his association with a talented, true friend: Gabe Stone."

"He said that? Can I borrow them notes for proof?"

Good long giggle.

"From then on, it became my obsession to *be* John Wilkes Booth. I loved it. The mind is a powerful thing, Mr. Stone. Once a frustrated, demure failure of a man, I became a confident, charismatic actor. You saw the way people cheered."

"But you still go by St. Helen in public, right? I mean, you were billed as such the other night."

"Sure. Think about it. I'm not intending to risk my life. Besides, John Wilkes Booth is dead, or so the world believes. This is my living tribute. How many can claim a true legend gave them the license to carry on their legacy beyond the grave, and paid them to do it! I'm part patsy, part decoy, and part celebrity. I'm a somebody. I always had his look, more so once I took the necessary steps – a painful sacrifice."

"Yes, I see the scars and marks. Why the hell would you do that to yourself?"

"I'm a believer in virtually becoming the person."

"Willing to go to such extremes?"

"Oh yes, as you can see, I self-inflicted identical wounds in case it ever comes into question. Even mangled my own thumb, scarred my neck, and nicked my eyebrow."

"So, you expect to get apprehended? You're warped."

"Maybe, maybe not. It's worth it."

"You're a blame crazy sod, St. Helen. You know that?"

"Could be, but I'm alive, more so than ever. I was nearly suicidal in the months prior. Missed my wife and children. I saw this as a sign, a gift from God, if you will, however long it lasted. I went to my mother's gravesite and asked for her forgiveness. From then on, I became this brilliant, empowered performer. I live vicariously through J.B. Wilkes' energy."

"I admit, Booth can be intoxicatin', but ain't you concerned? I mean, if no one accuses you of being Booth, why confess such incriminatin' revealments to Finis Bates?"

"I thought I was dying. Were they going to hang a dying man? It's a rush of adrenalin. Right up to meeting you. This makes me a part of his lore. To me, that's extraordinary. I wish it to continue, right up to the end."

By now, I had a headache you wouldn't believe. It was getting late, and we had walked for miles. "So, what now? Where will you go? Will you stay here in Granbury, and carry on the charade forever?"

"No," said St. Helen. (I wasn't even sure of his real name.) I'm off to Oklahoma. I have a few friends there, friends that will embrace me and my newfound identity, give me work as a painter."

"You're an artist, too? Same here."

"I know."

"How? Oh, right, you pretty much know everything about me."

"Enough," he admitted. "I truly am sorry about your wife and child, by the way. If it's any comfort, Booth teared up when he told me the story of her death. Made me weepy, as well."

"Thanks. That was so long ago. I know they're still with me." I really did grow to like this man. He was sensitive, kind, and talented. "If you don't mind my askin', what's your real name?"

"David E. George."

I wouldn't bet my life on it, but okay. "Nice to meet you, Mr. George."

"Likewise."

"If there's ever anything I can do," I handed him my card, "don't hesitate."

"Thank you. If there's no more to be said here, I'd like to begin my journey to Enid. Long ride. I'd like to get a good start."

"I understand. Where's your horse and carriage?"

"All the way back in town."

"Yikes, I'll walk with you."

"No, thank you. I'd rather be alone." He took several steps, then turned. "Mr. Stone, as long as we're being truthful, I'm just a house painter. Wouldn't be proper to pretend otherwise. I'm told you are a master portrait artist. Had your work in the Executive Mansion, did you not?"

"Yes, a portrait of my dear Abraham Lincoln."

"I bet it was spectacular." He walked away again.

"Mr. St. Hel...I mean George, where is J.B. Wilkes? Any idea?"

"No," he said, face forward with head slouched, hands in his pockets.

"One last question. Why keep it up, then? Why not go back to just bein' you? You're a delightful, talented gentleman."

"I'm no longer welcome in my own home, my wife is remarrying, and my children are happy for once. I'd rather be Booth, even on his worst day." He smiled, slashed a make-believe sword, and disappeared into darkness.

CHAPTER NINETEEN

PLACES UNKNOWN

If John Wilkes Booth was alive, I had no inkling where he was hiding. No sense wasting time with it. I traveled back to New Orleans to start my new life. The sum total of gold amounted to $117,458.97. That was the going rate based on the weight of it, according to the fella at the Union Bank of Louisiana where it's stored. I mostly left it all in there. I had this crazy notion of rebuilding the Cypress, but my Uncle Cal held the deed and title. I worked it through Bates to pay him eighteen thousand dollars, so's I could do with it what I wanted. That still left the majestic sum of a hundred thousand to live off. Of course, I could always sell some portion of the 200 acres later on down the road, if need be.

I rented a room at the old Lamothe House on Esplanade Avenue in the French Quarter, until solid plans were in place. Traveled back and forth to Franklin a couple of times to meet with an architect Finis Bates recommended, but things never panned out. Maybe I could have talked myself into it, or maybe I'd done well listening to my little voice. The moment the architect took a gander at the dilapidated old mansion, he strongly encouraged me to tear her down, start anew, or simply sell off the acreage for farmland. Soil was still good; structure, not so.

I once saw a man photographing the place for posterity, and was reminded of how the once-magnificent South had been reduced to ashes. S'pose the only thing incapable of destruction was the soul, the human spirit. Everything else changed, even the body. If you think of it, I ain't the little kid who climbed out the window and had powerful adventures in the dark of the bayou. I ain't the adolescent with the tent in his trousers, fixing to pounce on the first willing woman. Ain't even the 20-year-old who burned the midnight oil creating a waxy wonder. I's the one who watched it all, silently within. Reckon that's who I'll always be, even when my bones lay in some box in the soil. Comforting notion to outlast death, live forever.

Life is chock-full of wonder. I'd written Angus while I was in Granbury. Ain't mentioned the revelation about Booth being on the loose. No need to worry him. John surely don't know his victim survived; only a manageable litter ever did. Lincoln lived within the protective walls of the Presidio. What were the odds of the two of them hiding out in the same city? This was a big, wide world. St. Helen, or David George, said Booth could be anywhere, even foreign countries.

On a mostly sunny Saturday morning, I took a walk to the post office on Rue de Pontchartrain. The lady that worked the desk always brought hot, fresh beignets from Café du Monde in the French market. I reckon I could eat about a million of them fried sugar dough balls! Mrs. Anatole Malo (the counter lady) also offered me a café au lait – that's coffee mixed with hot milk. She's real friendly, and pretty, too. Fiery red locks, round hips, thin waist. Too bad she's got this husband named Martine, works down at the docks. So again, I's shit outta luck with the love life.

Keying my way to my mailbox, I opened door #44 and reached for the stack. Only fetched letters twice a week, Wednesday and Saturday, on account of it was a bit of a walk from my current accommodations. Buried among the bills was a post from Abe. This pleased me much. I was lonesome for news of his postbellum life. He ain't said much about day-to-day happenings, just that he sorely missed Mary and the boys, and wondered if it had been worth all the trouble to do what he done to stay alive. He talked about how his writing was his salvation. Urged me to continue to document the events of my own life, to see where I been, and where I'm a-going. Told him don't worry, I was.

259

Lincoln had become an exceedingly spiritual think-er. Spoke of the "Great Inheritance" we all had access to, we all got born with, and how we let our minds interfere with earthly cares, desires, and ambitions. I couldn't wait to hear more. He pontificated the heaven we all expect, a place where every creed and color live harmoniously, and how blame ignorant it was per-secuting, a-judging, and killing like we done down here in the solid world. "Nothing but hypocrisy," he offered.

After pondering his wisdom a while, I read to the bottom of the page: finally got the invite to head out to California for a visit! I couldn't wait to see my friend, and the city by the bay that Edwin prattled on and on about. Thanks to federal land grants, men had laid tracks all the way from New Orleans to St. Louis, then Kansas City, Denver, Salt Lake City, and finally, San Francisco. What a marvel that was! Just kept won-dering how much sweat and blood was lost building the thing. You think they commenced at one coast and worked all the way across, or started on both shores si-multaneous, shaking hands in the middle? I allow the latter.

After a week or more, the Central Pacific Railroad chugged me clean over the Rockies (highest mountains imaginable) and through many miles of forest, before reaching its final destination. The tracks opened to a vast, expansive stretch of hilly chaparral. I could see the beautiful Pacific Ocean that twinkled with the bril-liance of gold, or stars, or diamonds. (Okay, looky here – if it sparkled, that's what it looked like.) After all the dirt, sand, and taupe-color, the Pacific territory touted the greenest grass and trees, bluest water, and colorful buildings that filled the steep hillsides with their intricate facades. After dipping our toes in the Atlantic together all them years ago, I just know my Kate would have loved to see the counterpart. Jaw-dropping.

I's told that by the early 1870's, San Francisco was the nation's tenth-largest city. It looked the part, too: hotels, restaurants, parks, churches, synagogues, theaters, schools, libraries, and academies around every corner. When we reached the inner-city section, I noticed the streets was going ever which way and even straight up the hill. They's these magic buggies called Clay Street Hill Trolleys that pulled people right up the slope – no horses, no engines, no nothing! Inconceivable. Straight off, I liked it even more than New York. The topography was interesting, too. San Francisco had mountains, the gorgeous sea, vistas, parks, and trees. I wanted to see it all.

This operation called The Sausalito Land and Ferry Company connected folks with the other shores by boat, making it one giant community. It was such a different world for me, but one I was eager to further acquaint myself with. I had left everything in storage back home, but brought enough clothes and such to last a month – two big bags full. I figured if Abe kicked me out, I'd rent space in some nice ole lady's townhouse in the city. Why not? Shoot, I come all the way out, might as well set a spell.

On the way to the fort where Abe was living, I passed sections with so many Chinamen. Most was wearing pajamas and pointy hats that looked more like upside down music symbols, or tiny umbrellas. They was making delicious smelling meals, and bartering their wares under canopies along the endless side-walks. Some washed and folded clothes whilst folks waited. It was like I's sailed the ocean, and landed smack dab in the Orient or something.

I arrived at the great stone-walled structure on the cliff, fortified by brick and granite. Great war machines with gears, cranks, and levers protected her innards, and huge cannons rose high atop platforms. Langley was safe as could be. Again, the words "T.L. Road" got me past the Presidio gate. I bet they don't even knowed what that meant, just followed orders from a government higher-up. At the onset, only a handful of folks knew anything of the Grand Plan. I's sure hoping it stayed that way.

Sergeant Milo F. Mortimer escorted me through the front gate marked "Alameda," then up a wide dirt road called Funston Avenue. Rows of beautiful residences faced west to a large parade ground. Mortimer was aw-ful informative, saying General William T. Sherman had lived here as a young military lieutenant. I asked why the place seemed so scarce, and he informed me that many of the troops were deployed to fight in the Modoc Indian Campaign. Now we's targeting injuns? Guess you always gotta be massacring somebody to keep the army occupied and spend those taxpayer dollars.

I tested my theory, and asked what he knew about Angus Langley. "Hell," he said, "he's just this old man that we were told to protect. Figure he's related to some general or something. Why are you looking for him?"

"He's my uncle," I lied. "And yup, we's cousins twice removed from General Joshua Chamberlain. His brother's aunt was married to my father's sister's half-brother." I loved to lie, just for the fun of it.

"Oh," he looked perplexed. "Well, then...welcome."

Unattended, I walked up a short grassy embankment dotted with tiny buttercup wildflowers. I found my way to a row of red-brick rooms with matching red roofs, shaded by stately maples and elms. It looked like a university dormitory or chain of offices. Finches and swallows chirped happily, darting branch to branch, occasionally swooping to the grass for a snack of seeds and insects. The picturesque, serene water served as an inspirational backdrop for a man on a wood-post porch, sitting in a rocker. He had wavy, shoulder-length silver tresses and scant round spectacles. A wrinkled, pointy jaw jutted sharply from a double-wrapped scarf, and a wool shawl covered his shallow shoulders. He wore a button-down shirt with the sleeves rolled halfway up his thin, sun-cured arms, and indigo trousers called Levi's blue jeans, invented by a guy named Strauss to protect local kids from the elements. Before me was resident writer, Angus Langley – AKA Abraham Lincoln.

"Well, well. Looky who decided to drop by."

"Greetings, Angus," I said, fighting off a teary meltdown. I climbed wooden steps and approached him at the far end of the gallery. Struggling to stand, he hugged me hard as I knelt at his side. "You look wonderful, you ole fart."

"I look like somethin' the cat regurgitated, but thank you. They keep me unkempt and covered up, as if people got the eagle-eyes to see in here. How was your journey? Where are your bags?"

"Under inspection at security."

"Oh, pish-posh. Security. What are you packing, TNT? Never thought you'd encounter something like this, did you?"

"No," I was quick to admit. "The barracks are incredible, as is San Francisco. Edwin was absolutely right."

"How do you like my duds?" he asked, tugging at his suspender straps with his thumbs, then letting them snap at his gaunt midsection. "Add a wide brim hat and a pan, and I'm a miner forty-niner from Sutter's Mill, am I not? Speakin' of hats, remind me that I have a gift for you back in the room."

"Which winda is yours?" I inquired, looking at the endless row of dormitories.

"Window? This here is my building. I have the whole damn thing to myself. You think the Executive Mansion was large and drafty? I was hoping you'd stay a while, long as you want. Help me cook, keep me entertained, and fill the dead, silent air."

"They ain't cookin' for you?"

"No, they do, but have you ever had military grub? Besides, with these awful teeth, I can't taste much. Why do you think I'm so thin?"

"Nobody comes to keep you company?"

"No, no...they do. I just tire of listening to stories from snot-nosed sergeants about boot camp, chores, rules, and procedures. They're always bad mouthing authority figures. They should've served during the Great Trouble. That would've wiped the whining from their tongues. The brave men under Grant and Lee never caterwauled like that. And you wonder why I ask to be left alone to my reading and writing?"

"Ain't ya made friends? Even one?"

"Not like you, Rembrandt. You are one in a million. There's this fella I'm acquainted with in the city who seems to be part of the same place, same time. Name's Cicero, a savy businessman. Periodically rents a fine flat at the beautiful new Palace Hotel on Montgomery (he leaned on *fine*). We meet for a meal on the rare occasion. Says he travels a great deal, and always insists on paying. If you set a spell, I'll introduce you. Bet you two would really hit it off."

"Why do you think?"

"Oh, I don't know. Same interests, maybe. Southern culture, theater, politics, females. We met after a matinee at the Market Street Theater."

"You went out to the theater? What did you see?"

"*Our American Cousin*. You know, I never caught the end of that one." I sat mum, not sure what to say. "Only bending your feelers," he chuckled. "It was an Ibsen piece called *The League of Youth*. Funny story if you care to hear it. C'mon, sit."

"Sure," I said, plopping cross-legged right on the planks. Lincoln was the absolute master at long-winded, humorous tales.

"Well, the way the story goes is such: There's this Protagonist, in the play, I mean. He poses as a political idealist, wants to start a brand new party called the League of Youth. Aims to end the current, corrupt party of old fuddy-duddies. In scheming to get elected, he makes marital promises to scores of women that he can't keep, and finally gets run out of town. Chock-full of cynical humor and farcical intrigue. Right up my alley."

"Sounds like a winner."

"You'd think so, right? Well, here's the catch: The crowd got so into it, a ruckus ensued. Each party had loyalists in the audience who assumed they were being made fun of. People were shouting, shoving each other. Management finally shut off the gas lamps and sent us all on our way. It was a hoot. Men pushed each other stiff-fingered in the chest. Women gave their adversaries "what-for" at the top of their tone. Then came the all-out blows and tossing of chairs. Of course, the guards ushered me out right quick to a bar down the block. This fella and I recognized each other from the lobby, and struck up the most fascinating conversation. We've been acquainted ever since."

"Well, what's so funny about that?"

"Ain't supposed to be funny. Does every story I tell got to be funny?"

"No. Reckon not, but you said, 'funny story, wanna hear it?'"

"I did? Well, maybe I ain't finished. So, when we were at the saloon, these two termites walked in and asked 'Where's the bar tender?'" A pause. "Get it?... Bar*tender*...bartender?"

"Yes," I repeated the punch line, tee-heeing dutifully. "I'm a-feared your humor's sunk considerable in my absence."

"I have better ones, but they're lengthy and offensive. That's the culture around here, so it goes with the territory. I've become a crumb crude in my old age. Last rite of passage."

"Good for you," I says. "C'mon, try me again. Who else you gonna offend with tasteless humor? Have you replaced me?"

"Naw, trust me, no one can compare to you. Except maybe that fella I mentioned – Cicero. Elias H. Cicero."

"Oh, right. The East Coast businessman. Tell me, what sort of occupation affords him a hotel apartment at The Palace? Costs a pretty penny, don't it?"

"He claims to be an investor. One of them ne'er-do-well, international playboys."

"Did he recognize you?"

"I doubt it. Never spoke of it if he did. You done such a bang-up job fakin' my demise, I doubt folks are even capable of the notion. I get the once-in-a-while comment like, 'You look familiar,' or 'Anyone ever tell you look like President Lincoln?' But I just slough it off with a laugh, and it usually ends right then and there. I have armed guards that hide in plants and whatnot in case there's ever any hassle, but there ain't been one yet, and I don't rightly plan on it in the future. They follow wherever I go. Part of the severance package. Plus, using a wheelchair helps."

"You can't walk?"

"Sure, with a cane. Limited distance, though, before my knees and hips get to aching something awful. I'm six-foot-three, maybe not quite, anymore. I'm sure I've shrunk in my advancing years. Typically catch a hack or trolley ride, then walk the rest of the way." A muted whistle sounded in the distance. "Please, let's go inside. I have jasmine tea on the burner."

His sitting area was one big bookshelf – a library unto itself. He musta had every selection under the sun: from Homer, Shakespeare, and the Bible, to 'Oft Told Tales and Alice's Adventures in Wonderland. A veritable smorgasbord.

"Have you read 'em all? Your books, I mean?"

"Barely made a dent," he called from the kitchen.

"Need help?" I asked, fully reclined on a cushy leather seat.

"Nope." He come out the door in that wheelchair he spoke about. "Drinking glasses fit perfectly in the side tray attached to ole Betsy here."

"You named your wheelchair?"

"Well, you named your house."

"Touché."

He left the room and returned with a box wrapped in newspaper. "Sorry, the gift-wrap girl is out sick today." I opened the container and removed a Scotsman's cap with a band of plaid fabric tied around the brim. "You know what this is, don't you?"

"Uh, no, but I like it." I really didn't, but I wasn't about to hurt his feelings.

"That's the cap I wore to sneak into Washington when I first arrived. White House security kept it all these years. I want you to have it. Maybe dress wax Lincoln in it for fun."

"I would if it weren't for the fact your resin counterpart became a substitute corpse."

"Land, how could I forget? Where is it now?"

"Well, after he acted on your behalf durin' the funeral procession, he tracked his way to Springfield for burial."

"So, he's six feet deep?"

"Not anymore. There were attempts to steal your body. So's we replaced it with that of a unknown man that matched your description. My hope is the government had the good sense to dispose of it. Make candles or somethin'. Either that, or it's hidden deep in some federal archive somewhere."

He itched his upper lip where whiskers were commencing to sprout. "My, what a web we made, all so I can sit here on a porch and rot. So sorry, Gabe." Abe began to get glassy-eyed.

"Don't be," I touched his knee. "You gave this country the greatest gift imaginable: a chance for a future. For this, and the cap, I thank you." When I tried it on, it fell over my eyes, same as the beaver pelt hat I found on the floor at Ford's. "You know, I had the top hat you wore that day. Now I wish I would have held on to it."

"I loved that hat," he mused, wiping a rogue tear on his sleeve. "Where'd it go?"

"Heck if I know. Some do-gooder musta sent it to the Smithsonian."

"That was the last night I ever saw my Mary. And Taddy-boy," he expressed sadly, taking a rejuvenating breath. "I pray to the Father that she comes to her senses and joins me out here, now that Tad's gone. I know she would love California. Molly was always more inclined to see Europe, I reckon. Her taste for finery never did match my own. Perhaps that's the reason she distanced herself from me."

"Don't count on it." I tried to put it as gentle as possible. "Robert had her put away for mental instability, you know."

"I know, read it in the papers," he ruefully admitted. "That was a dark, dark day for the entire Lincoln clan. I immediately requested Bob's presence, but he declined. Made up some nonsense about a gal and a legal case in Springfield. Why wouldn't he come? What did I do wrong? Should I have not eschewed my duty, kept on as president? Would it have been nobler to die bravely, finishing what I started? I truly believed we would all reunite in time and live peacefully in Vancouver as a family. I've failed them."

"No." I assured him. "They loved you, you know that. As for the First Lady, I think the depression finally got to her. Woulda happened whether you were with her or not."

"Perhaps," he sighed. "You know, we had our moments like any other marrieds, but we loved each other. Even as we sat watching *American Cousin*, she reached over to me, wondering what Rathbone's woman, Miss Harris, would think of our hand-holding? Do I repeat myself? Well, enough. God is at the helm. Let's see to some tea, shall we?"

We sipped, talked, and even laughed. I helped fix a good hearty pot of chili with corn bread, and then more introspection by a crackling fire before bed. "Angus," I scooped the last bit clinging to the bottom of the bowl, "why didn't they put you in one of them large, private officer's mansions up top the hill, or along Funston Street?"

"They offered, but I said no. Too conspicuous. The more I wither like a faded old nobody, the better." For the first time, I noticed his left eye was a tetch lazy, and both gleaned expressionless. Wonder what he's thinking deep down? In his day, he was the greatest political mind this country had ever known. Now, he was an artifact, a relic, a dinosaur of a man.

What had I done to this once magnificent soul?

"I asked the staff to set up a nice room for you." Abe broke the silence. "There are towels, a pitcher of water, and probably a tray of fruit in case you get a hankerin' for a midnight snack. If you fancy something else, just leave the little card around the doorknob. Porters come by several times a night."

"Thank you." I had to speak up. "You know, sir, this may seem selfish, and I make no apologies, but I would save your life all over again if'n I had to."

"Bless you, Gabe," he said softly. "I would save yours, too."

Then I got a mammoth case of the guilts or the stupids. "Lincoln?"

"Yes?" he stopped short of the threshold, hand on the brass knob for balance.

"John Wilkes Booth lives."

A pause.

"How can you be sure?" he asked, frozen, not looking at me.

"Met a man in Texas," I admonished. "He told me Booth paid him to keep quiet. John even schooled this fella so's he could impersonate him. It's complicated. The guy knew everything, includin' key details about the family, the murder plot, escape, efforts to keep hidden. The accuracy chilled me to the bone."

Lincoln looked straight ahead, unresponsive.

"Sorry to say it right before bed," I continued remorsefully. "Hope you're able to sleep. Just thought you should know. Want me to bunk with ya?"

"Uh, no thanks. I live in an army fortress, remember?"

"Oh, right. Stupid me."

In typical Lincoln fashion, he broke his trance and half-smiled. "I appreciate you telling me. What a plot for a novel, huh? And yes, I'll be able to sleep, unless I wake up to pee. Bugger getting old."

CHAPTER TWENTY

PHEASANT UNDER GLASS

A thick, low-lying fog covered the city like a blanket, making my room feel darker than it should've been. I slept late, nearly to ten o'clock, but ole Angus was up and at 'em by five. He'd made a pot of steel-cut oats with blueberries, and brewed a fresh batch of coffee. In his memoirs for the day, he wrote of my arrival before returning to matters of a spiritual nature. It was Sunday, after all.

Now, I ain't here to preach, nor waste time with lengthy dissertations on Abe's religious belief system. I reckon most groups claimed him as their own at some point or another, including atheists. I will speak briefly to the fact that he ain't subscribed to the notion of original sin, but rather, insisted men were made "perfect, and in all the constituent parts of God's being – made in harmony with God's laws controlling man." He wrote about disobedience being the sole force that separated us from divinity, and how we shall return to a godly state once we rid ourselves of wicked, sinful notions. He and his God were entirely forgiving, loving, and believed in endless second chances – until we enter heavenly realms where the Father decided our ultimate fate. That's all I got to say on the subject. Period. The end.

Just grant me one footnote: Once, just when we finished discussing the veil of darkness being lifted from mankind, there came a break in the fog and the sun shined through as if God was in harmony with his message. Same durn thing occurred during his second inaugural speech, lo, them years way back. I reckon Lincoln and the Lord was tight as tonsils.

Golden Gate Park was a sanctuary of green in the center of San Francisco, carved out of unpromising sand dunes called "the outside lands" at the western city borders. Angus and I took an afternoon stroll by a man-made reservoir lake beneath the plentiful pines, alders and blue gums. The lawns were covered with birds – mostly seagulls – that caught rides on the cool breezes as they headed inland for lunch. Picnickers offered sandwich scraps freely before taking rowboat rides around the center island. By the squawks of the gulls, they were much appreciative.

"Are they gonna be here the whole time?" I asked about the two military personnel, ten paces behind us the entire time.

"Yes," he said from beneath the brim of a cowboy hat. "They are prime members of my posse." He was once again in blue jeans, vest, and a pinstripe shirt. Old West style.

"What's with the costume? And is that a handlebar mustache you got a-goin' on there?"

"Yippee-ki-yay, partner. You don't like it? After all those years I had a beard and no mustache, I thought I'd cross them up and sport the reverse. Maybe I'll do a full Fu Manchu!"

"Ya know," I took a closer look, "it works."

"You ever play Cowboys and Indians growing up? Or rodeo?"

"No. You?"

"Nope, weren't no such thing when I was a boy. Frontier explorer, maybe. I reckon I fantasized about plenty of other things though, from books. I would crouch by a fire and absorb, until my eyes started to sting. Get to laughing or something and have to muzzle myself not to wake my parents, sound asleep, six feet away. I could lose myself in the story, the rich characters. If I felt sour about something in my own life, I would take on the persona of the protagonist, and everything suddenly seemed all right."

"Strange you say that. You're the third person to share the insight, J. B. Wilkes bein' one."

"Booth, eh?" he puzzled. "What a play of paradox, a dichotomy. You and he were pals, and you and I are pals. Nobody would've believed it in a million years. You couldn't have thunk it if you were Herman Melville."

"I know somebody who thunk it."

"Who?"

"Madame Yvette, the voodoo psychic witchy-witch I met when I was 10. She foretold the whole ordeal: marryin' my Kate, meetin' you and John Wilkes, pullin' off the Grand Plan. Whole blame shebang."

"Do you feel it was all worth it? Was it a blessing or a curse?"

I thought a moment. "Well, a blessin' I reckon. I mean, Katie was the love of my life, and you been such a grand friend. Even Johnny somehow gave me self-confidence, newfound creativity, and not to mention steady work for years. Yessir – a blessin'."

"And if this voodoo witch, as you call her, brought this blessed message to you, then she is loved by the Father, as well. She was no evil demonic energy, but a conduit to truth, wisdom, and love."

"Powerful good notion. Never thought of it as such. See, this is why you were president, and part of why I enjoy your company so."

Leaves began to cascade. Wind ruffled the surface of the lake. We seemed to be taking a steeper incline, and even I was getting gassed. Just then, he stopped and clutched his chest, struggling to get air, and gasping deeply. "Angus, you all right?"

He dropped his cane. "Not sure. Give me a minute."

The guards ran up, a-shoving me aside. They made him sit on the hillside until he could regain his wind. "I think that's enough for today, sir," one said. "Let's get you back to the barracks," advised another. Perhaps his condition was more serious than he'd let on. He talked of his heart being a jumping jackrabbit, and the uncommon sensation down his left shoulder and arm. They handed me the cane and helped him away, throwing his gangly limbs over their shoulders. Lincoln had deteriorated so much since leaving office. He escaped murder, true, but the slow, grinding effects of war had already taken their toll. Though not yet 70, he looked at least 90. I'd stay overnight, perhaps re-evaluate the next day. Probably ain't in his best interest for me to linger long-term.

Lincoln made a Monday morning comeback. T'was almost a spring to his step as he plopped me down in front of a towering stack of buttermilk flapjacks, sausage, hash browns, and freshly picked raspberries. "My Molly would be proud, don't you think?"

Now, it only happened from time-to-time, but that day, I was in a pall of fog. I had one of them dull, dense headaches, and my mind was fuzzy and dizzy. I couldn't recall what day it was, and honestly, if you'd asked me the year, I don't reckon I'd a-knowed. Vaguely recall it was '72 or '73, but who knows? Some suggest it was 1880, maybe even 1900! I defend the latter fierce, would've remembered such a momentous year as such.

"How long you been cookin'? Since three in the mornin'?"

"Heavens, no," Abe barked. "Seven or so. You slept until nine o'clock. Don't you heed Ben Franklin's advice? 'Early to bed, early to rise' and so forth?"

"I'm showbiz folk, don't rise till the crack a noon. This is mighty nice of you, more than I could ever shove down."

"Well," he warned, "don't overdo it. I made a reservation for the Crystal Palm Court over at The Palace. Mr. Cicero is meeting us for supper and drinks around five.

"Splendid, any friend of yours is a friend of mine."

When Angus and I arrived at the Palace Hotel, we were met by plain-clothed policemen who walked us past the kitchen, through a waiter's galley, out the swinging double doors, and right into Heaven. Oh my goodness, *oh my goodness*! The Crystal Garden was a sight to behold if ever there was one. Huge, buttressed glass windows arched broadly, supporting an all-glass ceiling. Enormous crystal chandeliers with candles stuck in them (candle-iers?) dangled from the firmament. Dozens of potted palms, like great green tarantulas, spread their fronds in every direction. Massive, golden marble columns flanked the acreage of lush carpet and polished tiles. Bright red and white poinsettias adorned the round tables, atop ivory silk cloth (that you'd kick yersself for even thinking of spilling on). T'was Christmas season all right, as they's this 25-foot tree in the center, with enough candlelight to put the night sky to shame. Round, red glass orbs and bows gave the tree a fancy finish.

I pocketed a paper cocktail napkin with the insignia on it, to prove I ain't making it up, looped on spirits, or maybe even gone on to my heavenly reward. Furthermore, the menus ain't even got prices on them. You knowed you're up a creek when they ain't even telling you what the food costs!

After some beer and a glass of water or two, I had to remove myself to leak. Even the washrooms was fancified. *I been lots of places in my life, but don't this beat all!* Upon my return, Mr. Cicero had arrived, as I saw a second head at the table. His back was mostly turned, but at first glance, I saw he had slightly salty hair shaved close, like a seaman or something, and a pointy beard like a French artist. Appeared to have his billfold out, showing Angus some photographs. I rounded the table and took position to his right.

"Have a seat, Gabe," said Langley, "and meet our guest."

"Allow me to introduce myself," the stranger said. "Elias H. Cicero." We shook. I remembered those eyes, that grip.

"John Wilkes Booth," I gasped, suddenly pale and stupefied. He ain't got the mustache or that wild, wonderful hair, but this time it was him! "As I live and breathe." I wobbled and went white as a tablecloth, feeling like I's gonna tip. *Am I dead? Are we all dead? On paper, two of us already are!* Reckon I lost consciousness for a split second, because the next thing I knew, both men were supporting my weight with their arms. I slumped in my chair, breathing deep. "Johnny Booth, what in the…"

"Yes, it's true," he confirmed, wetting my face, and patting my cheeks. "It's me." I felt the familiar wave of nausea that last accompanied seeing him at Ford's.

279

"You all right?" asked Lincoln, or Langley, or whomever the hell he was. I's in such a fog. "Before this gets too overwhelming, perhaps we should shed some light."

They shared a look. Everyone was calm and cooperative. It was obvious there weren't no hatred or animosity, only resolve.

"As I said," Abe started, "we were at the Market Street Theater, briskly ushered away when a political ruckus broke out. Once we arrived at a nearby tavern, Mr. Booth and I became instantly aware of each other. Seemed our eyes were a smidge out of focus, but we knew. We remembered seeing one another at the ruckus, exchanging a brief point of view as we stood at the bar."

"Where was this, again?" I asked in my cloud.

"Gunther's Grille and Spirits on Market."

John jumped in. "Didn't take long to realize what this was: a meeting between ghosts. Imagine my shock."

"And mine!" Abe enforced. "We were presented with a conundrum: What do we do? Fight, flee, or find commonality? We took option three. Here we were, both in the same predicament. The world thought we were dead, and it was imperative we keep it that way."

"We ordered a drink, found a table in back, and talked."

"What was it you discovered?" I asked, shaken as shit.

"We were more alike than different," John said. "We agreed to disagree on the emancipation issue. My position had softened some over the years, but not entirely.

I'd come to my senses in the months that followed my escape, realizing I'd acted out of anger, impulse, loyalty, and even pressure from Vice President Johnson."

"Backstabbin' traitor!" I wailed, gulping water.

"No," said Abe, "that's another rule we agreed to. Everyone got a free pass after the war. No grudges, no revenge, no judgment. It was a troubling time of unspeakable emotion, no matter what side of the fence. We were all trying to fix the country we love. Opposite of love is not always hate, but indifference. When a couple can't mend a marriage, it's often the moment of numbness that does it in – the second they stop caring altogether."

"True," said John, sipping a brandy as I'd seen him do a thousand times. An odd comfort washed over me. "My passion remained, but my hatred was replaced by fierce patriotism," he went on. "I came to realize I wasn't numb, but rather lost in an all-consuming thought realm, suffocating any chance for rationality. I was trapped in a cage of sorts, heavily influenced by the characters I had portrayed. It was easy to commit acts of equal solemnity. If I may be spiritual for a moment..." *Johnny Booth, spiritual?* "...a good way to escape your cage is to die while you're alive."

Now it was my turn. "What the hell are you talking about?"

"I was dead, right? Shot and burned in a barn. That was my ladder back to God, so to speak. My rebirth. Only I didn't have to expire to experience it."

I'll say it again: there truly *is* hope for us all. "Okay, I s'pose I believe you. Miracles are possible every day. I've experienced it. But let's go back to that night at Ford's. What in tarnation were you thinking?"

"At the moment of truth," Booth recalled, "I was liquored and ready to perform. Made my show-stopping entrance, my narcissistic attempt at immortality. This was one performance Edwin, or even the great Junius, couldn't top. Frankly, the president was merely a sacrificial stage prop. Quite literally, thanks to you!"

I shut my eyes and rubbed my temples. "And you blindly accepted this?" I played devil's advocate and turned to Abe. "The sumbitch tried to kill you, and now your mortal enemy is a friend?"

"Well, far from friends, but we had no choice," Lincoln explained. "We're already dead, remember?"

"Yeah, yeah, I remember. And by the way, you always have a choice."

"All right," said Booth, "then ours was to accept the past and move forward. We healed our wounds and embraced our commonalities."

"Like what?" I yelped, confused, even perturbed.

"Well," Abe explained, "our mutual passion for our cause. Our love of theater, country, and family. How about the fact we were castmates in arguably the biggest drama in American history?"

"I suppose," I shrugged, still trying to grapple with the whole scenario.

Booth added his two cents. "Then there's the eerie Edwin connection. My brother and the president were mutual admirers, for what it's worth. Edwin even rescued Lincoln's son, Robert, from that train. Remember?"

"I'd forgotten about that," I admitted.

Lincoln injected his wit. "And ain't it a hoot that I was always the beard, no mustache, and John here was mustache, no beard? Look at us now!" They had a chuckle and tugged at their respective facial hair.

A waiter appeared. "May I take your order?"

"I'll have what he is having," said John, deferring to the slain president.

"Pheasant under glass," Abe smiled, looking skyward.

"Make it three."

We snapped our napkins, placed them in our laps, nursed our drinks, and continued the epic exchange.

"Hey," I said. "Wanna play Reveal-a-Nugget?"

"What in the U.S. Grant is that?" asked Cicero.

"It's a game where you tell the other fellas a secret," Angus informed. "You go on, Elias," he told Booth. "Gabe and I already played it plenty of times."

"I'll pass. Already revealed enough."

"No, you can't pass," I huffed. "Oh, all right, I'll go first. I bumped into another friend of yours, Elias. Granbury, Texas. Venture a guess?" I saw a smile unspool. He knew exactly whom I meant. "Guy by the name of John St. Helen. Had me fooled for a minute, but you and I were too storied for it to stick."

"Pretty good, is he not? I showed him all my tricks."

"Yes. I attended a Shakespeare performance at the Opera House. He was incredible. Much better than you ever were."

"Watch it," said John, flashing a sinister smile, "I killed once, I'll kill again."

"No you didn't," Abe and I reminded him in unison.

"Right. Well played, by the way. Well played."

"Thanks," I gloated. "Now then, St. Helen said you paid him thirty thousand to keep quiet?"

"Not exactly," Booth sipped. "I paid him 20 to return to Galveston with some tools and confidence. Go support his family. I sympathized with his plight. Theater can be a cruel mistress. Anyway, it soon became his misguided quest to emulate not only my style and my look, but my life! I agreed it might make him a better actor to climb inside my mind. Let him have his fantasy. We coexisted for quite a while in that wonderful little town, but when it got uncomfortable, I left. Here I was, incognito, while he was playing dress-up. Odd. I looked nothing like my old self, and he was the spitting image. Scarred himself and everything! Busted thumb, leg. It was macabre, but the fellow was desperate. He no longer saw himself as a frustrated drama teacher at a second-rate school, earning a meager wage, but as a legitimate star. So, how did it end?"

"He went on to Enid, Oklahoma under the name David E. George. Said he was goin' to paint houses. Stay with friends."

"Funny," Booth concluded, "when we met, he was David Ryan Ney of Memphis, or something or other. Then he called himself David E. Ryan, I believe. Who was in hiding, for godssakes, him or me? I could've learned a thing or two from the fellow about disguised identity, especially in Mexico."

"Yup, heard about that one," I chortled. "Okay, Elias, you're next."

"Wait." He raised his free hand. (The other was glued to his brandy.) "Wasn't that enough? Admitting to having schooled a man to *be* me, donating twenty grand, or whatever it was?"

"I guess, but you sorta got off easy."

Booth looked at Lincoln, who shrugged.

"All right, Stone, I'll throw you a couple little pebbles. As you know, I have always loved the ladies."

"That ain't no nugget...."

He stopped me. "I've also had women in my life named Mary, and Kate. Like you. And, I've been nuptialized, like you."

"Land! You got married, after the escape?"

"No, well before. I have children, too."

"No shit! More information, please." I was dying to get the details. Lincoln sat still, resting his eyes.

"Stone, there's much you don't know. I promise someday to send a letter that reveals so many nuggets; you'll be reduced to ashes under the weight of it. I'll be on another planet by then."

"Fair enough," I agreed. It was worth the wait.

"I only have one...small...request," Booth added.

"What's that?" I feigned a gulp, feeling like I's making a deal with the devil.

"Well, I never understood why you didn't do my portrait. There's one of Edwin, and of course, old Angus here. I'm hurt. I received dozons over the years from admirers, people I didn't even know. Most were amateurish, but it made me feel appreciated, validated for my talents. I'd be honored if you'd paint one."

"I'd be happy to," I said. "But where would I send it, Mars?"

"Don't send it anywhere." A crooked smile. "It's enough just knowing you'd painted one. Besides, it won't be worth much until you're dead," he winked.

We were gladly interrupted by a team of restaurant staffers that set a portable table at our side. Three plates with glass domes were placed in front of us. That woke up Angus. Piping hot steam billowed beneath our chins as the servers lifted the lids. The smell was divine. White meat fillets covered in mushrooms and wild rice, a hint of Cognac in the sauce. No wonder John Wilkes was so enthused.

"Cheers." He clinked with Lincoln, then me, then all three.

Angus made a special toast. "Nothing like the holidays to put aside differences, build new bonds, and celebrate God in all his disconcerting masks."God certainly celebrated that day, as we set aside deep divisions, age-old rivalries and grudges. We done healed history, reached back and brought new meaning to the trespasses.

We stayed, chatting for hours. The historical foes found kinship in the fact they had both, at times in their lives, felt alienated by society – if not family and friends. In their differences, they reached commonality. In their deaths, they found new life. At one point, a photographer set up a static camera on a tripod to take publicity photos of we three in front of the Christmas tree. Guards dashed out from behind pillars and plants to stop the proceedings, but Langley shushed them away. Somewhere, that picture still exists. Ain't seen it in forever. Bet that would be worth something to the cynics. The two ain't exactly looked like the folks engraved in the misled minds of American history scholars, but we three know the truth of it. That's all that matters.

It was the last time I saw John Wilkes Booth. Years down the line, he decided to give Mexico another try, but not before venturing south to a town they was calling Coronado, California. The city done built this place called the Hotel Del Coronado, right across the waterway from San Diego. T'was supposed to be a marvel in its own right. It was an enormous wooden structure with red tile roof – a city unto itself. Best beach in the whole U.S. of A., too. Folks flocked from all over the world to bask in its magnificence and stroll its sandy promenade. I always wanted to get down there, but never made it. Did see the great Salt Lake and Denver, though. And, of course, my original homeland of St. Louis.

As for my lawyer friend, Mr. Bates, he never shook hisself of the belief that John St. Helen was the real John Wilkes Booth. In fact, he was so convinced, he went and bought the mummified remains of St. Helen (David E. George) after he committed suicide in 1903. That marvelous impersonator kept right on entertaining even in death, becoming a well-traveled carnival attraction. S'pose he had that long successful career after all. Ain't that just like America?

My good friend Edwin continued his booming career, which never reached loftier heights than after the assassination in 1865. Seems the country became even more infatuated with "the good brother." The unstoppable thespian founded a private Manhattan club called The Players, which included the likes of Mark Twain, J.P. Morgan, William T. Sherman, and Grover Cleveland. He hinted in his final few letters that he had been in contact with Wilkes, and was salved and solaced to know John was alive and well, forever a prisoner of his own doing.

On a sad note, I heard about the recent passing of Miss Laura Keene. She died from tubercular hemorrhage at the young age of 46. The acting she done for me on the night of the Grand Plan was not her last, nor best, but surely most honorable. Being a comedienne, folks sorta stopped laughing after that, probably picturing her blood-stained dress every time she took the stage. The papers suggested she was some kind of jezebel, had some nerve kneeling at the president's side while he lay dying.

If they only knew.

She started a magazine called *Fine Arts*. It was her swan song to a life on stage. Thing is, she used it against Edwin, Sleepy Clark, and me in a colossal way. You likely been asking yersself, "How'd them rascals get off scot-free, pulling off the biggest bunko job in history, nary a snag nor hitch?" Sounds like a load of cow crap to me. Well, we ain't. In the interest of storytelling, I confess I skipped over an important event. In an issue dated October 1865, Laura published a copy of a scathing letter she sent to the three of us. (Honestly, I's only guilty by association.) The way things wound up is this: Them two asked if I wanted in on producing that revival of *Our American Cousin* at the Winter Garden Theater in New York. Now, although Laura ain't owned the property outright, it was sort of her vehicle – the play she's famous for. Well, when we ain't included her, she dug down deep into the vault of nasty wastys, and spilled the beans about the Grand Plan. She blew the whistle about the wax figure, the cover-up, and the funds paid to those involved. The whole blessed deal. Don't think the *New York Herald* ain't grabbed it up, pasted it all over the front page.

On October 2, Keene wrote, "*Our American Cousin* is my personal, private property, and should have been held sacred to me by every respectable member of our profession." She wailed on about it being in bad taste to deprive her of the use of this play, and how it brought shame and horror to the Booth name. (As if the Booth name didn't already give a person the willies.) Worst part was the exposé on Lincoln. Remarkable aspect was that the next day, the government printed a retraction, saying in no uncertain terms that the president was killed in front of countless witnesses, and how the whole deal was just sour grapes over the sudden change of perspective regarding Miss Keene as a public figure. They even went so far as to infer she was going bonkers from having witnessed such a horrific scene. Whole episode was tragic and somewhat terrifying. I shudder to think of the ramifications if people knowed the truth. Reckon the government was finally good to me for once, settling the conspiracy before it blew up in our faces. We'll all be long gone by the time somebody opens this can of worms again, reading this here journal. Till then, it's like I always said with a splash of sarcasm (undetectable in this here writing), if the feds say it's so, it must be so...

Rest in peace, Laura Keene. So sorry for the trespasses. Thank you for many moments of friendship and inspiration.

SCOTT WESTMORELAND

Anyhow, that's about the way of it. I lived in New Orleans all on my lonesome for what seemed like an eternity, until my head got to giving me too much trouble (frankly, they's times I ain't even sure of my own name). I had the infrequent female companionship, but never found anyone to replace my dearest Kate. Probably best that way, as I reckon she, Mama, and Amelia will be awaiting my arrival any day now.

By and by, I landed myself in a senior care facility, Jeune Visage. That's Paris language for "Young Face" Nothing young about the place except for the nurses. Reckon them gal's paps would string me up from the next convenient limb if'n they knew my occasional impurities. Something about svelte, shapely gams in white tights that makes you all...involved. I's still the same ole rascal. Maybe I shoulda used the word *scoundrel*, for a dash of cayenne, but I ain't that ruthless, am I? ---so's I'll stick with rascal. Anyways, sobers me right quick to think how my own little daughter would be old enough to be they mama. Like Lincoln told me once, it's the last rite of passage to be a crumb crude. Just a crumb, mind you, to keep things interesting.

Lawd, how life races by. Looks aside, the nurses are okay, I reckon. S'pecially this gal named Onyx. Gonna leave her some money so's she can care for her family and be the mother I ain't never had to her own tadpoles someday. I'll see to it that Bates gets her the funds when I'm finally flat in a box.

As for my dear Abraham Lincoln, he died that New Year's Day, just weeks after I returned home. They found him in his warm bed with a peaceful expression on his face. The way he deserved to pass. They took him home to Springfield, where he was finally reunited with Mary. She wept, and rubbed the top of his coffin, regretting her decision to remain apart all those years. She had many regrets, but this was surely her greatest. Mary watched as they lowered Lincoln deep down – some 15 feet – where nobody, but nobody, would ever disturb him again. This had long been my wish, maybe even before I's born, if'n you believe God sends us here with a Grand Plan to perform certain tasks or learn lessons.

Whelp, that's pretty much it. I mean it this time. I feel about a million pounds lighter now I's said my peace. Bet you're all a-sitting there thinking, "What the hell has he been talking about? Lincoln lived, Booth escaped?" Pure nonsense. But looky here, the more a body takes to wandering down the road, and meets enough folks along the way, the more he realizes life ain't experienced "out there," but rather, in the mind and spirit. We see things the way we wish to see them. Maybe this whole blame thing weren't no more than a hallucination? That buck durn near sent me to my maker. Yet again, I knowed in my soul it was real. I couldn't have dreamed it with such detail. Here's a few observations I *can* disclose with absolution: If a government has a vested interest in a thing, and they's enough money and publicity to back it, it becomes history. We put it in print ('cause that makes it seem official), convince folks it's the truth, and tell it again and again until it's gospel. Secondly, the doings of Lincoln and Booth worked in tandem. There was an underlying unity, just as it was between the North and South, black and white, and good and evil. You can't have one without t'other. Booth's malevolence was contributive to Lincoln's legend the same way manure is contributive to the fragrance of the violet. And that, my friends, is truth.

Yessir, everbody got a Grand Plan. We seen Abe's come to pass, Johnny's take more twists than the mighty Mississippi, and now you know mine. It ain't like I preserved the Union, became some rich and famous actor, or (on the dark side) killed for my convictions. But I *did* preserve the lives of two men, if only in my most heartfelt dreams.

Indeed, God had an eye on me. On us all.

EPILOGUE

Jeremy Gabrick Stone died on August 31, 1928. The precious manuscript remained in the protective care of his dear friend and nurse, Onyx Robinson Bing. A literate, Southern woman of color (rare for the day), she never released his confidential memoir, nor the box of astounding artifacts. "Your secrets are safe," she had assured him, and she kept her word. Unfortunately, the promise to watch her diet was never actualized, and she succumbed to a heart attack in 1958 at the tender age of 57. The unclaimed sum of $50,000 still sits in her name, at the First National Bank of Granbury, Texas.

She was survived by a husband, Clevon H. Bing, and two children, Griffin and Amelia, in tribute to the two fallen children from Gabe's journal. Her self-written epitaph read as follows:

Here lies the body of Onyx R. Bing,
The truly tremendous, remarkable thing

Is the people she met, and the secrets she'd keep.
Don't get no ideas of disturbin' her sleep...

Beloved wife, mother, and friend.
1901-1958

The journal, and accompanying evidence, remained carefully concealed in the family attic for generations. Onyx was never convinced of their validity, and much too affraid to seek a second opinion. Every so often, she revisited the memoir, Booth's portrait, and treasurebox, agog with the claims and possibilities. On one occasion, a faded photo fell from the pages: Three men linked arms in front of a massive Christmas tree, poker-faced as if they'd held the secrets to the universe. This, perhaps, the most compelling component of all, until ultimately lost to the surging waters of Hurricane Katrina in 2005, claimed by the Gulf for eternity.

AUTHOR'S NOTE

I have always felt a strong connection to Abraham Lincoln. In fact, I recently came across a box of drawings I'd done as a very young child; there were dozens of portraits, in full detail. I would look at his photo and find myself overcome with love, gratitude, and admiration. Interestingly, I was also drawn to Southern antebellum architecture, and culture, yet I never waivered from a firm allegiance to the Union blues. Dichotomy aside, I wanted to somehow reach back in time, save the beloved president from his tragic fate. In doing so, I uncovered secrets and stories that far exceeded my expectations (see After Words). I hope you, the reader, have a similar experience.

I'd like to acknowledge a few sources that offered monumental assistance: *My Thoughts Be Bloody, The Bitter Rivalry That Led to the Assassination of Abraham Lincoln*, by the brilliant Nora Titone, *Blood on the Moon*, another terrific book by Edward Steers Jr., and the haunting *The Escape and Suicide of John Wilkes Booth*, by Finis L. Bates. I highly recommend them. In addition,

I'd be remiss not to mention Ken Burns' *The Civil War*, one of the finest documentaries ever made.

My gratitude also to the many people that provided guidance, aid, and support. Without them, this book would not have been possible: First, my lovely wife, Karen---partner, front-line editor, and tether to sanity. To my beautiful children, Cooper and Gracie, who never cease to amaze and inpire. And to my incredibly loving and supportive parents, Shari, and Dave, who have seen me through every ebb and flow. I'd also like to thank my dear friends, fellow scribes, and co-conspiritors---Michael, José, and Marie, along with my editor, Lori, and patient art agents, Greg, and Ellen.

AFTER WORDS

The following letter was post marked 2 December, 1883, addressed to a J.G. Stone of New Orleans, Louisiana, U.S.A. It never reached its intended recipient, and remains in the private collection of Armella Marie Whitney (formerly of Baton Rouge, Louisiana), who claims she has received offers in excess of $100,000---the original bounty for Booth...

Dear Mr. Stone,

I hope this letter finds you well. My name is Elizabeth Marshall Burnby Wilkes. My husband was a friend of yours, and instructed me to forward this as promised. His full name was John Wilkes Booth. He had a long and lustrous career on the American Stage. For obvious reasons he went by the name John Byron Wilkes while living in the Far East. He died peacefully here in India last month, November 18, 1883, from a lengthy respiratory illness. He wanted you to know how sorry he was for decisions made; impulsive, violent acts against his country, and a noble man, Mr. Lincoln. He also wished to thank you for the years of service and friendship. We ask that you respect his wishes to be buried abroad, as he did not want to cause any further grief to the land he so dearly loved.

John was secretly married to Izola Mills D'Arcy in 1859, and had a daughter with her named Ogarita Rosalie Wilkes, born that same year. He also had a daughter named Sarah Katherine Scott (born December, 1865), after a brief affair in March of 1865 with a Mary Katherine (Kate M.) Scott, a journalist sent to Washington to cover the second inaugural of President Lincoln. His third child was Mary Louise Turner, daughter of Ella Turner of Virginia. Ms. Turner attempted suicide while pregnant with Mary, upon learning of the assassination of the president, and subsequent capture and killing of my husband. These were his beloved children whom received the majority of his estate.

John was not entirely the man portrayed in the newspapers, and surely, the history books. He was kind, charming, and a lover of children. Wildly talented, passionate, and sincere, he came to understand the gravity of his actions, and forgive and forget the hatred between countrymen. Although we did have Negro servants in Delhi, they were treated kindly, compensated fairly, and even considered friends, free to live life at their choosing.

Thank you, Mr. Stone. May God bless you, and may God bless the United States of America.

Sincerely,
Elizabeth B. Wilkes

BOOK CLUB QUESTIONS

1. What images emerge when you think of the antebellum South? Have you visited a plantation, or battle site? Ever pondered what it must've been like to live in the times of slavery?

2. Our protagonist Gabe Stone elopes at his own wedding to another woman. Did you root for him? What drastic decisions have *you* made based on love?

3. John Wilkes Booth is a notorious villain in American history. Were you able to put aside preconceived notions, and allow his character to shed light on his circumstances?

4. Volumes have been written about Abraham Lincoln, but Gabe Stone only comments on a very private side the president reveals to him. What were your initial assumptions about Lincoln before reading the book, and did they change as the story unfolded?

5. In an era when flim-flam and trickery were prevalent (consider the exploits of P.T.Barnum),

Gabe's artistic ability certainly altered history. Do you think hoax like this has ever actually happened? What about the conspiracy theories shrouding the Kennedy assassination or UFO cover-ups like Roswell? Or the current public perceptions regarding events caught on camera?

6. Many claims have been made about a real person named John St. Helen (read *The Escape and Suicide of John Wilkes Booth* by F.L. Bates). *Bounty* has its own unique take on St. Helen. Did you sympathize with him? Would you ever consider a mentorship of such magnitude if it changed your life in a profoundly positive way?

7. Do you believe in fate, free will, or a blend of both? Why?

8. If you could change some historical event, what would it be, and why?

9. Gabe Stone talks about the legends of Booth (darkness) and Lincoln (light) as being interdependent. In what way has tragedy or struggle positively enlightened your life?

10. If you could sit and share a meal with Lincoln and Booth, what would you ask them?

www.ingramcontent.com/pod-product-compliance
Lightning Source LLC
Chambersburg PA
CBHW020338180626
46812CB00001B/252